the
little
island
secret

BOOKS BY EMMA DAVIES

EMMA DAVIES

the
little
island
secret

Bookouture

Published by Bookouture in 2021

An imprint of Storyfire Ltd.
Carmelite House
50 Victoria Embankment
London EC4Y 0DZ

www.bookouture.com

ISBN: 978-1-80019-430-4
eBook ISBN: 978-1-80019-429-8

Chapter 1

Dear Miss Prendergast,

Isn't modern technology wonderful?

I'm sitting here, desperate with a sudden longing to reread one of my favourite books, and what do I discover? That the despicable child in Year Ten I lent it to has not only failed to return it, but worse, took it with him on his summer-long jaunt around Europe last year and lost it.

Whilst I approve of the mind-expanding travel, obviously, I cannot condone such flagrant abuse of my generosity, but, whichever, the end result is the same. I am without my copy of 'Stoner' by John Williams and so I have taken to the internet to try to remedy this situation. And you and your lovely shop popped up!

So, I'm very much hoping that you haven't, as yet, sold your copy of 'Stoner' and in fact can dispatch it to me at your earliest convenience and by the quickest available means.

It's entirely possible that you may save my soul.

And can I just say that your website is lovely. Very friendly, in a quirky, slightly weird sort of way, which I wholeheartedly approve of. I'd love to know if you're the same, although I guess you must be, seeing as it's your shop and your website. But, one last question, is that a cat I can see sitting in your shop window?

Yours, in a fever of anticipation,
Cameron Innes
(Only please call me Cam, everyone does)

Dear Mr Innes, Cam…

It is indeed a cat. His name is Bruce. I know, but it seemed like a good idea at the time, and that is his very favourite spot to sit. Heaven help anyone who wants to display a book in the window… ridiculous idea.

I am very happy to report that Mr William's 'Stoner' is indeed still in stock. Although, before I send it to you, perhaps you could confirm your position with regards to whether William should have left his wife for Katherine.

I wouldn't normally countenance adultery, of course, but in truth I couldn't possibly send this book to anyone who doesn't agree. It's one of the greatest love stories that most of the world has never heard of.

As to whether I am friendly, quirky, or slightly weird in any way… I called my cat Bruce, I shall leave you to draw your own conclusions.

Provided you can confirm your position with regard to William's marital conundrum, please forward your address and credit card details. I can confirm that I shall hasten to the post office this very afternoon.

Yours in gratitude,
Abigail Prendergast
(Abby, only my mother calls me Abigail)

Dear Miss Prendergast… Abby,

*My heart leapt with joy to hear that you not only have 'Stoner',
but that you have actually read it too. Are we the only two people
in the world?*

 And, he should absolutely have left his wife.

 *Credit card details and address are below. You have indeed
saved my soul.*

Yours in gratitude,
Cam

Chapter 2

Seven months later

'So, this is me,' I say, turning to push open the door to my shop. The bell gives its customary clang, an old-fashioned sound that tells you exactly what you'll find when you enter; a room full of charm. Of nooks and crannies. Of wood and brass, and floors that are uneven, and a bay window where my cat sits, occasionally turning a sleepy eye to the passers-by outside.

The shop even smells old, as all good second-hand bookshops do. The comfortable, slightly musty warm smell of old book-leather and paper too, warmed by the sun that streams in through the huge window to the front.

My heart is going like the clappers as I lead Cam inside. What will he think of my little kingdom? Will what I think of as character and quirkiness be viewed the same way? Or will he just think the place untidy and long overdue for modernisation?

'It's exactly how I pictured it would be,' he says, putting down his rucksack and gazing in wonder around him.

I follow the path of his eyes, watching his expression as he takes in the details of the room I've tried my best to describe over the last few months.

'That's the chair where Mr Ridley sits…' He points, laughing. 'And the picture that you have to straighten every morning as if someone has been dusting carelessly in the night. Even Brown Bear is exactly where you said he would be.'

He picks up the slightly dishevelled bear that is propped beside the till, waiting for his long-lost owner to reclaim him. He's been waiting a long time, but I haven't the heart to throw him away.

He pats the bear on the head. 'In fact, it's even better than I thought,' he adds, spinning to face me, his eyes firmly fixed on mine. And then I see his gaze widen to take in all my features: from my deep-brown eyes fringed with long lashes (my one redeeming feature) to my slightly snub nose and my cheeks, which I know are rosy despite my best efforts to calm them down. His mouth pulls into a wide smile and I feel my own mirroring it.

That's one thing you can't get from a photo; someone's smile. You can't really see how it changes their face or lights up their eyes.

I frown. 'Sorry, did you say something? I was miles away.' Miles away, but right here, lost in the enormity of seeing Cam, in real life, looking like he does, instead of as words on a screen. Words that are no longer mere text, but instead rich and textured by the soft lilt of his Scottish accent.

His eyes are dancing with amusement. 'Only that it's so good to see you.'

'Oh yes, me too, good to see you that is, not me, obviously.' My cheeks grow even rosier, I'm sure of it. His photo hadn't done him justice at all.

'It seems forever since we agreed to meet, but now that I'm finally here…' He wrinkles his brow. 'A weekend isn't long, is it? It's going to whizz by.'

I nod. 'I know.' I meet his eyes, suddenly saddened by the thought that Cam will be leaving again. His being here seems… I push the thought away. It's far too early to be thinking that kind of thing.

Cam looks around him once more. The shop is closed, it's half past six and I've finished for the day, and I can't help but wonder what he's thinking. I love the place at this time of the evening. The light in here is golden and I sometimes wonder if I can hear the books sighing and settling themselves for the hours ahead. The slightly expectant air the shop wears during the day replaced by something more cosy and comforting.

'Do you ever come down here when you're not open? At night?' he asks. 'I know I would. To sit among the books and read, or read to them, perhaps? I'm sure they like to hear stories other than their own just as much as the next book.'

He didn't wait for my reply. But then maybe he didn't need to. Perhaps my astonished look and gaping mouth has informed him that's exactly what I do. There's a corner where I sit, on an old armchair placed beside a small table with a lamp on it. It's there to illuminate what would otherwise be a dim and unwelcoming corner, the overhead lights in the shop too weak to reach across the top of the bookcases and drop down into that little space. I'd never sell a book from there if I didn't have the lamp lit, but there's also the added benefit that it transforms that little nook into a haven, a safe harbour against the world and all its problems. It's no coincidence that the armchair is occupied almost from the minute I open.

'I bring a blanket, and hot chocolate,' I reply. 'Although only in winter, of course. In the summer, I like the feel of the warm wooden boards against my bare toes.'

He nods as if it's the most normal thing in the world. It's one of the things I love— One of the things I really *like* about Cam; he's one of the few people I know who thinks that what everyone else labels as my eccentricities are, in fact, perfectly acceptable, even desirable. My mother thinks I'm odd and has taken to talking about my quirks quite openly in the company of others, often when I'm present, and most of my other friends, now married, quietly worry about my spinsterly state and don't quite understand why I'm not more like them. I love them all to bits, but the thought makes me shudder.

'Right,' I say brightly. 'Shall we?' I indicate the door to the rear of the shop, which leads to my flat. 'And then we can…' I trail off. I've seemingly waited so long for this moment that I'm not sure what to do now that Cam actually *is* here.

'Perhaps have a cup of tea?' says Cam, a wicked smile playing around his lips. 'Seeing as I've been on a plane, a train and an automobile to get here.'

I blush beetroot. 'Oh God, yes, yes! I'm sorry.' I bash a hand against my forehead. 'I wasn't thinking, I—'

'Abby…?'

I stop gabbling to look at him. At the slow smile which is still turning up the corners of his mouth. At the angle of his face, coloured golden by the afternoon sun, catching his eyes… unusually green.

'I'm just teasing.'

'Of course. You don't even like tea, do you?'

I knew that. I'd already got in four different varieties of coffee, especially for the occasion.

I walk purposefully behind the till, holding open the door which leads to a staircase via a short hallway. At the top of the stairs another small landing offers a row of coat hooks and I pause for a moment while Cam puts down his bag, so that he can remove his jacket. It's late August, but last week, squally showers seemed to mark the tail end of summer and the air is much cooler now of an evening. Today, though, has been perfect; sunny and warm. I had a feeling it would be.

I take a deep breath and lead us through to my kitchen. Beyond that is my living room, bathroom and two bedrooms. Plus, a tiny box room that I use as my study and general-purpose junk room. But more than these collections of rooms, it is my home, the one I share with my daughter, where we make our life, one not often punctuated by male company. This is a big thing for both of us.

The kitchen is my favourite room in the flat. It runs the full width of the building and sits over the shop so that the windows to the front look down into the street below. But it is also light and welcoming and full of character. Beneath the side window is a small round table where Beth and I sit to eat our meals, and to watch the world go by outside or chatter about our day. It's where I gravitate now, thinking that Cam might like to sit while I prepare some drinks.

Instead he puts down his rucksack beside the chair and looks expectantly around him. 'May I?' he says and, without waiting for my response, takes off across the room and through the door opposite to the one we came in.

I wonder if I should follow him, but what would I say? This is the living room. Obvious. This is my bedroom. Again, very obvious. And this is where I work. Which he will know like the back of his hand because it's where our correspondence first started all those months ago, a room I have described to him nearly every day. He's more than capable of working it all out for himself. So, I fill the kettle and set it to boil while I wait for him to return.

'I missed your email today,' he says, coming back into the room. 'Today, the office is…' He grins and I return it. It's how I start every email to him. *Today, the office is… sitting to attention, with a big brave smile on its face.* That one sent on the day when I was preparing to do the month-end accounts. Or, *today, the office is… a will-o-the-wisp, gossamer thin, adrift on the shimmering morning air.* That, from a day in the spring when the air in the park around the corner was soft, floating with cherry-tree blossom.

'I should have sent one this morning anyway,' I reply. 'Today, the office has ants in its pants…' I grin. 'I've been on tenterhooks all day, hoping that your journey went according to plan.'

'And now here I am,' he says.

'Yes, here you are.' I hold his look for a moment, before busying myself with the cafetière and mugs. 'So, what do you think to my little kingdom?'

There's a pause while Cam considers the question. 'I think you suit one another perfectly,' he says. 'And I can see what good friends you are.'

I laugh. It's true. And I'm happy that Cam has noticed.

A few minutes later, I place two mugs of coffee on the table and take a seat opposite Cam. 'Are you very hungry?' I ask. 'Only I thought we might eat out this evening, if that's okay. I can show you a little of the town when it's quieter. You'll get to see her gentler side.'

'That sounds perfect,' he replies. 'And I confess to having had a pasty for lunch from a station-side seller.' He blows out his cheeks. 'I've never eaten so much pastry in one sitting. So hungry, yes, but not ravenous.' He pats his flat stomach above the waistband of his jeans.

I nod. 'Great, well, Beth should be back soon. She's been at a friend's house this afternoon, which I suspect has involved a good deal of plastering each other in make-up and listening to horrendous music.' I cover my mouth with my hand. 'God, does that make me sound really old?'

Cam smiles. 'I can't wait to meet her.' He sips his coffee, looking at me over the rim of his mug.

It's another thing that's making me more nervous than I can say. Beth is like me in many ways, which makes her unlike most of her school friends. And when there's just the two of us, that's perfectly fine. But the thought of someone new to meet, and a man at that, is something that's caused both of us a great deal of anxiety. Still, she'd said to me only last night, 'If you hate one another when you meet, at least Cam lives so far away you're almost guaranteed never to bump into him again.' Remote Scottish islands do indeed have their advantages.

I lace my fingers around my cup. 'Well, this is… I was going to say odd, but maybe that's not quite the right word.'

Cam tips his head to look at me. 'Odd?' he queries. 'Why odd? Or not odd?'

His smile is so easy. Perhaps it's this that is adding to my nerves.

'No, I don't think I do mean odd, but…' I trail off again, fishing for a way to describe how I'm feeling that doesn't sound rude, or unwelcoming. 'Just that I don't really ever go on dates. Actually, I don't *ever* go on dates. And this isn't that, I know, but still… It feels strange. I feel strange.'

Cam looks round the room, taking his time, smiling slightly every now and again as he takes in some new detail. 'I don't feel strange,' he says. 'I know it's a little unusual that we know so much about one another yet have never met before. But, if you think about it, that makes it much easier than it would otherwise be.'

'Go on…'

'Well, I don't really go on dates either, but the ones I have gone on…' He pauses as if thinking about horrific or embarrassing encounters that might have occurred in the past. '…have been excruciating, because even though I probably knew within the first ten minutes of meeting the person that they weren't right for me, I still had to go through the process of finding out all those things we're supposed to, if only to confirm my suspicions. But you and I have already got all that horribly embarrassing stuff out of the way already. So now, we can get on with…' He colours slightly. 'Enjoying it.'

I squint at him. 'I think I know what you mean.'

He wriggles upright in his chair. 'Okay, so ask me a question about yourself. A question that you think I should know.'

'What, like favourite colour?'

'Exactly like that.'

I grin. 'Okay then, what's my favourite colour?'

'Autumn.'

'My favourite food?'

'Cheese on toast or honeyed cashew nuts if you're in the mood for something sweet.'

'My favourite book then?'

'I can't possibly answer that. You don't have a favourite book because you say it wouldn't be fair and you'd hate all the other books to feel they weren't up to scratch.'

I laugh. 'Okay, I get the point.'

Cam raises his eyebrows. 'See? We know so much about each other already. You even put one sugar in my coffee just now without even asking me.'

I stare down at his mug. 'Yes, I did, didn't I?' I think about his words for a moment. And then swallow. 'Which is fine. It's lovely, actually. But I still don't really know how I should be, what I should do.'

Cam chews the corner of his cheek as he stares at my face. 'Well then,' he says eventually. 'How about this?' And he leans across the small distance between us and presses his lips against mine. Softly and absolutely perfectly. 'Hello, Abby Prendergast. It's absolutely delightful to meet you.'

Chapter 3

He has no idea I'm watching him, but that's what makes it so wonder-ful. There's no pretence, no making sure I only see his good side. And I've thought about this moment for so long, in a way it's weird, but in others so much more than I ever dreamed it would be. I already know that his eyes are sort of green, sort of grey or, as Cam has described them, a mucky sort of khaki colour. Just as I know that his hair is thick and unruly, with a tendency to stick up at the front where he runs his hands through it. There's a curl which persists in hanging down over his forehead when the rest of it obediently sits swept back, and it's dark, almost chestnut, just like mine. Plus, he has dimples in his cheeks when he smiles and one in his chin, very Kirk Douglas.

What I didn't know, but have imagined over and over again, is just how all these parts of Cam fit together. How the curl sits on a forehead that is smooth and wide, how his eyelashes are almost ridiculously long, even longer than mine, so that when his eyes are open as they are now, the tops of his lashes almost touch the skin beneath his brows. How the curve of his cheek, normally so sleek, clinging to his cheekbones, puckers the moment he even thinks about smiling. But it's his mouth that I can't stop looking at. How the skin there is so soft, but fleshy too, generous... and the way in which he can smile with only one side of his mouth, the other side twitching up and down, almost as if it's amused at itself, giggling. But by far the best thing about his mouth is the way it feels on mine. And that is something I have long thought of.

Beth says something and Cam's head suddenly turns from her to include me in the conversation. I have no idea what they've been talking about. I'd been far too intent on my investigation of Cam's face and feel a flush of warmth hit my cheeks. His eyes meet mine, amused by my embarrassment as he catches me out, teasing as they sparkle under the light from the window.

The table between us is still littered with the remains of our breakfast, which we've eaten in Rumer's tearoom, just off the market square. It's where I quite often buy sticky treats if my colleague Gwen and I are having a particularly slow or frustrating day, but I've never been here for breakfast, and certainly never with a man. Rumer is going to want all the details come Monday morning, and if she doesn't get them will hound me until I spill them. She's already given me several meaningful glances since we've been here. But, having eaten, we now have the whole day ahead of us and it's bright and sunny. In fact, it's perfect.

I shake my head. 'I was miles away, sorry,' I say. 'What did I miss?'

Beth rolls her eyes and dabs a finger on her plate to pick up the stray flakes of pastry from her croissant. 'Honestly, Mum, what are you like? We were talking about going punting. Cam's never been and…' She drops her head, a little shy. 'It might be quite nice, don't you think?'

'I think it sounds lovely,' I reply, smiling. 'If you discount the fact that I've haven't been on the river in years, let alone manned a punt, or whatever it is you do while on one. It could be a huge disaster.'

'Or the greatest day ever,' replies Cam, emphasising the last word as he smirks back at Beth in a parody of a sulky teenager.

She laughs. A golden sound on a golden day. It's enough to make me want to go punting even if it were blowing a gale or the temperature, three below.

'Reassure me that you can at least swim,' I say.

'Abby, I live on a tiny island.'

'So, that doesn't necessarily mean you can swim.'

'True, but I was born on Kinlossay, don't forget. And, as island custom dictates, we get thrown in the sea when we're only six weeks old, to check that the legend still stands. We islanders are born knowing how to swim, or so they *say*…'

I look at him sideways. 'That's never true.'

'Which bit? That we get thrown in the sea or that we're born knowing how to swim?' He puts his hand over his heart. 'I'm heartbroken that you don't believe me.'

'I thought all babies could swim?' says Beth. 'I've seen videos of them in a documentary before, all swimming underwater. They're not afraid at all.'

Cam stares first at me and then at Beth. 'What? You mean we're not special? And the stories we've been told aren't true?' He fakes an anguished cry. 'They *lied* to us…' He lifts the back of his hand to his forehead as if he's about to swoon, but then he drops it, straightens up and grins. 'I learned to swim like pretty much everyone else did on the island – at primary school, where we had a half-hour lesson, two times a week in the outdoor pool. Brrrr.' He shivers. 'With Miss Pettigrew holding a long stick and poking us if we put our feet down.'

I shake my head in amusement. 'That's an even worse story than being thrown in the sea.'

But Cam shrugs easily. 'And somewhere between the two lies the truth. But yes, I can swim, so you needn't fear on that score, Abby.'

His eyes are soft as he speaks. 'And I will take the greatest care of both you and Beth. There will be fun, an amount of laughter, a modicum of shenanigans, but no death by drowning, I promise.' He turns to Beth and gives a courtly bow. 'Well then, shall we?' he says.

She gets to her feet, dusting more pastry flakes from her top and moves out from behind the table. I don't think I've seen her quite so animated in a long while.

'Can I just say, Beth, that those are damned fine dungarees. In fact, the damnedest, finest pair of dungarees I've ever seen.' Cam holds his hand over his mouth in an aside to me. 'Is damned a swear word?' he whispers, wiping imaginary sweat from his brow as I shake my head, laughing. I don't think I'd care in any case, I could listen to him talking for hours; the way he rolls the words around on his tongue, the sounds so different from those I'm used to. It's like poetry or music, notes dancing in the air.

He gestures that Beth should lead the way from the tearoom and I watch as my daughter walks ahead of us at least a foot taller than when she came in.

The river is only five minutes' walk away and we wander alongside it for a while, ducking heads under the whips of the willow trees which sway gently in the breeze. The river is quiet this early in the morning, but as on any Saturday when the summer-holiday season is in full swing, it will soon team with life and shouts of laughter.

There are several places where you can hire boats, not just punts but rowing boats too, and I head for the farthest away, where the prices are a little cheaper and the river likely to be a little less crowded as time moves on. It's nice, simply wandering, the conversation flowing as easily as the water. I walk a lot, most mornings before the shop opens in fact, but rarely by the riverside. It's a place for people, you see. For friends, for families, for lovers, and if you're none of those things then it's easy to feel out of place and even easier to feel alone. Today though, I feel neither of those things.

I realise my error, however, as soon as we arrive at the pontoon where the boats are tied together, waiting for hire. It's the widest part of the river, and they're arranged in rows, cheek by jowl, extending from the bank out almost into the middle of the river. And this early, when few punts have already been hired, those by the bank are immoveable to all intents and purposes. The only way to access an available boat is to walk across the floating 'deck' formed from the flat sterns of those in the line. This fact is nimbly demonstrated by the boat owner, in a fluid, confident movement that makes no acknowledgement of the fact that the surface on which he walks bounces alarmingly with his every step. And it's clear that if we want to hire a punt, this is the only way we're going to do it.

Cam gives me a look that says he is no more prepared for this than I am, but which acknowledges the illogical but stereotypical view that men are naturally more capable of this sort of thing than women. He walks towards the water's edge and then pauses.

'There must surely be an etiquette for situations such as this,' he says. 'Is it every man for himself? Or do I chivalrously take your hand and run the risk of dragging you into the river with me when I fall?'

From beside me, I hear Beth tutting in amused fashion as she steps onto the stern of the boat nearest the bank and saunters across to where the boatman is waiting with a guiding hand to help her down into the punt.

Cam stares at me. 'Did you know she could do that?' he asks.

I swallow and shake my head. 'Nope.'

He grimaces. 'And now we're going to look complete wusses if we don't follow suit, aren't we?'

'I'm afraid so,' I reply, nodding. 'I can't believe she did that.'

'So, what do we do? Go on three, or…?'

I eye the row of boats in front of me. 'Something like that,' I mutter, stepping out onto the first of the line. It tilts alarmingly.

The boatman is grinning, holding out his arm towards me, and I can only imagine what he's said to Beth. I'm about to take another step when Cam lands beside me and any semblance of balance I had deserts me entirely. I'm left clutching both his arms, begging him not to move as my centre of gravity shifts first one way and then the other. And only when he's standing absolutely still can I contemplate moving.

'Come on, Mum!'

I raise a ginger hand, to ward off further comment. 'Yep… coming,' I reply. 'Eventually.'

'Okay, Abby,' says Cam. 'We've got this. We're young, fit, reasonably, let-me-at-life kind of people. We're totally able to do this.'

I risk a sideways glance. 'Speak for yourself. I don't want to be let at life. I want it to invite me to an evening beside the fire, where we can eat hot buttered crumpets and read. Not dice with death and look a complete arse while I'm doing it.'

'Will it help if I promise not to look at your bum under any circumstances?' says Cam.

I throw him a look. 'No.' But he's doing that thing again with his eyes and I really wish he wouldn't. Having my knees turn to mush at this particular moment is really not going to help.

I raise my hand again and smile. 'Coming,' I call.

And this time I do. On the back of a very deep breath, and a wing and a prayer, I practically run across all twelve boats, and throw myself on the mercy of the boatman. He catches me with practised ease and swings me down into the boat, where Beth sits, laughing helplessly.

'Nothing to it,' I say, nonchalantly as relief hits me.

From the bank, Cam is ostensibly watching to make sure I made it into the punt safely, at which point he attempts to saunter across the boats towards us. A fixed grin is plastered on his face, which appears ever more manic the further he comes. He drops down into the boat with an easy smile, leaning towards me as he does so.

'Think I got away with that,' he says in a stage whisper. 'Nothing to it.'

I nod solemnly. 'Yep, you nailed it. Piece of cake.'

He turns to look at Beth. 'Right then, how do you drive this thing?'

The boatman hands Cam the long pole that will propel us through the water, with brief instructions as to its use. The trick is in finding a rhythm, he says. To drop the pole straight down to the riverbed, to wait until the boat has moved a little way beyond it, and then push off gently, using the pole as a lever. Pass the pole back up through the hands and then begin the process all over again. I'm more than relieved when Cam elects to 'drive'; I'm not sure I could even stand on the back of the boat, let along perform all those manoeuvres.

Progress is slow to start with, and Cam admits to the lack of propulsion being down to the fact that his legs are shaking but, after ten minutes or so, he finds a rhythm and we pick up a little more speed – still sedate, but smoother and, importantly, in a straight line. Cam divulges that his legs seem to have got the hang of things, and after a few minutes more he declares it to be great fun.

The conversation slows too, but that's okay. It's enough to watch the world go by, albeit from a different point of view than usual. In fact, it's lovely, seeing Cambridge the way that countless visitors do. I'm usually so caught up in the day-to-day urgency of life that I miss this. But it's important and I should do it more often.

In this way the colleges of Magdalene, St John's, Trinity and Clare drift by.

'It's by far the best way to see them,' I say. 'Although, of course, I've never taken my own advice,' I add quickly. 'The trouble is that when you live here, you get used to seeing all this amazing architecture, and after a while you stop "seeing" it at all. You forget that what you're looking at is extraordinary and beautiful and the most incredible achievement.'

Cam nods. 'I'm not used to seeing buildings. At home there's sky and the sea and more sky and more sea, but very few buildings. Pockets of them, but they cling to the ground, skulking almost. Not like these, who stand up straight and tall, demanding to be seen in the strongest possible terms.'

'I can't imagine what that must be like,' I reply.

'Then you must come, Abby. One day, you absolutely must.'

I'm very conscious of Beth sitting beside me. What must she be thinking? I've never seen anyone who has scored such a hit with my daughter, or so quickly before. But this is one visit that has been months in its coming, and the future that Cam speaks of isn't somewhere I can think about going just yet.

He shades his eyes against the sun, sighing as the magnificent splendour of King's College builds and then starts to retreat as we drift past. He's almost leaning on the pole, lost in contemplation of the sight before him, when he suddenly realises that the pole is static, but we are not. Too late, he tries to pull it upward but the distance between the two increases with every second, and the longer he and the pole stay connected, the more acute the angle at which he's leaning. And just at the point when I think he can't possibly sustain it any longer, Cam does the only thing he can if he wants to remain on the boat; he lets go.

For a moment there is absolute silence as we watch our continued passage down the river. Behind us the pole stands rooted to the spot, standing almost perfectly perpendicular, stuck in the mud on the bottom of the river. And then, all at once, there is movement. Cam kicks off his shoes, which land carelessly in the boat, and then his hands are at his waist, unbuttoning his jeans.

'Cam!' I swivel round, flicking a look at Beth. 'What are you doing? You can't…'

But he already has, and a hot flush hits my cheeks as Cam thrusts down his jeans and steps out of them.

'What?' he says, laughing. 'How else are we going to get the pole?'

I'm flustered now, as much for my sake as for Beth's. 'Yes, but…' I gesture vaguely at his legs, toned and tanned.

'I'm wearing boxers,' he adds. And he certainly is. They're bright yellow with blue polka dots on them, although I'm trying hard not to look.

And in the next moment, in one smooth movement, Cam's fingers grip the lower edge of his tee shirt and tug it upward. His muscles ripple, flat stomach contracting as the cloth is pulled over his head. The next second it lands in my lap and almost before I register the faint smell of soap, Cam has turned and executes a perfect swallow dive into the water.

There is a second when he is gone but then he bursts through the surface, head and shoulders, bubbles and droplets shaking free from his tousled hair.

'Shit… God, it's freezing!'

He meets my eye, his face split wide by a grin and then he turns, arcing his arm over his head and swims fast, away from us.

By the time he reaches the pole, the constant current of water has loosened it from its home in the mud, and sent it tilting towards him, it's topmost point slowly closing the distance between the sky and the water. He plucks it from the riverbed and begins to swim a one-armed front crawl back to us.

Beth cheers with excitement, leaning out of the boat with her arms outstretched to take the pole, heaving it onboard once she has it. Cam pulls himself around to the other side of the punt, causing it to lurch wildly as he pushes himself up against its side. Then, as I pull, his body reaches a point where he teeters for a second, balanced on the punt's edge, and then the river releases him. He slithers to the bottom of the boat like a wet fish.

I don't know where to look first, or rather where *not* to look, but Beth doesn't seem to be suffering from such qualms. She's already reaching down to help him upright, giggling at the sight of him. He shakes like a wet dog, his hair sending freezing droplets of water in our direction, and our screams join the sounds of the birds wheeling overhead.

'Well, that went well,' he says, grinning as he begins to shiver despite the heat of the day. He wriggles backwards until he's able to sit on the other seat and holds out his hands for his jeans. I wonder at which point I should tell him about the paddle tucked neatly underneath Beth's legs. Placed there for just such an eventuality.

'I can't believe you have to go tomorrow,' I say.

It's evening now, late, and the dusk has long since settled around our shoulders. There's just the two of us here, sitting on the roof terrace, looking out over the city that is either preparing to sleep or to party. A bottle of wine stands on the table behind us, where the remains of our last meal together also lie. I don't want to count tomorrow's breakfast, I can't bear to think of it. Or the drive to the station, where I'll have to wave Cam goodbye.

For a moment he simply stares out across the tops of the ancient buildings, myriad lights winking, but then he turns and takes my hand in his.

'You're very lucky, living here,' he says. 'And I'm so very glad I've seen it.'

'I do feel lucky,' I say. 'I used to come here every weekend as a child. Things were a little less official then, and my grandad used to let me help out, serving customers and all sorts. I never dreamed that one day it could be mine, but his death came at a time when Beth and I had nowhere to go. He saved my life by leaving this place to me. I guess in a way it made his loss slightly easier to bear.' I smile across at Cam, giving his hand a squeeze.

'And it's been lovely, hasn't it? Keeping the real world at bay, even if only for the weekend.'

'It's been amazing,' I reply. 'But tomorrow, it's back to the daily grind.'

'Not quite,' replies Cam, a wistful expression on his face. 'Because it won't be the same daily grind any more, it can't be.'

I tip my head on one side, puzzled. 'How so?' I ask.

'Because the world has changed, Abby, can't you feel it? Two people, among countless of millions, have met, and that changes everything. Yes, tomorrow will come, and the weekend will have been and gone, but tomorrow isn't an end, Abby, it's just the beginning.'

Chapter 4

October

Today, the office is… sailing on stormy seas, steady as she goes.

Dear Cam,

I wish you could hear the wind, it's crazy! Especially sitting up here at the top of the building. We had a storm in the night that would have shaken the bats from the belfry, if we had any that is, or a belfry for that matter. But as I lay there listening to the elements hurl themselves at the windows, I couldn't help wondering whether the same wind was blowing against yours. It's fine here now though – blue skies – but, despite my happiness at this change to the colour palette, the wind has also torn away the last of the leaves from the trees and the ground was laden with their bodies this morning. My beloved autumn is all but gone!

Anyway, what are you up to today? Have you forgiven Alfie yet for volunteering your services to help his sister make Halloween costumes? But the party sounds like great fun, I wish I could be there!

Blimey, is that the time? I'll catch you later. Duty and the provision of Gwen's eleven o'clock cup of coffee call.

Abby xx

Put like that it all seems rather romantic, when the truth of it was that the window panes were rattling so hard, I thought they were going to break. But I smile as I read through the message before sending it. It wouldn't be the first time I've lain awake thinking about Cam.

Ten minutes later, I have a tray laden with two mugs of coffee, and the last of the Jaffa Cakes. I swore I wouldn't eat any more but then I figured that since they were here, I might as well finish them. Then simply not replace them, at least that's what I'm telling myself anyway.

There is a reassuring sound of voices as I descend the stairs into the shop. Business has been better this week, thankfully. The summer trade seemed to disappear early this year, and I know I shouldn't pray for rain, but perversely we often do well when the weather isn't so good; folks look for places to browse, to while away a bit of time, and we're a good fit for that.

I slide the tray onto the edge of the counter as Gwen is saying goodbye to a customer. She has a fixed smile on her face, of the type which, if I know Gwen, will disappear the moment the man is out the door. I wait for the tinkle of the bell as he leaves.

'Cheeky so-and-so,' she says in a low voice, rolling her eyes. 'Why is this so expensive, when it's only a *novel*? Well, sir, that would be because it's a novel by William Boyd and it's a signed first edition. Besides, it's a book and is therefore sacred. What is wrong with these people?'

I smile and pass her a coffee. 'But he still bought it though?'

She narrows her eyes as if peering for his figure on the lane outside. 'Yeah… minted by the looks.' She takes the mug and swallows a huge mouthful. 'Although not a bad morning, actually. One lady cleared out our entire stock of Monica Dickens and a couple of the other Persephone titles as well.'

Gwen snaffles a Jaffa Cake, tossing her gleaming hair over her shoulder as she does so. Gwen is gorgeous. Tall, willowy, with bright-blue eyes, raven black, shiny, glossy *obedient* hair and perfectly shaped full lips, which, as usual, are painted a dark voluptuous red. She also has a beauty spot in the gap under the left-hand side of her nose, which makes her look witchy and mysterious. Coupled with a virtually encyclopaedic knowledge of authors and their books, and a caustic wit which has me in stitches most days, and it's easy to see why I love her to bits.

'Right then, boss,' she says. 'What's next? Do you still want to do that window display?'

I tip my head to one side. 'I'm not sure, what do you reckon? I'm worried it's too early and we'll look a bit—'

'Well-organised? Prepared? Festive? Full of cheer?'

I grin. 'I was going to say eager, grasping, out of place.' Actually, Christmas can't come soon enough.

'Abby, it's November next week. The market is going to have its first Christmas fair the week after. And don't forget I'm addicted to fairy lights and anything else that's bright and shiny.'

'So that's a yes, then?'

'It's definitely a yes. What have you got to lose?' She gives me a sly look. 'Besides, I have a feeling you're going to particularly enjoy Christmas this year. I think it's only fair and decent of you to share that over-spilling of joy with everyone else.'

My happy glow, a near-constant companion these days, burns a little brighter at her words. I sigh. 'Oh... Christmas on Kinlossay, Gwen, wouldn't it be perfect?'

'Do you really think he's going to ask you?'

'No, but it's the thought of it. That one day, perhaps he might.' I stare out the window at the familiar scene. 'Anyway, I wouldn't be able to go this year even if he did ask me. It wouldn't be fair to lumber you with everything here and I haven't made any arrangements yet or...' I trail off. I've had this conversation with myself on many occasions, and I probably should get the thought out of my head. Nothing can come of it, after all. And it's enough to know that this year Cam will be with us at Christmas, in spirit, if nothing else.

I drink my coffee, pushing the plate of Jaffa Cakes in Gwen's direction. 'Okay, so that's enough daydreaming for now. If we're going to do an all-singing-all-dancing Christmas window, we'd better make a start. Can you bring the books through? I'll go get the box of decorations from upstairs.'

'What about Bruce?'

I turn to look at my fat black-and-white cat, stretched out in the window, where he's sprawled across a copy of a Delia Smith cookbook. 'He can stay there. I'll pin a huge tartan bow around his neck, and he can be a living art installation.'

Gwen gives me an incredulous look. 'Bruce, with a bow? Good luck with that.' She darts a look at the window. 'Uh oh, incoming at twelve o'clock.' She plasters a smile on her face. 'Morning, Mrs P!'

My mother hates that Gwen calls her that. It's absolutely why she does it.

'Hi, Mum, how are you?' I move from behind the counter to give her a kiss.

She looks around her. 'Better than you, by the looks of things. This is the third time I've been in here and no customers. Are you sure you're doing okay?'

'Mum, we can't be thronging with people every minute of the day,' I say patiently. 'It's actually been pretty busy this morning.'

She purses her lips. 'Well, then, if that's the case I won't keep you, but I just popped in to ask about these tickets again. Are you planning on coming, or not? I really don't know why you're being so reticent.'

'Because I'm sure Patrick's very nice, Mum, but I'm not interested in going out with him. I'd die of boredom for one thing, but worse, if Tilda has her way, she ends up my mother-in-law. I know she's your friend, but I can't think of anything worse.'

My mother frowns. 'Abby, that's very uncharitable. Tilda only wants what's best for you, and her son, of course, but—'

'Mum, Patrick's wife has just left him. I'm really not sure that makes him the fantastic catch that you're both making him out to be.'

'He's a systems analyst, Abby. With a very good pay-and-incentive package and a gilt-edged pension. You could do a lot worse.'

'I don't even know what a systems analyst is, for heaven's sake. And before you say that he and his money could take me away from all this, I like my little shop. No, I *love* it.'

'I don't know why, when it's practically falling down around your ears.'

I ignore her. It's an age-worn argument. 'I'm not giving this up for anyone. Anyway, Beth would hate him.'

'You don't know that.'

'I do.'

She glares at me for a moment and then smiles at Gwen, who instantly raises her hands and walks away to tidy something.

'Keep me out of this,' she says as she goes.

'Look, Abby… It's an evening at the theatre and a few drinks afterwards. Where's the harm in it? You could do with a night out. Stuck in the flat with just you and Beth, day after day. It's not good for you. You should be out there, making friends, meeting potential suitors. They're not going to come in here and throw themselves at your feet, you know.'

'Maybe I don't want them to, Mum. Have you ever thought of that? And I do go out, I do have friends.' It's not a complete lie. 'And finding a boyfriend isn't the be-all and end-all of my existence.'

She flutters her eyelids, closed in consternation. 'You're going to end up on your own,' she admonishes.

'Fine!' I retaliate.

I see her face soften then. 'Oh, Abby… you don't really want that.'

A sudden prickle of tears feels ominously close. 'No, no, I don't,' I say quietly. 'But please, Mum, I'll find someone when it's right. And that time will come.'

'So, you don't want to come to the theatre then?'

I shake my head. 'No, sorry, I don't.'

Her eyes search my face for a moment, looking for any sign of weakness, any doubt at all that I meant what I said. 'Right, well then, I'll let Tilda know. Poor Patrick, I imagine he'll be very disappointed.'

Out of the corner of my eye I see Gwen moving back towards the desk with purpose. 'Shall I go and get those books, Abby?' she asks. 'And we'll need all the lights too. Where did they end up, can you remember?'

My mother looks first at Gwen and then back at me. 'Well, I can see there's no point in trying to persuade you to change your mind. I'll let you get on.' She gives Gwen a tight smile. 'I'll see you at the weekend,

Abby.' And with that, she turns and goes, the shop bell tinkling into the silence she leaves in her wake.

I blow out air from between my cheeks. 'Thanks, Gwen.'

She throws me a sympathetic look. 'Well, honestly. Why do you let her boss you around like that?'

I give her a weak smile. 'Because she's my mum?'

Gwen wrinkles her nose. 'Yeah, fair point.' Then she opens her arms for a hug.

'Well, that sucked all the joy out of doing the Christmas window, didn't it?' I say, pulling away. 'I'm not sure I'm in the mood now.'

Gwen looks at me, sympathy mixed with exasperation. 'Why don't you tell her about Cam, Abby?'

'Because what would I say? That I've met a man on the internet? You know what she's like as well as I do. I'd never hear the last of it. It's not the way things are done in her book. "Modern technology is all very well, but in moderation and when it's appropriate." She says *Tinder* in the same voice she reserves for my cousin Julie's boys and, as we both know, they've well and truly gone off the rails. I'll be accused of virtually selling myself.'

'So, explain. Tell her how you and Cam began to email. That it started off as just another mail-order transaction, but then it grew as the months went by. If you think about it, it's almost the same thing as meeting someone through work, and she can't argue with that, surely?'

'And all she'll do is point out the horrors of conversing with someone you haven't met. She'll tell me all the horror stories about young girls who thought they were chatting with someone their own age, who then turned out to be some predatory pervert. She'll say he's pretending to be something he's not.'

'But you have met him. And he didn't turn out to be anything other than lovely. Cam's everything you expected him to be.'

I give her a long look. 'Gwen, you don't know that, you've never even met him.'

Gwen puts on her best no-nonsense face. 'No, but I know you, Abby Prendergast, and you don't give your heart away to just anyone. If you think he's special, then that's what I think too.'

I sigh. 'Is it that obvious?'

She raises her eyebrows. 'What? That you're totally and utterly besotted? Yes, it is. But that's not a bad thing. In fact, isn't that the whole idea? Abby, forgive me, but this all sounds far too much like you're making excuses. Come on, tell me. What's the real reason you don't want your mum to know about Cam? Because I know there is one, even if you don't want to acknowledge it.'

Gwen has known me for too long for me to try to evade her question. She'll know instantly if I'm not telling her the whole story. And she's right, my reticence is partly because I don't want to admit to something myself. I rustle up a smile. One that lets her know I've been rumbled.

'Okay, Miss Marple, there is something, just as you suspected, and I'm still giving myself a hard time over it. I know I should want to tell Mum, because even though she drives me up the wall on an almost daily basis, she's also my mum and I love her very much. But the truth of it is that I'm having a hard time admitting to myself how special Cam is to me, and I can't bear the thought of anything changing that. I don't want to hear my mum's concerns or criticisms, or have her tell me that it's a relationship doomed to failure because we live several hundred miles apart. I know all that. I just don't want to hear it from someone else as well.'

'Oh, Abby.' Gwen's face is full of contrition. 'I know it's human nature to do it, but don't think about the end when it's only just beginning. Cam hasn't given you any reason to think that, has he?'

'No...' I trail off, thinking about his words. Words that I've hugged to me every night since. 'Quite the reverse.'

'Well, then. And you're both adults, not lovesick teenagers. You both know the score. Besides, it wasn't as if either of you set out for this to happen. It's simply one of those lovely serendipitous things that comes along every now and again. That's *why* it's so lovely, because it's grown out of nothing, no agenda, no anticipation of what might happen, a friendship that grew, and didn't stop growing. Isn't that just the way it should be in an ideal world?'

'I suppose. But it's not only the whole distance thing that complicates this, is it? There's Beth too.'

'Ah...' Gwen stops, clearly thinking. 'Abby, please tell me you're not still feeling guilty that her dad isn't on the scene? It was a toxic relationship that you had to free yourself from so don't you go thinking it would have been better if you'd stayed with him. Never mind what your mother says.'

I shake my head. 'No, I don't think that. I'd rather be a single mum forever than be with someone just to give Beth a father figure in her life. But I'd also be deluding myself if I didn't acknowledge that I'd like nothing more than to be a proper family.'

'You are a proper family, Abby.'

I smile at the admonishment in Gwen's voice. She's always been my biggest champion as far as my relationship with Beth goes. 'I know that,' I say warmly, thinking of my daughter. 'But I also know that deep down, Beth would like a dad too. It's hard enough being eleven, without being different from her friends at school.'

'And that brings added pressure to any romantic encounters you may have, yes, I get that. But I thought you said Beth got on really well with Cam.'

'She did. In fact, I can't believe how quickly she took to him. You know how wary she normally is around people she doesn't know but—' I break off as a trilling noise sounds from my back pocket. I ignore it. 'But in a way that makes it harder, because if things don't turn out the way I want them to, it isn't just me who's going to feel it.'

Gwen rubs my arm. 'But that's always going to be the case, Abby, you know that. And you do everything you can to consider Beth. You don't have a string of one-night stands or parade a succession of men through the flat, but at some point you have to start thinking about what you want for *your* future. Don't let fears for Beth put you off taking the risk on a relationship that could turn out wonderfully.'

'You're such a good friend, Gwen,' I reply, smiling. 'What would I do without you?'

She rolls her eyes. 'I'm only telling you things you already know, so none of that. Besides, I've been married for ten years, your love life is the only excitement I get.'

'That's not true.'

She blushes then, not something she does often. 'I know… I'm just trying to make you feel better.' She points to the pocket in my jeans. 'Speaking of which, aren't you going to look at that?'

'What?'

'The email that just arrived from Cam. Don't think I don't know he has his own ringtone.'

'You weren't supposed to know about that,' I reply, screwing up my face.

She waggles her finger in my face. 'Aha! Not as discreet as you thought you were, are you?' But she grins. 'Go on then, read it.'

She waits while I pull my phone from my pocket and quickly scan Cam's latest message.

'See? Look at you. You only have to read his reply and you have the biggest smile on your face. Hug that to you, and see where it goes, Abby. It could be the most perfect place you've ever been.'

She walks back behind the counter and stuffs a Jaffa Cake in her mouth, whole. 'Right then, missus, Christmas window. Me, the books, you, the decorations. Come on.'

I grin. 'Yes, boss.'

And strangely enough, I've found myself right back in a Christmassy mood.

Dear Abby,

Make sure you hold that tiller steady, I don't want you or Beth falling overboard!

The weather here today is… wait for it… raining. But it does make me glad I was born with webbed feet. We all have them up here, they come in very handy. That's a joke, by the way, in case you're wondering. My feet are lovely as it happens, very… functional.

Gin's feet however are very big, very hairy and extremely muddy right now. I swear that dog seeks out every puddle there is and delights in sloshing through them. Is that a spaniel thing do you think, or do I just have the most scatter-brained dog on the island? Our climate here is described as temperate, which really means that it rains nine days out of ten, but it's still beautiful, Abby. The beach was pale silver and gold when we walked this morning. The rain hadn't come in yet and a weak slanting sun glinted across the ripples of sand, and the pools of water. Even days like this still take my breath away.

And yes, I am still speaking to Alfie, but only because I made him promise to help man the bar on Christmas Eve so that his sister can do all her baking. And that is definitely something that needs to happen, Fiona's Christmas spreads are legend. Maybe next year you'll be able to taste them for yourself!

I love Christmas here. Mainly because it goes on for weeks, but perhaps because when you have to make your own entertainment you get pretty good at it. In fact, you spend as much time in everyone else's houses as you do your own, but it's always been that way. People come and go and that's part of it, like one big happy family. It can get a bit much if you're hungover, especially if my dad throws another of his whisky specials, but then at least you have some fellow sufferers to sympathise with.

Tell me about your Christmas, Abigail Prendergast. I want to know all the details. I bet you're a sucker for a string of fairy lights or two? I can just picture you, all tucked up in your little shop, like a shining beacon of light against the dark...

Chapter 5

December

Today, the office is bristling with anticipation, tempered with patience and goodwill to all men.

'Come on, Beth, get your shoes on, we'll be late otherwise.'

She lifts her head from the book she has her nose stuck in. 'Late?' she says. 'How can we be late? The shops have been open all day.' She's sitting at the kitchen table, where she's been ever since we ate tea.

I throw her a look. 'Figure of speech,' I say. 'You know what I mean. And your book will still be here when you get back. The sooner we go, the sooner we'll be finished.'

She closes the cover slowly, sighing, but gets to her feet. 'And you promise we can have a hot chocolate from Rumer's?'

'I promise.'

I watch as she fetches her Converse from the cupboard and brings them back to the chair so she can put them on. There's just time enough to take one last look at my emails before she's ready. Cam often emails around about now. But there's still nothing.

Moments later we're descending the stairs into the shop, where Gwen is holding the fort until I get back. There are already customers milling around and I really hope they want to shop, not just soak up the bonhomie and the chance of snaffling a seasonal treat. Gwen's bright-red outfit is suitably festive and perfect with her colouring. She manages to look both jolly and siren-like at the same time.

'We'll be about an hour, Gwen, if that's okay.' I purse my lips. 'Maybe an hour and a half, but message me if you get inundated.'

'Go,' she replies, making wafting movements with her hands. 'Go and enjoy yourselves, I'll be fine. And if it gets busy and folks get impatient, I shall ply them with mulled wine and chocolates.' She checks her watch. 'I'll start warming it, just in case.'

The street outside is already busy, thronged with shoppers, many of whom are clutching bulging shopping bags. Lights twinkle from every shop window and coloured lanterns criss-cross the streets. It's a beautifully cold and clear night, and a little whirl of happiness dances inside of me.

'Shall we see about Granny's present first?' I ask Beth as we make our way down into the main shopping area. 'There's that lovely shop along by the church I wanted to look in. The one that sells recycled cashmere.'

But Beth isn't really listening, she's caught in wonder at the lights and decorations in the square. She turns her attention back to me. 'I suppose. But aren't gloves and stuff a bit boring?'

'These ones aren't. We'll have a look. If they are then we'll decide on something else.'

'Okay, and what about Grandpops? Can I buy some of those toffees he likes?'

I nod. 'It wouldn't be Christmas without them,' I reply, smiling. They've been Beth's gift to her grandfather from the moment she was able to make choices over such things.

She walks beside me for a moment, winding her scarf tighter around her neck. 'And what about Auntie Debra?' she asks. 'Is she having yet another stinky candle?'

I nudge her arm. 'Some of them aren't that bad,' I reply. My sister has a penchant for lighting scented candles in her home. And some of them are so pungent that it can take days for the smell to leave my nose after we've visited. 'Maybe…' I grin at her.

We cross the street and begin to cut across one edge of the market square, heading towards the church on the opposite corner. I'm about to step out into the road again when Beth pulls at my sleeve.

'Mum, wait a minute.' She directs my attention to the centre of the market square, where her gaze rests on a large group of people gathered beneath a huge sparkling tree. 'Is it the carol singing?' she asks.

I'm about to answer when the first bars of 'Silent Night' ring out, the brass band sounding rich and clear in the evening air. I automatically follow Beth towards it.

'Can we stay?' she asks. 'Not for all of it, just one or two carols.'

We shouldn't really. If I know Beth, one or two will turn into three or four and before you know it, half an hour will have passed, with not a present bought. And I promised Gwen I wouldn't be late. But I can't pass up the opportunity either; hearing Beth sing, especially at Christmas, is a gift all of its own.

We shuffle closer until we're as much a part of the crowd as anyone else. And now that we're nearer, I can see that the choir from St Luke's School are here too. A teeny bloom of guilt flowers deep inside me. I would have loved for Beth to go there instead of the local comprehensive, but the fees were way beyond my means.

The brass band are reaching the end of their introduction and a second later the air is filled with a single lone voice, its tone pure and sweet as it rises, soaring into the night sky. After a few bars the rest of the choir join in and a lump automatically forms in my throat. It's such a beautiful evocation of the season.

The first verse is coming to an end and, to my surprise, as the second starts, the audience begins to sing along, directed by some unseeing hand at the front. Beth starts softly at first, waiting until the people around us catch on and lend their voices and it's there, in the swelling sound, that she finds her confidence. She doesn't show off, her voice is no louder than anyone else's, but she doesn't need to; the hauntingly beautiful notes she sings are all she needs.

She turns to check I'm behind her, happiness and excitement glowing on her face. This is where Beth truly shines, it always has been. I lay a hand on her head to tousle her hair, catching the eye of a woman across from us as I do so. She's a mother too, I can see it in the warm smile she gives me, the understanding of the pride I'm feeling, and why. She nods, just a fraction, but it's acknowledgement enough, and my heart swells even more.

I'd be quite happy to stand here until the singing ends but the pull of all that I need to do is becoming more urgent. Eventually, after the fourth song has ended, I tap Beth softly on the back. She turns, cheeks rosy and eyes bright and, with a reluctant look of longing, she moves with me away from the crowd.

'Sorry, sweetheart,' I say. 'I'd forgotten this was on today or I could have arranged things with Gwen so that we could stay for the whole thing.'

'It's okay,' she says. 'But it was lovely though, wasn't it?'

'Beautiful…' I reply, trailing off. 'You know, you should have auditioned for the end-of-term concert,' I say lightly. 'You'd have knocked spots off everyone else.' The concert isn't for a couple of weeks yet, held in the last week before the school breaks for Christmas.

Beth's smile fades a little.

'There wasn't any point,' she says. 'The Year Sevens never get a part.'

'Well, there has to be a first time for everything. Maybe if they'd heard you sing, they'd have broken with tradition.'

I could wither under the stare Beth gives me.

'They wouldn't, because everyone knows that Emily Robinson and her gang always get picked. And you don't mess with them unless you want your life making a misery.' She slips her arm through mine. 'Come on, let's go and see about Granny's gloves.'

But despite Beth's attempt at changing the subject and putting a brave face on things, I know how disappointed she is. It's her first year at secondary school and she had such hopes of the opportunities it would bring her. Sadly, though, a large part of the term has been about discovering that she's no longer the big fish in a small pond, as she was in her last year at primary, and instead is now a very small fish in a very big pond. It's been a hard lesson to learn in many ways.

Once outside the shop, Beth rests her head against the shop window, where jewel-like coloured swathes of cashmere nestle against one another, decorated with pinecones and fake snow.

'I like those ones,' she says, tapping the window lower down in front of her. 'Don't you think the colours are lovely? I bet Cam would like them.'

'Cam?'

She turns. 'Well, you'll need to get him a present too, won't you? I didn't think this shop would have things for men as well.'

His name reverberates though my head. 'Oh, well, I hadn't really thought…' I have, I've done little else. 'I don't even know whether we're buying one another presents,' I add. That part, at least, is true.

'Why ever not? You've got to get him a present, Mum.'

'Yes, but if he doesn't get me one too, it could be a bit awkward.'

She turns away from the window to give me one of her looks, one that she perfected quite some time ago. The type which clearly states that adults are incredibly stupid sometimes. She could well be right.

'Well, why don't you ask him? Then you'd know, wouldn't you?'

'I have, but he hasn't answered yet.' My reply sticks slightly in my throat. After weeks of vacillation, I finally did just that. I can feel the weight of my phone inside my bag.

'Oh… When did you ask him?'

'The day before yesterday.' I'm trying really hard to keep my voice light.

She frowns and then rolls her eyes. 'He's probably forgotten. Men are good at that, and well known for being hopeless when it comes to Christmas presents.'

I smile at her eleven-year-old wisdom. Would that it were that easy. Cam hasn't just failed to answer my question, he hasn't replied to my email at all. 'I expect you're right,' I say.

She nods. 'Anyway, I still think you need to get him a present, whatever he says.'

'Okay, but I would imagine that living where he does, Cam has lots of pairs of gloves.'

'Yes, but those aren't gloves, they're wrist warmers. Don't you remember him saying that he gets very cold hands when he's reading. I bet those would help.'

I focus on the object of Beth's attention. Hues of heathery blues and green, velvety soft.

'Let's go and have a look inside,' I say.

*

We make it back to the bookshop within seconds of our allotted timeframe. Beth takes one look at the number of people inside and automatically holds out her hands to take my bags, while I slip off my coat. Threading our way through to the rear of the shop, I flash Gwen a smile before dumping my things in the small cloakroom that sits next to the kitchen.

'Thanks, sweetheart, I won't be long,' I say, kissing Beth's forehead at the foot of the stairs. She'll be okay, it's a routine she's well used to. By the time Gwen and I have said goodbye to the last of the shoppers and I've closed the front door against the night, Beth will be tucked up in our sitting room, swaddled in a blanket, with her head back in her book.

A tray filled with small glasses sits on the end of the counter. All are empty and redolent of the mulled wine they once held. In fact, the whole shop smells of spiced fruit. I carry them back though to wash up later before returning to relieve Gwen.

'Has it been like this the whole time?' I ask, smiling at a man who walks past the desk with a bundle of books under his arm.

'Pretty much,' she replies. 'But mostly browsers, sadly. A few folk looking for something to read themselves, but one or two more gifty type things have gone. The rather lovely A.E. Housman edition, the signed Ben Aaronovitch as well.'

I nod. 'I was hoping that would go.' I check my watch. 'Thanks ever so much, Gwen. You get going now, though, I can carry on from here.' I grin at her. 'Besides, you've done all the hard work.'

She dips her hand into the tub of Quality Street that also sits on the counter and pulls out an orange octagon. 'Sustenance,' she replies. 'I've still got Ellen's two to buy for, and toy shops at this time of year are not my idea of fun.'

I give Gwen a warm smile that acknowledges the bittersweet task ahead of her. She and her husband are still childless despite several years of trying.

She unwraps the sweet and shoves it in her mouth. 'I'll grab my coat.'

I take out my phone from my back pocket and wait until the screen automatically lights up. There are no new notifications. And it's nearly eight o'clock – Cam doesn't normally email after about half eight, the last two hours of the evening are usually when he reads. The day is almost over.

I open up my email app anyway. Every now and again my phone does a weird thing where it stops sending notifications. That'll be it, it's happened before. I wait as the program connects, checking for new messages, and my heart skips a little as I see one drop into my inbox.

'Is everything okay?' asks Gwen, slipping her arms inside her coat. She peers at me.

'Yes, fine,' I reply. 'I just thought it was Cam, that's all. But instead an email from the Inland Revenue help desk, reminding me of the numerous wonderful webinars they produce.' I pull a face. 'It doesn't have quite the same appeal as an email from Cam.'

I smile, but Gwen's hands remain on her hips. Her eyes are slightly narrowed and she's giving me the look that I've never been able to avoid. The one that sees right through me.

'Don't pass it off, Abby,' she says. 'I know you're trying to make light of it, but when did you last hear from him?'

I bite my lip. 'On Monday… and I know that's only two days ago, which is nothing really, but—'

'It's unusual for him.'

I nod. 'I've got used to it, that's all. I expect he's just busy.'

'He might be, but then I guess even when *you're* busy, which is pretty much all the time, you still find the time to email him. And I would imagine he's the same. It's more likely that they've lost their internet or something. Maybe a storm blew in and knocked everything out. When you live on a remote Hebridean island that probably happens all the time.'

'Yes, I bet you're right. That must be it.'

Except that in all the months we've been in contact I can't recall that ever happening before.

'What other reason could it be, Abby?' She pauses a moment. 'What? You think he's suddenly gone off you?'

My gaze lowers to the floor.

'Abby, that's daft, that's—'

'Why is it?' I counter. 'Maybe I got it wrong, Gwen. Perhaps he's been having a think about things and has decided there's no future in it. We live nearly five hundred miles apart, for goodness' sake. And besides…' I trail off, not wanting to sound even more pathetic.

Gwen's eyes search my face. 'Oh, I get it. You don't believe he could possibly be interested in you. Not really.'

'It's as valid a reason as any,' I reply. 'He might live on an island, Gwen, but I'm sure there are women there too. Why pick me?'

'Well now, let me see. You're gorgeous, you're funny, intelligent, articulate, weird – in a good way – and a damn fine human being to boot. What's not to love?'

I blush. 'I know you're only trying to make me feel better, but I'm serious, Gwen. Our relationship has been based on emails and one short visit. We know virtually nothing about each other, not really, and if you wanted to end something… maybe something that perhaps should never have started in the first place, wouldn't it be easier to stop emailing?'

She shakes her head. 'For some people maybe, but not Cam. He's not like that, Abby, and you know it. Admittedly, everything *I* know about him has come from you, but I can't believe he would treat you that way. You're seeing shadows where there are none, and I bet if you got in touch some other way, you'd find out that there's a very simple explanation.'

'But that's just it, I'm not sure I can get in touch with him. I don't think I have anything other than his email address, which is stupid, but—'

'Doesn't he have a mobile?'

'No. I know it seems weird, but he says he doesn't need one. Either the signal's rubbish or it's quicker to go and talk to someone. It's a small place. I can't imagine how different their life must be from here.' I frown. 'I might have a phone number from one of his very first emails. I could check.'

'What about his friend?' Gwen wiggles her fingers. 'I can't remember his name.'

'Alfie,' I supply. 'But I don't even know his last name.'

Gwen buttons up her coat. 'I'm sure you'll find something. Do it when you finish here, okay?'

I nod.

'No, promise. Put yourself out of your misery. It's silly worrying about it like this when it will be something of nothing.'

'I will, I promise.' I smile at her. 'Go on, go, otherwise there will be no time left. I'll see you tomorrow… Oh, and Gwen?' I point to the red Santa hat that still sits on her head.

She rolls her eyes and grins, pulling it off and stuffing it under the counter. 'What am I like?'

My heart is in my mouth as I turn the key in the front-door lock some while later. I've been kept relatively busy but that hasn't stopped me checking my messages every ten minutes or so. But it's okay, by the time I've locked up properly and got back upstairs he'll have emailed.

Except he hasn't.

Well then, by the time I've made myself a cup of tea, he'll have messaged.

Except he doesn't.

By the time I… I growl with frustration at myself. For goodness' sake, Abby, stop it. Stop making these stupid deals with yourself. He isn't going to email and you're going to have to do what you promised Gwen you would. Find out what's happened and set your mind at rest instead of driving yourself nuts.

I check on Beth, but she's exactly where I thought she'd be, so I take my tea through to the office. Just this morning it had been bristling with anticipation. But when I'd written that message, I had meant the office was waiting expectantly for the hopefully numerous sales that would be made during the day, not a day of anxious waiting for Cam to reply. And now my email seems tinged with some strange foreboding.

As soon as the PC boots up, I head online to check the weather but, although Cam's little corner of the world appears cold, there's no sign of storms or anything out of the ordinary. Nothing that could have knocked out their means of communicating with the wider world.

I sip my tea and open my email programme. I don't want to look. Because I know in my heart of hearts that there won't be a new message there. And to look will only provide me with confirmation that for some reason, Cam has decided that whatever it was we've had this past year should end. He's probably right; it was silly to think that anything could come of it. But he's the first thing I think of when I wake in the morning, and his face the last I see before sleep claims me at night. I don't want it to be over.

Deep breath, Abby, come on, don't be daft. Search for his landline number. Just do it and get it over with. I stare at the screen, at the folder in my inbox where all Cam's emails sit. One I keep just for him. I open it up and slide the scroll bar all the way to the bottom, to that very first email. And I smile, I can't help it. I've read it so many times, but it still brings a warm memory of the day I opened it; a Thursday in the middle of January, cold, dispirited, with thoughts of a long winter ahead now that the excitement of Christmas was over. And for a moment a little spark of something had ignited and transformed the day, the year.

There's no number on that first message. I hadn't thought there was, but on the third, a few weeks later, one appeared. And without stopping to think any more, I pick up my phone and dial it. It takes a moment for the call to connect and I picture it as a shining line in the dark, whizzing its way through the skies to reach him. But all it does is ring out, over and over.

I hold out my phone, disconnecting the call, the shining line I'd imagined falling away in a shower of winking stars, like the tail end of a firework. Think, Abby, think. There must be some other way to contact him.

And then it comes to me. Alfie, Cam's friend, whose sister and her husband run the local hotel. I have no idea what it's called, but there can't be many on the island. And if I have to, I'll call every one. I check my watch again. It's still early enough, and it might be a weekday, but they'll be open, surely? I navigate back to the internet and type in my search. There are holiday cottages, a few B&Bs, but only one hotel.

It takes an age for the call to connect and when it does, the voice that answers sounds hollow, as if coming from somewhere deep inside the earth. And I can hardly hear it against the background of other noise that surrounds it.

'Hi… I'm sorry, I wondered if I might speak to Alfie, if he's there?'

There's a long pause. 'Alfie? No, he's over at Morag's, with the rest of them.'

'Oh…' I have no idea what this means. I try again. 'Sorry, this might be a bit of an odd request, you see I don't really know Alfie, I'm phoning from rather a long way away, but I know of him, through his friend, Cam, and it's Cam I'm trying to reach, actually. I have his number but it's just ringing out and—'

I break off as a weird sound travels down the line, like a breath cut short, a faint click breaking it in two.

'Who is this, please?'

'My name's Abby. I'm a friend, and—'

'Oh, lass… I'm sorry…' I listen for a moment more, letting the words wash over me before I realise that the line is now silent.

'I see,' I say quietly. 'Thank you for letting me know.'

Chapter 6

Christmas Day

It's always odd waking up in a strange bed, but when it's the bed you slept in as a child, in the room that used to be yours, it's even weirder. And I could really do with today not being weird. Christmas Day isn't going to be the way I had thought it would be at all.

Across the hall, Beth will still be sleeping, the stocking that she's had since she was little nestling at the foot of her bed. She's always been a good sleeper. When she was younger, I used to feel quite smug when I heard tell of harassed mums whose children were up at four in the morning. I never had such issues. Even at Christmas, Beth would wake around six thirty at the earliest, and would trail her stocking across the floor and creep into my bed, where she would snuggle against me and open her presents from Santa. Now, it's only ten past four and more than anything, I wish Beth were tucked into the crook of my arm. Then I wouldn't feel so alone.

I turn over and stare at the glowing green numbers on the clock beside my bed. In six hours, my sister, Debra, and her husband, Ian, will arrive with their two overexcited children, a carload of presents, and the day will officially begin. From then on in it will be noisy, chaotic and exhausting, but full of laughter and love too. And I would usually enjoy every second of it. Today, though, someone else will be taking my place. A walking, talking version of me, but not me, I can't seem to find her any more.

Another tear has slid down my cheek. They seem to do that almost without me noticing at the moment, and I reach up to wipe it away. I can be reading, or cooking tea, not really aware that I'm even thinking about Cam, but the fall of a tear reminds me that he's never far from my mind. I sit up and reach for my book, turning resolutely to the chapter I was in the middle of reading, and thrust all other thoughts from my mind. I vowed that today there would be no more tears and I'm determined to keep my promise.

When I come to, a warm body is curled next to mine, almost falling off the edge of the single bed. The hands on the clock have crept forward and it's now just gone six. I wriggle to the far side, feeling Beth automatically take up the extra room this provides. How I'm feeling is tough on her too. How can I tell her why I'm so upset when it's been such a surprise to me as well?

'Happy Christmas, sweetheart,' I murmur, touching my lips to the top of her head. I feel her stir, her limbs soft and warm against mine.

'Hey, Mum,' she says, her voice sleep-laden. 'We don't have to get up yet, do we?'

'No, not for a bit. Go back to sleep.'

She snuggles deeper and within seconds I hear her breathing regain its rhythm of before.

And I close my eyes too, trying to focus on the day ahead.

*

'Hi, Abby, how are you doing, love?'

I pause to check the bedroom door is closed and smile at the sound of my friend's voice. 'Gwen, what are you doing ringing me? Get back to your family this instant. And I'm fine.'

'What? I can't ring a friend on Christmas morning any more? Besides, everyone's in the kitchen already getting sloshed and as I need to stay sober to cook the turkey, I thought what better way to excuse myself than to ring you.' She stops as a loud shout echoes in the background. 'And is that fine-fine? Or fine as in that pretend thing we all do when anyone asks?'

'You're not anyone,' I reply. 'And I'm okay, Gwen, honestly. It's going to be tough, but everyone's here and we're going to have a lovely day. Anyway, I probably won't have a minute to myself to think, you know how energetic Debra's boys are.'

'That's true.' I can hear her smiling down the line, probably recalling my tales of past Christmases. 'But I hope you know that you can ring me, if it all gets too much.'

'Gwen,' I say firmly. 'You are not to spend your day worrying about me, I'll be perfectly all right. It's silly feeling like this anyway and...' I break off, I don't think I can say any more.

'Telling yourself how to feel doesn't work, Abby, you know that. How you feel is how you feel. Have you thought any more about getting in touch with his friend?'

'No.' My reply is instant. 'In that I have thought about it and decided not to. I think it's best if I just get on with things. Really. It was... well, whatever it was we had was wonderful while it lasted, but it obviously wasn't meant to be. I have to move on, Gwen. Getting upset isn't helping anyone – me or Beth.'

'She'll be okay, Abby.'

'I know. But it's Christmas, that's what's important right now. And after that, life will go back to being the way it was before. And that's okay, that's—' There's an explosion of noise from downstairs. 'Listen, Gwen, I've got to go. It sounds like Debra's arrived.'

'Yes, go on, you go. And have a wonderful day, Abby. Take care, honey.'

'You too, Gwen. Happy Christmas. And thanks, for everything.'

I end the call and get to my feet, smoothing down the cover on the bed where I've been sitting. I tuck my hair behind my ears, checking in the mirror that my face looks okay. The reflection that stares back at me looks a little pale, but otherwise? I pinch my cheeks a little, opening my eyes and mouth as wide as they can go to inject some life back into them. Then I pull open the bedroom door.

'Right then,' I call down the stairs. 'Where're my two favourite boys? Come here, I need a big Christmas squish!'

The carpet has almost disappeared under a sea of wrapping paper, ribbon and discarded packaging, but there are also lots of happy faces around me, replete, and relieved that another Christmas has been a success.

I'm sitting on the sofa, squidged between my mum on one side and Ian on the other.

Beth is cross-legged on the floor in her customary spot in front of the Christmas tree. She's chief disher-out-of-presents, a job that she loves. It makes me even more proud that she enjoys watching everyone else open their presents as much as receiving them herself. As I watch, she turns and wriggles onto her belly to peer underneath the bottom-most branches. She takes a moment to check the tags on the presents there and withdraws empty-handed.

'Mum, where's your present from Cam? I can't see it, but there's nothing else left for you, sorry.'

I look up, startled by his name, here, where it has no right to be. I smile at Beth. 'I left it at home, sweetheart. I can open it another time. Besides, I've had so many presents already.' There's no way I could unwrap it here, in front of everyone. In front of people who have no idea who Cam is.

The postman had caught me unawares three days before Christmas. I had stared at the brown-paper parcel, addressed in a bright-red pen with a little sprig of holly hand-drawn onto the paper beside my name, the last thing I'd expected to receive.

I don't want to open it because inside is the last little bit of you. And once I do, you'll be gone forever. It's the thread that binds us.

Beth darts an apologetic look at me, as if suddenly realising the effect her question would have. She hastily pulls forward another gift; there's not many left now.

'Grandma, this one's for you,' she says, handing over a small oblong present, wrapped in cheerful paper adorned with robins. It's the one Beth and I bought together, from the little shop beside the church; the one where we bought Cam's present too. I turn my head away slightly.

I'd tried so hard to leave thoughts of you at home, but I can't, you're with me everywhere.

'It's from Mum,' Beth adds. 'Although I picked out the colour.' She watches, wiggling with excitement as my mother begins to tease off the paper. As the last fold is undone, the soft bundle falls into her lap.

'Do you like them?' Beth asks, her face expectant. 'Because there were so many different ones, it was really hard to choose.'

My mother picks up the gloves to examine them. Quite probably the twentieth pair of gloves she's received over the years, but she nods and smiles, first in Beth's direction and then in mine. 'And cashmere too,' she says. 'They're beautifully soft, thank you. And such a lovely colour.' Beth nods in delight, already peering back under the tree, her latest present-giving duty discharged.

'Who's Cam?'

I might have known I wouldn't get away with it. I swear my mum's prospective relationship antennae are permanently engaged when it comes to me. But she could at least have asked her question quietly, not loud enough for the whole family to hear. My sister is already glancing up from where she's attempting to wrestle some batteries into the remote controller for one of her boys' new cars.

'Cam?' I reply. 'Oh, just a friend.' I focus my attention back on Beth.

'A boyfriend? Cam? Is that short for something?'

I nod. 'Hmm, Cameron. He's Scottish.' I lean forward to touch the next present that Beth has pulled from under the tree. 'Oh, Debra, this one's for you.'

But my mum is not so easily pacified.

'So how come we don't know anything about this Cam person?' she asks, giving me a searching look. 'You've kept that very quiet.'

'Mum, there's nothing much to tell. He's a friend, that's all.'

'Oh, I see…' She gives Debra a knowing look. 'Is that why you didn't want to come to the theatre with Patrick?'

Beth looks mortified. I can feel her looking at me, squirming because she never intended her comment to attract so much attention. I need to end this conversation, and fast.

'Yes, it is,' I reply. 'But I don't want to talk about it here, Mum, now's not the time. Come on, Deb, open your present.' I turn my head away from my mother's relentless gaze, eyes pleading with my sister to change the subject.

She lifts the brightly wrapped box to her ear and gives it an experimental shake, then sniffs it. 'Oh, is this what I think it is?'

'Give us a little hint,' adds Mum. 'At least tell us if it's serious.'

'No, it's not serious,' I state. 'I hope you like it, Deb.' She's already got half the wrapping off.

'Oh… Don't tell me you've already frightened him off.'

A look of panic comes over Debra's face. My dad sits forward.

'Annabel,' he says. A warning.

'No, I haven't frightened him off, Mum. He's dead, if you must know. He died two weeks ago.'

A yawning cavern of silence opens up. And just when I'm wondering if the sides are so steep, none of us will ever be able to climb out, one of Debra's boys, Scott, sneezes, and a big thick bubble of snot is left dangling from his nose.

'Urgh, that's disgusting,' shouts Rory, his brother.

And suddenly everyone moves. Ian jumps up to fish a hankie from his pocket, Rory snatches up his toy and moves it further away from the threat of bogeys, and Debra rips off the rest of the wrapping from her present and wrestles open the lid of the box within.

'Oh, that is *gorgeous*!' she declares, holding the candle she discovers under her nose and inhaling deeply. 'Ian, smell this, isn't that lovely?'

Her husband nods in agreement, still mopping up his son's sneeze. Whether he can actually smell it or not is irrelevant.

'Ooh, let's see,' says Mum, flicking a glance at me I'm not supposed to see. She follows Deb's overly dramatic sniffing and proclaims the candle to be one of the nicest she's ever smelled.

Emergency over. Everyone as you were.

I smile at Beth, trusting she can see the reassurance in my eyes. 'I think you can fish out the next pressie now,' I say. 'It's Grandpops next.'

*

'Have you had a nice day, sweetheart?' I ask.

We're back at home now, sitting curled up on either end of the sofa, our toes wriggling against each other with a blanket thrown over our knees. It's my favourite time of the day, just Beth and I, reading, accompanied by the restful tick of the clock. The lights twinkle on the tree, the street below us is silent and on the little table in front of us is an empty mug of hot chocolate and a glass of Baileys.

She looks up and smiles. 'I have…' She trails off and I know what's coming next. She's just like me. 'But it's even better to be home. Granny's house is a bit loud at Christmas, with everyone there.' There's a sheepish grin. 'And there's nowhere quiet to sit either.'

'And what's the point of getting loads of books for Christmas if you can't start reading them?'

'*Exactly.*' She swings her legs down and slides over so that she's sitting next to me. 'How 'bout you, Mum?'

I put my arm around her and bring her closer. 'I still feel full up,' I reply, patting my stomach. 'Granny likes us to eat well, doesn't she? But yes, it's been a nice day.' I drop my head against hers. 'And thank you for my present too,' I add. 'Inspired.'

She looks at the book resting in my lap. 'Do you like it? I wasn't sure if you would want something you already knew.'

'Ah, but that's the beauty of Miss Read; it's like coming home to an old friend, especially at Christmas. I love it. And this is a lovely edition, too. I hope you didn't use up all the pocket money you'd saved.'

She gives me a sheepish look. 'Granny lent me a little bit,' she says. 'But I'm not supposed to tell you.'

She's silent for a moment, her fingers twiddling with the label on the edge of the blanket. 'I'm sorry about mentioning Cam,' she says, quietly, a little wobble in her voice.

'You don't have to be,' I reply, slipping my fingers into hers. 'You didn't do anything wrong, Beth.'

'No?' Her eyes are full of doubt. 'But it was awful, the way everyone wanted to know about him. I just wanted...' Her voice fades away. 'I thought you were thinking about him, you see, and that it might be nice if you opened his present.'

'Which was a lovely thought. And you were right, I was thinking about him.' I squeeze her hand. 'But I wasn't really in the mood to tell everyone about him, not when he isn't here any more. Does that make sense?'

She nods.

'And you mustn't mind Granny, she wants to see me happy, that's all, and she thinks that means married off, or with a boyfriend at least.'

Beth looks up at me, a tiny frown wrinkling her smooth forehead.

'I liked Cam,' she says, hesitant.

'I liked Cam too, sweetheart,' I reply, flicking her nose gently. 'I really liked him, but it wasn't meant to be, that's all. And I'm not about to go looking for anyone else to replace him. Why would I want to, when I have you? We're perfect as we are, just the two of us.'

She snuggles back up, and we sit for a few moments more before, as I knew she would, Beth reaches for her book.

'I might go to bed now,' she says, 'and read for a little bit longer.'

'Not too long,' I reply. 'I don't think I'll be far behind you. I'm tired too.'

She pushes herself up from the sofa and leans down for a hug. 'Night, Mum, happy Christmas.'

'Happy Christmas, sweetheart.'

I watch as she leaves, leaning forward to pick up my glass and drain the last mouthful of liquid from it. The liqueur blazes a trail down into my stomach. And then I sit back, staring at the window and the silent street outside; shops mostly, but flats too, just like this one, countless other families enjoying countless other Christmases. I place my glass down on the table as my phone buzzes with a message. My heart sinks a little when I see the words written on the screen.

Are you okay?

It's from Deb. I know she's mainly asked out of concern for how awkward things had been earlier in the day, but also because, like for everyone else in my family, the mention of Cam had been a complete surprise. So, it's also a request for information, and I don't think I can do that just now.

I stare at my laptop on the seat of the chair opposite me. There's only one person I want to talk to. I pull it closer to me, running my hand across the lid. This is crazy. But, apart from anything else, Cam's emails to me were a comfort, a warmth that surrounded me every day, and absolutely what I need right now.

I lift the lid and settle it on my lap.

You're going to think I'm nuts… Maybe you already do, I don't know. And now, I can't ask you. But neither can I stop talking to you. There's still so much left to say.

But, in a way, maybe you are still there. Because I can't see how you could possibly have ended. You were always so full of life – so where did that go? Where did you go? How can all that energy, the spark you carried inside of you not be there any more? It doesn't make sense. Admittedly, I never paid much attention in physics when I was younger, but even I know that energy can't disappear, neither can matter. It can change form, become something else, but not end altogether. So that's what I've decided; that maybe you're now part of the table leg in my kitchen, or the books on my shelves, who knows, but I reckon you're around somewhere, you have to be. So I think I'm going to carry on writing to you, if that's okay…

I pause for a moment to look at what I've written, almost fearful, as if somehow everyone will know what I'm doing, and I'll have to explain myself.

You see, the thing is, Cam… The thing that's most ridiculous, actually heartbreaking, about all of this, is that I never got the chance to tell you how I really felt (feel?) about you, and now you'll never know. It's silly really. I mean, how can you love someone you've only met once? And why is that so easy to say to you, when it's been so hard to say to anyone else in the past? That makes it sound as if there's been loads of other men (there hasn't), but something has always held me back. There was Beth's father, of course, and I wouldn't have married him if I didn't love him, but even that wasn't like this. And the few men that came after him were okay; they were nice, they treated me well, and there wasn't any specific reason why I ended it with any of them. Just that I knew they weren't right, that I would be settling for something that was so much less than I knew it could be. Does that make sense? But with you… It felt so absolutely more than I could ever have hoped for. And for some goddamn reason, I never told you. And I should have.

And now the thing that hurts the most is that I don't know how you died. And if whether knowing how much you were loved would have made it any better in those final moments. That isn't to say that there wouldn't have been other people you'd be thinking about, of course you would; your family, Alfie. But would it have helped, knowing that I love you? Would it have been a comfort?

Anyway, what I really wanted to say was just, Happy Christmas, Cam.

Love Abby xx

Chapter 7

February

Today, the office is channelling Eeyore; grey, gloomy, and without a doubt very much in need of a pot of honey.

'Oh dear God, is it ever going to stop raining?' Gwen heaves a sigh from where she's standing beside the shop's front door, hands on her hips, surveying the water running down the street outside. There's not a customer in sight. 'I could make another cup of tea,' she offers.

I groan. 'I'm awash as it is. Sorry, you have one if you want.'

She pulls a face. 'I don't, it's just… so *miserable.* But I need something to do, and if we don't have any customers soon, I'm going to have to get the duster out.'

'You and me both,' I reply. 'And for goodness' sake, whatever you do, don't suggest a cake from Rumer's. My willpower is at an all-time low and I will bite your hand off, as well as the cake.' I come out from behind the counter. 'Even Mr Ridley hasn't been by this morning.' I stare at her in horror. 'Oh… you do suppose he's all right?'

She smiles. 'He's fine. I saw him coming out of Boots as I was on my way in. He grunted at me, as usual, so I would say he's probably displaying unparalleled good sense and staying inside.'

I look at the window as a thought comes to me. 'Seeing as even Bruce has eschewed his usual spot in the window for his cushion beside the radiator upstairs, why don't we avail ourselves of the opportunity and take the window apart?'

Gwen wrinkles her nose. 'But we only did it last week. Does it need changing?'

I think it was raining that day too.

'Well, it's a bit…'

'Shit?' Gwen grins at me.

'I was going to say lacklustre, but…' I stare at the street outside. 'I want the spring, Gwen, and it might be only February, but today, I think we should have it. There are snowdrops coming up in my pots on the roof terrace, and the other day I spotted daffodils in the churchyard. Only stalks, admittedly, but they're there.' My voice lifts as I warm to the idea.

I'll do anything to take my mind off the persistent drip of water in the bucket on the landing upstairs. Or the letter from Richard at the stationery shop. It might be a good idea to start an action group in case the council do go ahead with rates rises, but I can't bring myself to think about it today.

'Let's fetch everything growing and spring-like and hopeful that we can find and while we're at it, we can spring clean the window too. It hasn't had a good going over since before Christmas.'

Gwen's eyes light up. 'How about Cicely Mary Barker's books? That set we had in a couple of weeks ago is so beautiful. And the market had some potted primroses the other day. I'll even volunteer to go and buy some if you like.'

'Oh, yes… perfect! Take some money out of petty cash and I'll grab the cleaning stuff and start emptying the display while you're gone.'

I've always loved the windows here. Unchanged since I was a small child, we're one of the few shops along the street whose front hasn't been modernised. The mahogany surrounds are expensive to maintain, but nothing could ever look as good as they do with their beautifully finished boards, which line the inside of the bay and cover the whole of the display area. Polished up, they look amazing; rich and gleaming and, even though they show the dust a little more than painted boards would do, I wouldn't swap them for the world.

Removing all the books doesn't take long at all, and I pile them beside the till. Gwen has volunteered to rehome them on her return and a few minutes later, she deposits six primroses on the counter as well as a suspiciously familiar paper bag.

'Sustenance,' she says, peeling off her raincoat carefully to avoid dripping water all over the floor. 'In case we're in danger of fading away.' She holds up her hand. 'And before you say anything, I got the healthy ones.'

'Does Rumer sell anything healthy?' I ask. 'Because the last time I looked they were all cakes and pastries and muffins and…' I break off, catching Gwen's eye.

'They're date flapjacks. Perfectly healthy,' she replies with a grin. 'But if you'd rather not have one, then…'

'Eat mine and you're a dead woman,' I reply, climbing into the window.

It's all I seem to do at the moment – eat. The nights are the worst. Long hours when Beth is tucked up in bed and there's no one to talk to, my laptop silent beside me.

I frown at the pile of cat hair that has collected in the front corner of the window. It's always the same and I shouldn't allow Bruce to sit there, really, but he's one of the best advertising gimmicks I have. I'd have a dog if I could; Beth would absolutely love one. It's simply not possible living in the flat, but the curiosity that people hold for a shop cat never fails to amuse me. Imagine what they would think of a dog. I swear as many people stop to look at Bruce as they do the books in the window, but once there, it's amazing how many people find their eyes straying to something of interest. Many a sale has been made in this way. But Bruce's fur is insidious stuff; it gets everywhere, mostly up my nose.

Still, at least it isn't warm today. The expanse of glass heats up mercilessly on a hot day and it can feel like being in a sauna when you're changing the window display. It's also fairly ineffectual trying to clean the glass on days like that; the polish dries so fast that all you're left with, apart from a very red face, are a bunch of streaks and smears on the surface. Today, though, I give the glass several enthusiastic squirts of cleaner and pick up my cloth, stretching on tiptoes to reach the topmost parts.

I jump as Gwen puts a cold hand against the bare skin of my back. Joining me in the window, she takes hold of the bottom ribbing of my jumper and pulls gently downward.

'Good job it's quiet out there today,' she says. 'The books are not the only thing on display.'

I look down to see several inches of flesh showing in a strip above the top of my jeans. 'Now I know why no one is coming in,' I reply, stretching back up. 'I shall rely on you to preserve my modesty while I do these top bits,' I add. 'I'm nearly done.'

She waits until I've finished before picking up the can of wood polish and squirting a little onto the back boards of the window. We've done this so many times before, there's a rhythm and an order to it – window panes first, back boards next and lastly the 'seat' of the window itself. We don't begin to add books until it's all gleaming.

'You know, I was thinking,' says Gwen. 'Have we still got all the ribbon we used for that Easter competition a few years ago?'

I rub at a particularly stubborn streak. 'I think so, why?'

'I thought maybe we could use it. Hang streamers or make paper-chain-type things; the colours were so lovely it would really brighten up everything. We'd look like a splash of light in the dark.'

'Brilliant idea,' I say decisively. 'Although don't ask me where it is, in the storeroom somewhere, I think.' I stand back a little to survey my work. 'I like the thought of being light bringers.'

My phone emits a little trill from my back pocket. The sound is unexpected, curious. And it takes me a moment to work out what it means.

I lift my head, Gwen has heard it too.

She looks at me, confused. 'But how…?'

A bloom of heat hits my face. Followed by a wave of grief so fierce I have to put out a hand to steady myself.

'That's Cam's ringtone,' Gwen says, brow furrowed, checking if she's understood. 'For when a message…'

I nod silently. Stuck.

'But how can he have replied?' she asks, her voice barely there. Her eyes are wide as she looks at me, checking, wondering.

I swallow. Cam is dead, I remind myself. There's no way that this can be him. I push down the spark of hope that has flared amid the confusion of emotions. 'He hasn't,' I reply. 'It will be a mistake.'

She frowns.

'My phone does weird things sometimes. It doesn't mean anything. It's probably played the sound when it shouldn't have. I mean it's not like Cam can reply to any of my messages, is it? I know that.'

Her eyes lock with mine; shocked, compassionate, sad. And then, something else… Too late I realise what I've said.

I want to cry. To run away and not have to admit to what I've been doing. But Gwen is far too good a friend to ever let me get away with that. My eyes fill with tears.

'I've still been emailing him, okay?'

'Oh, Abby…' Warm words, her hand on my arm. Both of which send the tears spilling down my face.

I dash them away. 'I know! You don't have to tell me how stupid it is. But it makes me feel better.' I stare at the rain, running in rivulets down the window panes. 'I'd got so used to talking to him, telling him stuff. And I miss it, Gwen, I really miss it.'

She nods, a glimmer in her eyes.

'Sometimes it wasn't even so much what we said, more simply knowing that he was there. That there was someone to share things with. And that hasn't changed, Gwen. Every time I see something interesting or beautiful, or hear something funny, read something amazing, my first thought is that I must remember to tell Cam. It happens all the time and it's driving me nuts. It's such inconsequential stuff, mostly, and yet somehow it isn't, it's absolutely the stuff of life too. And I know I share things with you a lot of the time, and some of them with Beth as well, but there are some things that, well, only Cam would understand. Sorry,' I add.

But I can see that I don't have to explain, Gwen knows exactly what I mean.

She sniffs. 'How long?' she asks.

I drop my head. 'Since Christmas,' I reply. 'I needed to talk to him. There was still so much I had to say, it seemed the right thing to do. Then once I'd started, I couldn't stop because it would be like losing him all over again. Or him losing me…'

She holds out her arms and I slide between them, not caring that we're on display to anyone who passes by.

'Aren't you going to look at the message?' Gwen asks as she pulls away.

But I shake my head. 'No, I don't think I could bear it. I want it to be him so much, but it can't be, can it?'

Gwen is silent for a moment. She's still holding my arms and gives them both a brisk rub. 'I think you should though,' she says carefully. 'Only… What if his account has been hacked, Abby? That would be awful.'

I stare at her. That hadn't even occurred to me. And I suddenly can't bear the thought that someone else could have been rifling through Cam's account, our messages. I pull out my phone. The screen is lit with the first two words of the message.

Hi Abby… It says.

My name, in stark black letters against a pale-blue background.

Gwen nods at me. 'Read it,' she says. 'You have to.'

My heart is beating fast. Not a heavy thudding, but a light fluttery thing. Dancing? Or trying to fly free? I know it won't be a message from Cam. I know it deep inside and yet…

'I'll do it if you want,' Gwen adds. 'And if it's some crank, I'll delete it. You won't even have to see it.'

There's merit in what she suggests, but… Is it really that wrong to want to hang onto hope for as long as I can? *Don't be so stupid, Abby.*

And now my heart is in my throat, my voice no more than a breathy sound. I shake my head, a tiny movement as I press my thumb against the home button on my phone, then another touch to see my emails.

Hi Abby,

Sorry… I just wanted to say hi, that's all. A bit daft really but…

Anyway, hi, how are you doing?

I stare at the words on the screen. But they don't make any sense. I scroll, up and down, several times, but there's nothing else there, only my message, sent this morning. And the reply. No name, nothing.

'Who is it from?' asks Gwen, peering over at my hands.

'I have no idea. It's not signed.' I look up at her face, relief flooding through me. 'But at least I know his account hasn't been hacked.'

She gives me a quizzical look.

'Well, he – the person – knows. They know that Cam's gone; they're asking me if I'm all right.'

Gwen's expression is a mixture of sympathy and sorrow.

'What?' I ask.

She swallows. 'Abby, love, you don't know that. Think about it a moment. Whoever has replied has read your email. Possibly more than one. I don't know what you've written to Cam over the last few weeks, I don't want to know, but I'm guessing that to anyone reading them it would be pretty obvious what's happened. This person is simply responding to that. Asking you a leading question in the hope that you'll reply. It could be anyone.'

I falter. Is that true? I look back at the message. Even though I know the message hasn't come from Cam, am I simply holding onto the hope that there is still a connection? As the seconds tick by, I know Gwen is right.

She gives my arm another rub. 'You know, maybe you should talk to your family about how you're feeling. I know you didn't want your mum to know about Cam when he was still alive, and I can fully understand why. But by not letting them into the world that you two created, now you're even more on your own. Or at least it feels that way. How can you expect them to understand how much you're grieving when they don't even know who for?'

She softens her expression. 'Wouldn't it be better if they knew? At least then they'd be able to support you, and you'd be able to let your feelings out, instead of holding them inside of you all the time.'

'But what would I say to them? It's stupid. Falling in love with a man you've only met once. And now falling apart because he's gone.'

'It didn't feel stupid to you, Abby.'

'Maybe that's where I was going wrong,' I say. 'Maybe it should have done and then I wouldn't be in this mess.'

Gwen's smile is warm. 'Love *is* messy, Abby, haven't you learned that by now? But since when did that ever stop any of us?'

I lift my chin a little. 'Anyway, I have spoken to them, sort of. I told Debra, after what happened at Christmas, you know, when Beth let slip about him. No one said very much at the time, but Deb messaged me later in the evening. She asked me about him then.'

'And what did you say?'

'I told her everything. How Cam was a customer to start with, how we began emailing one another, how we met.'

'What did she say?'

'Not much. She was sympathetic, of course, but you know how it is when someone dies, Gwen, people find it so hard to talk about. Grief is such a taboo subject. If we'd had a fight, or Cam had turned out to be married, or one of the other hundred and one reasons why relationships break up, it would have been easier. But as it was, she didn't know what to say. I could tell she wanted to know how he died and I don't even know that. It's ridiculous when I think about it, I can't expect other people to understand.'

'She is your sister though, Abby, I'm sure she does. She would have seen how upset you were.'

I pull a face. 'I know. And she did get it, sort of. But she's much more attuned to my mum's way of thinking than mine. You only have to look at our lives to know that. She married, aged twenty-three, to Ian, who's an accountant. They have a lovely house in suburbia, with the requisite front and back lawns, beech hedging, and hydrangeas. They have two boys who go to the best local school, a Labrador, and two rabbits. Ian drives an Audi, Debra has an SUV and they go on holiday three times a year.'

Gwen raises her eyebrows. 'And what's all that supposed to mean?'

I sigh. 'It doesn't mean anything. But look at my life compared to hers. I met a man, got pregnant at nineteen, only to discover what a mistake I'd made, leaving me to bring up a three-year-old child alone. I live above a tired shop in a draughty flat, with a leaky roof terrace, where I try to grow a few dead things in pots. My daughter goes to the nearest comprehensive, because when we moved here the last thing I considered was what school catchment area we were in. And I drive an ancient Ford Fiesta and am on first-name terms with everyone at the local garage. I can't remember the last time we went on holiday. And given all that, it's no surprise to anyone that I picked to have a relationship that was virtually impossible. It's exactly what they expect from me.'

'Life isn't one-size-fits-all,' Gwen admonishes, gently.

I drop my head again, sighing. 'Sorry, Gwen, that wasn't meant as a pity fest. I love my life, you know that. But that I loved it more when Cam was in it, and much as I love my family too, they don't really get where I'm coming from on this one. Besides, how can I expect them to understand when it's still a mystery to me? Falling in love with Cam took me completely by surprise.'

Gwen cocks her head to one side. 'So, what are you going to do?'

'Carry on as best I can. I've had plenty of perfectly good years without Cam in my life. I need to get used to how it was before, that's all. And Christmas is over and done with, the New Year is here. I mean, it's February already, for goodness' sake. It *will* actually be spring soon, bringing with it all the things I love about this city. And then it will be summer, and with any luck, madly busy, and life will go on happily as it always has. I still have you, and Beth and...' I pause to look around the shop. 'This place, with the chair where Mr Ridley sits and Brown Bear and everything else that makes it so special.' I tuck my hair back behind my ears. 'And in the meantime, we're going to pretend that the rain isn't still falling endlessly and we're going to make the brightest, most joyous window there's ever been.'

Gwen looks sheepish. 'I didn't actually mean in general.' She reaches out to tap my phone. 'I meant about the message.'

And despite the situation, I smile. 'Oh... Well, the sensible thing to do would be to just ignore it, wouldn't it?'

'Yes, Abby it would,' she says firmly, making sure she catches my eye. 'It will be from some creepy guy, or worse. Anyone who hacks into an email account can't be up to any good, can they? And if you reply, they'll probably infect your computer with some hideous virus or, or... Well, anyway, it's not a good idea.'

I nod. 'You're absolutely right,' I say, thrusting my phone back in my pocket.

But the thought of the message still haunts me.

Hi, how are you doing?

Chapter 8

I'm still staring at my phone when Beth comes into the kitchen the next morning. Or rather clomps in, her feet moving as if they're sticking to the floor. I've read and reread the email over and over again since yesterday and, unsurprisingly, it doesn't seem to have changed one iota, or provided me with any more clues. It sits, mocking me, taunting me, whispering to me every time I put down my phone, calling me to pick it back up again. Which I do, of course.

I push the phone to one side and pick up my mug from the table, taking a swig of coffee before smiling up at Beth as she comes to sit down opposite me. I had to wake her twice this morning, which is most unlike her. I push the rack of toast towards her.

'Stone cold,' I say. 'Just the way you like it.'

She mutters thanks and half-heartedly plucks a slice, adding it to her plate. But instead of buttering it, she simply stares.

'What the matter, love?' I ask. 'Still half asleep?' I wouldn't blame her, it's that sort of day. Not raining like yesterday, or at least not yet, but dark and mizzly, clouds hanging low in the sky.

'Yeah, probably.' She picks up her knife, rolling the handle between her fingers.

I watch her for a moment. She's not normally so reluctant to eat her breakfast. In fact, more often than not, she eats half of mine as well.

'So, what have you got first thing then?'

'Drama.'

It's her favourite subject. Which you'd never know from her tone of voice.

'That's good then. At least it's not maths, not if you're feeling tired,' I remark lightly. 'How are the auditions going, anyway?'

She pulls a face and looks away.

'Ah,' I say. 'Like that, is it? But you've got ages yet, Beth, I wouldn't worry. It's not until Easter, and we've half term to go yet.'

She glances back up at me and finally begins to butter her toast, but her look is long enough to see the slight reproach in her eyes. I groan inwardly; I could kick myself. In my turmoil over the message yesterday, I had forgotten that Tuesday is normally the day that Beth stays late after school for drama. Except that yesterday, she'd come home at the normal time.

'Was after-school rehearsal cancelled yesterday?' I ask. 'Sorry, love, I've completely lost track of the days.'

Her knife stills. 'No, it was on… I just didn't go.'

'Oh?'

'Well, there's not much point, is there? When all I do is sit around the whole time. And by the time Mr Matthews gets to us, there's like five minutes left.'

I study her face. 'Is he not a very good timekeeper then?'

'More like he can't be bothered. Not with us, anyway, the Year Sevens. We're not the stars of his show, are we? Not like his precious Year Tens, Emily and all her pathetic groupies. Honestly, you'd think they owned the place the way they swank around school, picking on everyone. And Mr Matthews won't do anything to upset them. It's like he's scared of them, or something. And Emily's not even the best singer.'

That's not the first time I've heard Emily's name mentioned in less-than-flattering terms. In fact, I've heard it far more than I should.

'But that's a ridiculous stance to take, especially for a teacher. Talent has nothing to do with age.'

'Yeah, Mum, I know.' She gets up and dumps her school bag on the table, buckling it up, ready to leave. 'But you're the only one who thinks so.' She opens her mouth to say something more and then thinks better of it, instead swinging her bag onto her back and walking towards the door.

'Beth, you haven't eaten your breakfast yet.'

She comes back to claim her piece of toast and carries it with her.

'Bye, Mum, I'll see you later.'

'Bye, sweetheart. Have a good day.' But the door has already closed.

It was different when she was in primary school. There, she was looked up to for her talents, encouraged by the teachers and admired by the younger pupils. And the curriculum was more relaxed, there was altogether more singing, more dancing, altogether more creativity of every sort. But at secondary school, even in her first year, there's very little room for anything outside of academic subjects. And even less now, it seems.

Cam had been musical too. He played the guitar and the piano, and when he was here, during those two brief days last summer, he heard Beth sing. I don't think she realises how much she does it, around the house, in her bedroom. And then on Cam's last morning with us, just before leaving, he had broken into song himself and the two of them had larked around for quite some time, singing hits from the musicals. The look of surprise on Beth's face had rapidly turned to elation and it's the only occasion I can recall when someone in her immediate environment has ever encouraged her. Apart from me and Gwen, that is.

Maybe this is part of a wider problem. Beth's environment, the same as mine, doesn't consist of very many people. There's my family, Gwen, and a few other friends. When you're quiet and self-contained, and have your head shoved in a book most days, that doesn't seem to matter. But sometimes – at times like this, in fact – it matters very much indeed.

I bite my lip. I've always known that there'd be a time when I would need to push myself very firmly out of my comfort zone, for Beth's sake. She needs to experience things. She needs people around her, and maybe I do too. Perhaps that's what Cam had been to both of us, a link to another world, one that could open up new possibilities, new places to explore.

I stare back down at my phone, very well aware that hope is a dangerous thing. My head is whispering, What if Cam isn't dead? What if he'd had second thoughts about us? What if he had come to the conclusion our relationship was doomed, that it could never grow and become anything more? That it was kinder to end it, rather than stutter on, trying to persuade himself that the inevitable wasn't just around the corner?

And people do weird things in situations like those, they don't always behave rationally. And come to think of it, how well did I actually know Cam? Perhaps he wasn't as caring as I'd thought. Perhaps, in fact, he was downright callous. After all, our relationship had grown through our emailed correspondence, it was the means by which we communicated. Therefore, had Cam sent word that he wanted to end things with me, I would have emailed back, wouldn't I? I might have kept emailing him, become a nuisance, or at least made it difficult for him to be resolute in his decision. So, what could he do, other than come up with a foolproof means of ensuring that I would never contact him again? Because what would be the point in emailing a dead man?

Except that I had…

I shake my head. This is all so ridiculous. I'm thinking up things that have no basis in fact. I'm dreaming of a possibility that I hope might be true but know in my heart of hearts can't be. That's all it is, clutching at straws. And yet the thought that Cam might still be alive is in my head now, and I can't un-think it.

I still can't bring myself to open the Christmas present he sent me. It's a link to the time when he was alive. When he sent it, Cam was living and breathing. I imagine him folding the gift lovingly inside the paper, sealing it carefully and smiling as he takes it to the post office, perhaps imagining the look on my face come Christmas day when I opened it. The present is a paradox, like Schrödinger's cat, both dead and alive. But once I open it, once I gaze upon it, it moves out of its shadowy realm of possibility and becomes reality. The little bit of Cam sealed inside that lived and breathed will fly free and be gone. And Cam will truly be dead.

And this message is exactly the same. But I have to find out. Absolutely and irrevocably. For Beth's sake as much as mine.

I pick up my phone, heart beating wildly, and check the message again, inwardly laughing at the possibility that something might have changed. Imagine the irony. But it hasn't, the words are still the same. I stare hard at the screen, take a very deep breath and type.

Sorry, who is this?

And then I get up quickly, swallowing the last of my coffee before carrying the dirty plates to the sink and pushing them under the sudsy water. It's just gone half past eight, high time I was down in the shop.

*

Gwen collars me the moment I appear and I can see she's dying to talk to me about yesterday's message. She sits down behind the counter, pushes her glossy hair back from her face and pats the stool beside her.

'Right, quick, in case we get interrupted. How are you this morning? Did you find out where that message had come from?'

A little flicker of shock fires in my stomach. *How does Gwen know I replied?* But then I realise what she means.

'No, there's no way to trace it. I suppose I could report it to Cam's email host, but have you ever tried dealing with those companies? It's torture. Besides, I don't even know that Cam's email address is being used for anything untoward. It's more than likely someone mucking around. Like you said.'

'You don't have to follow it up, Abby, but perhaps you should report it. Just in case. If nothing is done about it, then at least you did what you could.'

'I guess so. Yes, perhaps I should.'

'And there's no one you can get in touch with, on the island, I mean, to let them know?'

'Oh, well…'

Gwen's face is instantly contrite. 'Sorry, I wasn't thinking. That would be awful, wouldn't it? No, you can't go through that again,' she declares. Her eyes are sweeping my face, assessing what she sees. 'You do seem a little… brighter this morning.'

I sit down and use the business of straightening the paper bags under the counter as a means of hiding my expression. 'Yes, I think maybe I am,' I reply, praying that she doesn't see through my subterfuge. I'm like the proverbial cat on a hot tin roof. And the agony of not checking my emails every two minutes is killing me. I can't, you see, because Gwen would spot that in an instant. It's how she clocked that there was something going on between Cam and me in the first place. I've turned off his special ringtone too, so there'll be nothing to alert her to new messages either. Or me, of course.

I should tell her, but somehow I can't, not until I know. I'm already aware I'm deluding myself. I smile, as brightly as I can manage.

'I think it might be deleting that message yesterday,' I add. 'Almost like it was the end of something. Drawing a line underneath it and deciding to move on.'

'There's no rush,' she cautions. 'Grief isn't a precise thing, Abby, don't forget that. It's good if you're feeling better about things, but be gentle with yourself. There'll probably be as many bad days as good, and that's okay.'

I pull a face. 'Just when you thought you'd had enough of my crying all over you.'

'Don't be silly, you can do that any time you like. But it *will* get easier.'

'And in the meantime, I'm sure I'll find plenty of other things to worry about.' My smile isn't quite so bright. 'Shall I put the kettle on?'

Gwen's eyes narrow. 'Not so fast,' she says. 'What other things to worry about?' She gives me another searching look.

'Nothing serious. Beth was a bit down this morning, that's all. But I think perhaps it's another thing that's made me realise I need to start over.'

Her eyebrows raise a fraction.

'Something Beth said. That I'm the only one who thinks she has any talent. It isn't true, of course, she was saying that to make a point; she's having a bit of a tough time at school, I suspect. But I think she was referring to the fact that lately Cam, being musical himself, has been the only other person who understood how she feels, who's lavished compliments on her about her singing. It made me realise that my being on my own, perhaps it's limiting her too. Limiting the number of people in her world.' I blow a puff of air from between my lips. 'I should probably try to change that, except we both know how fraught the whole dating thing can be.'

She nods. 'Very true, but…' She pauses, as if working out the best way to put things. 'Beth is growing up and at some point, you *do* have to start doing what's right for you. You've always been very careful with your relationships and the impact they could have on her. And in Cam's case it looked as if it would work out wonderfully, only—' She breaks off. 'Sorry, foot-and-mouth disease. She may not like everyone you get together with, but knowing you, you'll deal with everything in a very caring, considerate and tactful way. And if any problems crop up, you'll work your way through them, like you always do. Don't let fear of what *might* happen put you off from experiencing what *could* happen. But there's no rush, go at your own pace.'

'I know. I think that's pretty much where I am with things. Although when I'm pulling my hair out in several months' time, please remind me of this conversation.'

She laughs, looking up as a customer enters the shop. 'I'll never let you forget it. Right, sit here, I'll go and get that coffee underway.'

I wait until I can hear Gwen clattering about in the kitchen and my customer is busy browsing before quickly pulling my phone from my pocket. My heart is suddenly racing… Fight or flight?

It's Alfie. I don't know if Cam ever mentioned me, but I'm a friend of his, was a friend of his. His best friend.

And I'm sorry, I probably shouldn't have sent that message. I
realised that the minute I pressed send, because what must you
have thought? So, I'm sorry if I shocked you or upset you. It's just
that… I was having a really bad day. And I wondered how you were
doing, that's all.

Sorry…

Stupid, stupid, stupid… How could I have been so stupid? My throat tightens with the rush of grief and disappointment that suddenly fills it. It's not Cam. Cam is dead, Abby. He's dead.

I jump up from my seat and rush to a bookshelf on the other side of the room. Anything to hide my face from the world. Deep breaths. Steadying breaths. You're perfectly fine, Abby, nothing has changed. You knew Cam was dead and this is… This is better. It means that no one has hacked into Cam's account. It isn't some weirdo, but a friend, that's all.

And gradually the heat from my cheeks recedes and my heart begins to regain its usual rhythm. Gwen appears with a tray of drinks, and I take out a couple of books, pretending to study them. The customer comes to the counter, and while she pays Gwen for her book, I rearrange a couple more until I'm sure I have myself under control.

But I can't get the message out of my head, and I suddenly feel that the day will be spent treading water, waiting until the time when I can send a reply.

Another customer comes in, a regular, with books he'd like me to take a look at. They're good books, and I buy all but three. He gives the rest to me anyway.

The phone rings, a sales call from a company seeking to sell advertising space.

The postman arrives with a couple of parcels. We joke about the weather. He's still wearing his shorts.

And then Gwen pops to the loo.

Hi Alfie,

Yes, I do know who you are, Cam used to talk about you often and, well, hello, I suppose. This is so weird…

But it's okay, don't apologise. I'm not really sure how I felt when I got your message. Shocked, yes – actually just that odd thing your heart does, like skipping a beat when something makes you jump – but after that, I felt stupid because I half hoped it meant that Cam was still alive.

The morning wears on.

I put together an order for some stationery supplies and then pop out for some more Sellotape when I realise I forgot to add that to my list. I make another drink. I serve customers until lunchtime.

Oh, Christ, I hadn't even thought about that. Abby, I am so sorry, I don't know what to say. Forget I ever got in touch, it's me that's stupid. I suppose it's just that you look for things to help, don't you? And Cam talked about you all the time, obviously, but I didn't realise how my message would make you feel.

Once Gwen returns from her break, I spend the early afternoon matching up this morning's deliveries with outstanding mail orders in the office upstairs. I don't check my personal emails for at least twenty minutes.

Hang on… how did you get onto these emails?

I pick up the first order and enter the details that will create a delivery note for the parcel. I wrap it carefully, sealing the note inside and stamp the outside of the box with my logo.

Cam's mum has been going through his things. She brought me his laptop because she thought there might be some photos on it, or other stuff, that the family would like. Or I would. She asked me if I knew how to get into it, that's all…

I jump to the Royal Mail website and log in to my account, enter the details for my parcel, select the appropriate postage, and wait until the label prints.

So how did you get into it?

I select the next order and repeat the process. Then do it again another five times. I work on the new orders that have come in today, and by the time I've finished that, it's almost time for Beth to appear. I go back downstairs and make a cup of tea for myself and Gwen and a hot chocolate for Beth. I check my phone before I carry the drinks through to the shop. Nothing.

Beth arrives home from school, freezing cold, and snatches up her drink with a grateful smile. She seems okay now. She leaves to make a start on her homework, pops down a little later with a question, and then goes back up to the flat and I don't see her again until teatime. I wait through the rest of the afternoon in an agony of suspense. Talking to customers, chatting with Gwen, although an hour later I can't even recall what we spoke about.

I knew the password. Look, Abby, I've done nothing wrong. I just…
God, this was such a mistake, but I miss him, okay? I wanted to feel
that he was still around. Jesus, don't you ever reread his emails?

I almost burn the sausages. Beth asks if I'm okay and I tell her that
I've got a headache. And then when she's watching a film, I tell her
I'm going to have a bath. I close the door and cry out loud against the
sound of both taps running. And when the bath has finished filling, I
climb into it, and watch numbly as my tears drip one after another into
the rapidly cooling water. I read Cam's emails all the time, of course I
do. Some days it feels as if I do nothing else.

Yes, all the time, but they were OUR emails. Not anyone else's.
They were private. Have you read them all?

The more I think about it, the madder I become. How dare he read
our emails? Especially now. They were part of a world that Cam and I
created, a world with just us two and no one else. But now someone
else has intruded, someone who had no right to be there, rifling through
our conversations, poking about in our memories and taking them for
his own. I understand that Alfie was hurting, but these emails are all I
have left of Cam and now they feel sullied and tainted by his intrusion.
Another thought comes to me.

Anyway, how do I even know you are who you say you are? You
could have hacked Cam's email. You could be pretending to be
Alfie, and be sympathetic and upset that Cam's died and all the
time it's some stupid ruse to get me to send you my bank details
or something.

It's not, Jesus.

So why did you email then?

I told you why. Apologies, but I thought I'd check and see how you were doing. And I really don't need an interrogation, Abby, I know exactly who I am. I wasn't expecting to have to prove it to anyone, least of all you. I thought you of all people would understand.

I do understand. How dare you accuse me of not understanding when you can see exactly how Cam's death has affected me? For God's sake, I've been emailing a dead man because it's the only way I can get through the day! And now even that's been ruined. How can I email him now, knowing that anything I send might be read by someone else?

Abby, I'm sorry. I shouldn't have said that. I swear I won't read any more emails. But you have to believe there's nothing untoward going on here. I'm just Cam's friend…

Then act like one and leave Cam's memories of me alone. And don't contact me again. This isn't doing either of us any good.

Abby, I'm sorry, please…

Abby…?

Chapter 9

'Sorry, Gwen, what was that? I completely missed it.'

'So I see.' She laughs at me from across the shop floor. 'I don't think you've heard a word I've said. Wherever it is you've been for most of the morning, I hope it's somewhere nice.'

I try, for the umpteenth time, to pull myself together. How long it will last, I'm not sure. I seem to keep drifting, and it's not as if it's something I even want to think about.

'Not especially,' I reply, pulling a face. 'Sorry.'

'Well, that would explain the curious array of facial expressions I've seen you wearing. Is it anything you want to talk about?' She pauses, and then tuts. 'Don't tell me, if it's not one thing, it's your mother. Is she still hassling you about Patrick?'

I give a complicit smile. That's not the reason my mind had been elsewhere, but Gwen doesn't need to know that Alfie's words have been ringing in my ears for the last two days. 'Moving on,' I say, clearing my throat. 'What did I miss?'

Gwen comes over to the counter. 'I wondered whether you'd had a chance to look at the calendar yet. Sorry, Rhys is getting hassled at work to book some holiday or he'll miss out.'

'I hadn't. But let's do it now,' I reply. At last, something that might stand a chance of taking my mind off everything else. I pop up to my office and return with my diary, spreading the book open on the counter. I turn to the first couple of pages that show the year to view.

'When are you thinking?' I ask.

The two pages are almost blank, save for a few notations spaced throughout the year which show the school holidays. There's only one other mark, and I rummage in the pot by the till to find a rubber. Somehow I don't think I'll be travelling to Kinlossay any time soon.

I'm about to erase the entry when Gwen stills my hand. 'Don't,' she says gently.

I look at her, an unspoken question on my lips, but she shakes her head.

'One day, I think you might like to go,' she says. 'Leave it there, as a reminder.' She flashes a quick look at me, before directing her attention back to the book. 'So, Rhys would like his two weeks in the sun sometime, if that's still okay? How about the end of June or early July, so I miss the school hols?'

'Either's fine with me,' I reply. 'I don't have anything planned. And Lottie will be back from uni by then. She messaged me at Christmas to ask if I could bear her in mind again this year, so I'm sure she'll be happy to help out.'

'Good, then I won't feel so bad about going away and leaving you in the lurch.' She taps a date in the diary. 'How about these two weeks? And then there's at least a week between me being back and the schools breaking for summer, in case you want to go somewhere straight away.'

I pencil in Gwen's choice. 'Perfect,' I reply. 'I'm not sure what Beth and I are doing yet. We might stay here as usual. That's just as nice.'

Gwen is quiet for a moment, ostensibly looking at the rest of the year. 'Try to get away,' she says. 'I think you should.' And in the silence that follows is everything Gwen doesn't say, as loud as if she'd spoken the words.

My breath feels a little shaky. 'And what about the rest of the year? Do you want to sort that now?' I ask.

'I'll check with Rhys, first,' she says, straightening up. 'And see what he wants to do. But it will probably be a week in late spring and one in the autumn sometime, as usual. It was the summer break he wanted to get sorted.'

'Okay, sounds good.' I close the book and push it to one side. 'Where do you think you'll go this year?'

A dreamy expression comes over her face. 'I'm hoping we can go back to the Amalfi coast. Oh, Abby, it's so beautiful...'

It's no surprise to me that Gwen loves that area. She looks as if she could have been born there. With her looks and her style, the Italian Riviera is the perfect destination. And I can see the appeal, just...

She laughs. 'I know,' she says. 'You'd much rather be in the middle of nowhere, with a good book and a bacon sarnie.'

'And what's wrong with that?' I challenge, but she simply rolls her eyes.

'Nothing, if you like wet fields and rolling mist and endless rain.'

I grin at her. It's an age-worn argument; Gwen is not a fan of the English countryside.

'I like peace and quiet,' I say, but I know I'll never convince her.

She checks her watch. 'I might pop out now and get my lunch,' she says. 'Do you want anything?'

'Other than to eat my body weight in Rumer's cakes? But no, I'd best not. Thanks anyway.'

I smile at her retreating back as she leaves. Gwen is the polar opposite to me in many regards, maybe that's why we get on so well.

I head through to the kitchen to boil the kettle, ready for a cup of tea when she gets back, and have just laid out the mugs when a pointed cough claims my attention.

'Sorry, Mr Ridley,' I call, hurrying back through. 'I didn't think you were quite ready yet.'

He's been sitting in his usual chair for the best part of an hour, a pile of books on the floor beside him. He has the most extraordinarily eclectic taste of any of our regulars, and I smile when I see which title has claimed the prize today. It's a copy of Thoreau's *Walden*.

'Good choice,' I comment as I take the book from him.

He studies me intently for quite a few moments, and just when I think he might be about to say something, he takes out his leather purse and pulls a note from it instead.

I hand him his change before wrapping the book and sealing the bag with a small strip of Sellotape. He takes it silently, slipping it into his shopping bag, which also accompanies him wherever he goes. And then he touches a hand to his hat and turns to leave. My smile follows him almost to the door, where he turns at the last moment.

'Do you know it was the conversation you had with your colleague which helped me decide which book to buy,' he says.

I'm so surprised to hear him speak a whole sentence, I'm lost for words.

He takes a couple of steps forward. 'I can't remember when I last read *Walden*. Too long,' he adds. 'Have you read it?'

'I have,' I reply. 'And *Walking*, although *Walden*'s my favourite.'

He looks at me curiously, quite unashamed at the intensity of his gaze. 'I don't think I've ever told you this, but I met my wife on the Amalfi coast.'

It's quite possibly the longest conversation we've ever had.

'No, I didn't know that,' I reply. 'Was she on holiday too?'

He shakes his head. 'No, she was born there, just outside of Positano. She'd lived there all her life.' He breaks off to raise a small smile. 'Until she met me.'

I lean a little further forward over the counter. 'And you brought her back here to live?'

'I did,' he says proudly. 'She'd always wanted to see England. All my friends told me that it wouldn't last, that she was using me as her ticket over here, but I knew they were wrong. Her name was Liliana, but I called her Lily. And she may have had Italian blood but inside beat the heart of a true Englishwoman.'

My hand is laying over my own heart, I realise. 'That's so lovely.'

'We honeymooned on a farm in deepest Devon, and two days into it while we were out walking, through the fields, and along the narrow lanes, fragrant with the smell of wild honeysuckle, she turned to me and said, "Thank you for bringing me home, Peter." And we never looked back after that. Fifty-two years we were married, until she died.'

He bends down to take the book from out of his bag and I'm grateful for the interruption, wiping a finger surreptitiously under one eye.

'I don't get out much now,' he says, straightening. 'I'm not as mobile as I used to be for one thing, but that's why I decided on this book, you see. You reminded me that it's been too long since I visited the proper countryside, and I thought reading this again might remind me of the reasons why I love it. I can go there in my head at least.'

'Then I'm glad,' I say, knowing that doesn't really cover it at all.

'So, you stick up for yourself,' he says. 'With your colleague. The Amalfi coast is beautiful, but the middle of nowhere is much nicer.' And then he smiles, a cheeky, crinkled smile that forms ravines down his face but which lights up his eyes too. I've never noticed before what a bright blue they are.

And as I smile back, still reeling a little from our conversation, I see the direction of his eyes shift, just a little.

'Oh, would you like one?' I say, pointing to a row of bookmarks which are propped in front of the till. 'You can help yourself, they're all free.' I come out from behind the counter to straighten them a little, pulling them forward from the clutter of other things that have found their way there.

His eyes rove the selection on display. 'I usually use a little piece torn from a newspaper, but perhaps today, I could take one of these home with me.'

I smile warmly. 'Mr Ridley, you've bought enough books from us in the past, I'd say you've definitely earned one, several in fact.'

'No, just the one will do.'

He peers a little closer, deliberating long and hard over which to choose, and for some reason I find this incredibly touching. It's such a small thing and yet he appears immeasurably pleased by the prospect.

His finger lingers on one in particular: a linocut of a pastoral scene which was sent by a publisher to advertise one of their new releases. 'I think this one would be entirely appropriate,' he says, trying to separate the little oblongs of cardboard from one another.

I come to his rescue as he fumbles slightly, causing the rest to tip forward, almost spilling.

'I should really have a little clear out,' I say. 'Things often get dumped here when there's not really any other place for them to go.'

He nods, taking the bookmark from me, turning it over and back again. Satisfied, he looks up. 'We get so used to things being a certain way, we stop seeing them after a while.' He taps Brown Bear on the head. 'This little chap, for example. I've often wondered why you keep him here.' He gives a slight smile. 'I've even seen you pick him up, dust round him and then put him back again. Where did he come from?'

'He was left behind one day, nestled in the gap between a row of books and the shelf above, but he looks too well-loved to have been forgotten. I think his owner must have been pulled away before they had time to retrieve him and I couldn't bear the thought of them being parted, so I put him here in the hope that the little boy or girl might come back one day and find him again.'

'But they never did…'

'No, quite sad, really.'

Mr Ridley thinks for a moment, his eyes fixed on the soft brown fur. 'He's been here rather a long time though, how long has it been?'

'Too long,' I say smiling, echoing his words from earlier. 'But Brown Bear is almost part of the furniture now. Although these days perhaps I leave him there as a symbol of hope.'

'Yes, I thought so.' He hands me both his wrapped book and the bookmark. 'Would you mind popping the bookmark inside for me? I'm rather all fingers and thumbs.'

I nod and do as he asks, carefully resealing the bag when I've finished.

'You know,' he says, 'you mustn't let hope stand in the way of things. You can wait too long in the hope of something coming to you. Sometimes you have to get on and do. When I lost my Lily, I wasted too many years hoping she would come back. My grief had become a part of the furniture, just like Brown Bear here, and that's not right either.' He patted the bear's head fondly. 'He is rather too lovely to throw away though. Perhaps move him around from time to time, I think that would be better.'

He bends to replace his book with the rest of his shopping and, giving me one final smile, he touches a hand to his hat in farewell. 'Oh, and I left some books there. Would you mind—?'

'Don't worry, Mr Ridley, I'll put them back for you. It's my pleasure.'

'Thank you.'

I stand for quite some moments after he leaves, a curious smile on my face. Twice a week, for as long as I can remember, Mr Ridley has visited my shop. He sits with a pile of books at his feet, reading through each before deciding which one he wants to take home. And on every occasion, once his book has been paid for, he leaves with scarcely a word. Not about the pile of books he's left for either Gwen or me to reshelve, or anything else for that matter. I wonder what it is about today that has made him change? Or tell me such beautiful details about his life?

I turn around and pick up the soft toy that has lain unclaimed for all these years. Perhaps it has brought a little hope, after all. Clutching it to my chest, I survey the shop, looking for a spot which might suit him. I decide on a little display shelf that sits above two waist-height bookcases on the far side of the room. By shuffling along a spider plant and another book, there's enough space for him to sit on the end. I stand back to check his new position. Yes, that will do very nicely.

Walking back to the counter, I take my phone from my pocket and flick open my emails, rereading the last one I'd sent to Cam. Perhaps…

I'm shaken from my reverie by the sound of the shop door opening.

'Hello, Abby.' It's my mum. 'I'm not stopping, I just popped in to bring you these.' She hands over a pack of chocolate biscuit bars and a multipack of crisps. 'They were on buy one, get one free, but there's no way me and your dad can eat them all. In fact, I shouldn't really have bought them at all, I just fancied a little treat. Anyway, I'm sure you can make use of them, for Beth's packed lunches perhaps?'

Funnily enough, they're both Beth's favourite. 'You know, these last for ages, Mum, you don't have to eat them all in one go.'

'I know, dear, but…' She pauses, as if reconsidering. 'No, you take them, I've got plenty.'

'Okay, thanks, Mum.' I pop them through to the back. It's one of the ways she has of showing me she cares without drawing attention to the fact. I've been known to be a little spiky in the past when reference has been made to my single-parent, and therefore terminally poor, status. A ridiculous default defensive mechanism, as if I have to justify myself. This way, Mum still gets to help us out without alluding to the fact that she is and manages to neatly circumnavigate my ill grace in one fell swoop.

'Are you staying for a cuppa?' I ask. She often says she isn't stopping and then does.

'No, no, I must get going. I said I'd meet Tilda for lunch. She's got a voucher for that new place that's opened on the corner of Peas Hill and we said we'd give it a try. Just something light, nothing fancy. Although I've heard they have an excellent dinner menu too.'

I smile. 'And how is Patrick?' I shouldn't tease her, but sometimes I can't help it.

She sighs. 'Abby, dear, I do wish you'd reconsider. He's still on his own and had a totally miserable Christmas by all accounts. Plus, now I know more of the detail, it seems his wife didn't just leave him, she left him to swan off with a man she's been having an affair with. So, you see, it really wasn't his fault, and he's such a lovely young man.'

I can't see how that makes it any better, but I don't say so. 'Mum, I'm not really sure it's a great time for me, I—'

'On the contrary, dear, I should say it's exactly the right time. I know you'd been speaking with this man you met online, and now that's ended. But some company might be exactly what you need. And no one says it has to be anything serious. But I really don't see how you're ever going to meet anyone otherwise. You work all hours and when you're not working, you never go anywhere.'

I can feel Brown Bear's eyes on the back of my neck.

'Look, Mum, if I agree to meet Patrick, and I mean *if*, then I'll only do so on one condition: that I don't have to answer endless questions about him or how we got on. It's bad enough meeting new people, without feeling like I'll be subject to interrogation as well.'

All too predictably, her eyes light up. 'So, can I tell Tilda that you said yes? She'll be thrilled.'

'*She'll* be thrilled, or Patrick will?' I ask, my eyebrows raised.

She tuts. 'You know what I mean. Patrick will be thrilled, and Tilda will simply be pleased for you both.'

I narrow my eyes. 'And not dinner, or anything formal. Maybe a walk or something, I don't know.' I can feel hot panic beginning to sweep over me. 'But I'm not going anywhere where I can't escape if I want to.'

'Heavens, Abby, you make it sound like such an ordeal.'

I think back to how I felt when I'd agreed to meet Cam. And I *liked* him. I *wanted* to meet him. 'I don't like things when they're so contrived.'

She rolls her eyes and then checks her watch. 'Right, I must get going, but I'll see what I can do.'

I'm still standing in a daze when Gwen returns.

'Is everything all right?' she asks. 'You look as if you've lost a pound and found a penny.'

'I think I've agreed to go out with Patrick,' I say slowly. 'I'm not quite sure what came over me. And that's not all. I've just had a *conversation* with Mr Ridley.'

She baulks at my words, eyes wide. 'Blimey, I'll go and put the kettle on.'

Reappearing moments later, she comes to stand in front of me, taking a firm hold of both my arms. 'Who are you, and what have you done with my friend, Abby?'

I groan. 'Don't, it's no laughing matter. Although Mr Ridley was lovely, Gwen. I wish you'd been here. He'd heard us chatting about where you're thinking of going on holiday, and when he came to pay for his book, he carried on talking.' I give a wistful smile. 'It was so lovely… He told me about his wife, and where they met. They were together for over fifty years before she died.'

'Aw.'

'I know. She was Italian, from just outside of Positano, actually, but apparently never more at home than among the glories of England's countryside. But that wasn't all he said. He spoke about hope… and grief too. How you can let it become part of the furniture. I don't know, it's silly maybe, but it got me thinking.'

'Well, I can see that.'

'And then when Mum came in and asked about Patrick…'

'You very rashly agreed to meet him?'

I grimace. 'Something like that. I don't know, Gwen, but it's like I said the other day, maybe it's time I *did* push myself a bit, get out there more than I do now. And so, when Mum came along…' I trail off, sighing. 'Patrick might be really nice, and I won't know will I, unless I find out? But I made it clear that I didn't want the whole dinner-date thing, which is too nerve-wracking for words, and that once we'd seen one another on no account was my mother to pester me for details.'

Gwen can't hide the smirk on her face. She knows there's about as much chance of that happening as a pig flying across the sky. But then she smiles. 'Abby Prendergast, I'm proud of you,' she says.

It's on the tip of my tongue to tell her about Alfie and his emails, but it's over and done with now. Maybe it's the onset of spring, maybe it's Mr Ridley's words of wisdom, or maybe it's the realisation that it's time to move on from my grief. But, whatever the reason, I suddenly do feel a little lighter, and it feels good.

Chapter 10

Oh no…

I jump back from the window in case I'm seen. Not that this will make any difference. Patrick is striding up the street towards the shop and I'm fairly certain there's only one place he's heading for.

After I'd told Mum I'd meet up with him, I'd fully expected to hear from him that day, but I hadn't, and now nearly two weeks have passed. Not that I'm complaining. But I'd thought when he did get in touch, there would be an email, or a phone call, not an in-person visit. I am really not ready for this.

Worse, it's not like I can run and hide. Gwen is on her lunch break and although it's the middle of the half-term holiday so Beth is with me, I daren't leave her in the shop on her own. Oh God, that means he's going to meet her too. I risk another glance out the window, wondering if I have time to either quickly explain to her, giving her the option of escaping out the back, or actually bundle her out of the shop. Either way I'm still going to have to face him, something that's further complicated by the fact that I haven't mentioned Patrick to Beth yet.

I tut with irritation. What was he thinking, coming unannounced like this? I move back so that I'm standing slantwise to the window and less likely to be seen. Perhaps he's going to veer off at the last minute and disappear down one of the little side streets. Or even walk on by. I can hope.

Bugger. I turn my back and practically run to the nearest shelf, plucking off a selection of titles at random, so that at least I look like I'm in the middle of something. Plus, if I'm holding a stack of books he might be less inclined to stay.

I'm still facing away from the door as it opens, and it takes all my willpower to force myself to turn around. My face wears its customary smile, ready for a greeting, as if he were just another ordinary customer.

'Hello,' I say cheerfully. 'Oh… hello,' I add, as if suddenly recognising him.

He's obviously come from the office. He's wearing a long navy woollen coat, open at the front, with black leather gloves and a striped scarf at his neck completing his outdoor wardrobe. But underneath I can see a navy suit, the trousers cut tight on the leg, which only serves to emphasise his enormous shiny brown shoes.

He takes off his gloves. 'Abby, hi!' And then he leans forward and kisses me on the cheek, like he's done it countless times before, never mind the pile of books in my arms. I'm so stunned, I barely register the waft of expensive lemon-scented cologne. And then he looks me up and down. Actually does that really obvious once-over thing, and smiles. 'You look lovely,' he adds.

What, like I dressed up?

I give myself a stern talking-to. Abby, this is not the right attitude to take. Stop it at once. I rearrange my facial features so I don't look quite so dismissive, but I have no idea what to say. I needn't have worried, however, Patrick is obviously far more adept at small talk. He pulls off his scarf and looks around.

'So, this is your little shop, is it? Blimey, I didn't think people read books any more. I thought it was all on gadgets these days.'

He may well be right. Every day it feels more and more that way, but I'm damned if I'm going to agree with him. 'No, people still read the real thing.' *Abby, don't roll your eyes, that would be really rude.* 'And there's something about second-hand books, don't you think? I mean, new ones are lovely too, but second-hand… Well, they smell so nice for one thing, and then there's all that history – Who has read it before you? Is there a message written inside? – I love all that stuff.'

Patrick looks a little perplexed. 'Sorry, I'll have to take your word for it. I don't read, I'm afraid. Well, for business obviously, but otherwise, I never seem to have the time.'

I nod. 'Ah well, each to their own,' I reply faintly.

'I probably should have come in before, but the last couple of weeks or so have been rather demanding. System crashes everywhere! Still, I'm here now. And lovely to see where you are, of course. I shall enjoy picturing you here among all these quaint books.' He beams a smile at me as he looks around once more, his gaze ending up on the counter, where Beth is sitting, reading.

'And is this your little girl?'

I close my eyes for a second in horror and trail after him towards the till. Beth looks up, staring at him as if he has two heads.

'Er, yes, my daughter, Beth.'

'It's very nice to meet you.'

He holds out his hand, which Beth shakes, looking like she'd rather stick pins in her eyes. I can almost hear her voice: *Er, hello, I'm eleven, not a three-year-old.*

'No school today, though?' he asks. 'Not pulling a sickie are you, so that Mum gets some free labour?' His laugh seems incredibly loud.

'No, it's half term,' I explain. 'Beth often helps out during school holidays. She likes reading too, as you can see.'

His face falls. 'Oh, is that going to be a problem?'

'Is what? Sorry, I don't…'

'Well, when I whisk you away? Who's going to look after her?'

'Oh, I *see*… No, it's fine. I have an assistant as well, Gwen. She's popped out for a moment, but is here every day, so Beth will be fine.'

He gives me a puzzled look. 'Yes, but presumably she doesn't work evenings too?'

'No, but…' I pause. 'Sorry, I'm not really following you. I thought we were going to grab a coffee somewhere, or walk by the river, or…'

'A coffee?' He looks rather affronted. 'I thought we'd agreed dinner. Benedict's, in fact. What do you say to that?'

It's only the poshest, most expensive, most nerve-wracking restaurant in the whole of the town.

'Um…'

'Now, I've provisionally booked for Saturday, because Mum thought you'd be free, but obviously if that's a problem, I can rearrange.'

I hesitate, a fraction too long.

'Ah, so, the childcare *is* a problem?'

'No, it's not, my sister will come over. It's not that, it's… I didn't think we'd be going out for dinner,' I say, trying to be firm. 'Something a little less formal, I'd thought.'

'But Benedict's is the best! No, sorry, I can't take you anywhere that's not up to scratch. But it's on me, of course.' He pauses at the point where I know a hot flush has hit my cheeks.

I'm not sure whether to be offended, or relieved by this last comment. But it still doesn't change things.

'The reservation is for eight, but if I pick you up at seven, then we can pop for a drink first.'

The prospect is becoming worse by the minute.

'Or do you need longer than that to get ready?'

I frown. 'Sorry?'

'Well, I'm assuming the shop will be open on Saturday. But if you close at five thirty, that only gives you an hour and a half to complete your preparations. Is that enough? I know what you ladies are like.'

Preparations? What does he think I'm going to be doing, brewing up a potion? Although that's not such a bad idea... eye of newt, and toe of frog...

'Seven's fine,' I say. Anything to get him out of the shop.

He winds the scarf back around his neck and then claps his gloves together, before pulling them on in a weirdly flamboyant way. 'Excellent. Well, that *is* good news.' He beams a smile at me and then at Beth, also winking at her for good measure.

I lift the books in my arms in what I hope is a 'well, I must get on' gesture and step back to allow him more access to the door. His final lunge to bestow me with another kiss is thwarted as I engineer a slight slippage of the topmost paperback, a move I'm rather proud of, and then with a quick check of his watch, he's gone.

I watch him stride back down the street for a few moments, just to be sure he's actually going to stay gone and then return to the counter, where I lay down the books I've been carrying. Beth is standing staring at his rapidly retreating figure.

'Who on earth was that?' she asks. 'Jeez, Mum, he was a right weirdo!'

You can always trust an eleven-year-old to get straight to the point and I couldn't have put it better myself. In fact, my head is so full of thoughts all yelling at one another that I don't even remind Beth about her language.

'Tilda's son,' I reply, almost a whisper.

She stares at me. 'But I thought Patrick was married.'

'Yes, he is. But he and his wife have… Well, they're not together any more and Granny thought it might be nice for him and me to get to know one another.'

She gives me that look, the one that knows exactly how this has come about, however I try to spin it.

'Why doesn't Granny listen?' she asks. 'You've told her you don't want a boyfriend.'

'I know, love, but she wants what's best for me. Same as all mothers do.' I touch a finger to the tip of her nose. 'Are you hungry?'

Beth cocks her head at me. 'Why…?' A single word, drawn out so that it has at least five syllables.

'Because, I don't know about you, but I could do with something gooey and chocolatey right now.' Lunch had been a very virtuous salad, I reckon I deserve it. Besides, it might take away the nasty taste in my mouth.

Beth's eyes light up. 'From Rumer's?' she asks, grinning as I nod my head. I open the till and take out a ten-pound note. 'Do you want to pop out and get us something? You have whatever you like, and I'll have a salted caramel brownie, please. And a flapjack for Gwen.'

I stand by the door watching as she walks down the road, scanning it anxiously for any sign of Gwen returning. I pounce on her the moment she comes through the door, pulling her towards the back of the room.

'Gwen, quick, before Beth comes back. Patrick's just been in and—'

Her eyes widen. 'Patrick? And I missed him?' She pulls a face. 'Damn!'

'Never mind about that. Gwen, what am I going to do? He came in to invite me out and… This is going to sound so silly, and I didn't think about it before, but now that it's actually happening, do you think Cam would mind?' I nibble anxiously at the corner of my thumbnail. 'Me going out with someone else.'

Her face is instantly contrite. 'Oh, Abby…' Her eyes are soft on mine. 'No, I don't think he'd mind. From what you've said about his sense of humour, he'd probably find it funny that you're getting yourself into such a pickle over it.'

'Do you think?'

She nods. 'I do. Because I know he'd want you to move on with your life, Abby. To be happy.'

I press my lips together. 'It just feels—' I break off, tutting. 'This is ridiculous, but it feels almost like I'm committing adultery. Can you even commit adultery with someone's memory?'

She smiles. 'No, I don't think you can, but I know what you mean. He'd probably be far more concerned about the type of man you were going out with than the fact that you were dating at all. And if you think about it, that *is* what's important.' She eyes my face. 'Can I put my shopping down now?' she asks, lifting both arms slightly to draw my attention to the two bags she's still holding.

I nod and smile. 'Sorry.'

'So, what did you think of Patrick?' Gwen asks a few moments later as she returns to the room.

I roll my eyes. 'Urghh, where do I start? The whole thing was toe-curlingly cringey. He started by saying how quaint this place was, and not in a nice way, more condescending. And that he didn't think people read books any more.' I break off, frowning. 'Actually, the way business is going, I'm inclined to agree with him, but I wouldn't give him the satisfaction. Anyway, that's not the point. The point is that *he* doesn't read, Gwen. How can you not read? He's too busy, apparently, because he has this mega-important job and works all hours. And he was a bit forward and awful with Beth.'

Gwen is struggling to hide a smile. 'Oh dear... Anything else?'

I shoot her a look. 'That will do for starters.'

I look up as Beth comes back through the door. She drops two paper bags on the counter before smiling at Gwen and shrugging off her coat.

'Can I eat mine upstairs, Mum? Only I've got a double doughnut and you know how much of a mess I usually get in with those.'

I smile, memories of past jammy disasters flashing past my eyes. 'Yes, go on, good idea.'

I wait until I hear her foot creak on the top stair before looking back at Gwen.

'Abby, I'm sorry to say this but you know Patrick might be finding this as difficult as you. And being tongue-tied and embarrassed came out as arrogant and crass.'

'Or maybe he *is* actually arrogant and crass.'

'Maybe... but you won't ever know unless you find out.'

I groan as she grins at me, knowing she's playing devil's advocate. 'I knew you were going to say that. And I know it's true. *Probably* true. But how am I ever going to spend a whole evening with him?'

'He might surprise you.'

'Yes, that's what I'm afraid of.'

Gwen laughs. 'What's one evening, Abby? If your date is a total disaster then, well, at least you'll know. But if not, and – first impressions notwithstanding – there beats the heart of a really nice man, then... Look, I'm not sure whether I should say this or not, and don't take it the wrong way – sorry, I hate it when people say that, but you know what I mean – just that like you said, maybe what Cam's passing has taught you is that you've got to take the chance. You've got to open up to possibilities because you never know what life is going to bring you.'

I sigh. 'I hate it when you're right.'

Gwen screws up her nose. 'Hold that thought. And in case I'm wrong, and your date *is* awful, then you can enjoy telling me what a loathsome human being I am and that you should never have listened to me.' She breaks off to grin at me. 'Either way, I'm obviously going to need a blow-by-blow account of everything that happens.'

'Gwen,' I protest, poking her arm. 'You're as bad as my mother.'

'I have no reply for that.'

I smile as the postman comes in, pulling his little trolley. Only one parcel today and a handful of letters. I flip through them, praying for a couple of orders at least, when I come to one which bears the school stamp. I'm not expecting anything; the reports don't come out until Easter. My finger is about to slip under the fold on the back of the envelope when I hear the flat door open above, and quickly shove the letter back among the pile. It can keep.

'Was the doughnut up to the usual standard?' I ask as Beth comes down the stairs to join us.

'Even better,' she says, flashing a look at Gwen. 'So, if you do go out with Patrick on Saturday and you have a horrible time…' It's a question.

I raise my eyebrows.

'Does that mean I get another one?'

'No, it does not,' I reply, pretending to be cross. 'It means *I* can have a double doughnut.' I grin back at her. 'A double doughnut *and* a salted caramel brownie.'

'You haven't eaten that one yet,' Beth replies, pointing to the paper bag still on the counter.

'No, I know. I'm savouring the thought. There's a flapjack there for you too, Gwen,' I add.

'Oh thank God,' she replies, pouncing on the bag. 'I'm starving.'

'I was telling Gwen all about Patrick's lovely visit,' I explain to Beth. 'And she says I should still go out with him. What do you reckon? Do you mind me going out with Patrick?'

She thinks for a moment, giving the question proper consideration. 'No, I don't mind, as long as it makes you happy,' she replies. 'And *if* he turns out to be nice.'

'Well, if he's not, that will be the end of that,' I say.

'Okay,' she says, happy enough.

And that's that. But even though it's a silly thought, I still can't help wishing that I could somehow have Cam's blessing.

It isn't until much later when I've locked up the shop for the night and am sitting in the kitchen, trying to decide what to cook for dinner, that I remember the letter from the school. With Beth safely in the sitting room watching TV, I carry it back from the office where I'd left it earlier and begin to read.

Dear Mrs Prendergast, it begins…

I'm writing to you in my capacity as Beth's form tutor because I wanted to share with you a few concerns I have over Beth's behaviour. Concerns which have also been raised by several other members of the teaching staff…

Chapter 11

This is going to be a disaster. I know it, Beth knows it, but we're both trying to pretend that everything will be fine.

'I should have gone out and bought something new,' I say, staring at my reflection. It's not really showing me what I want to see.

'Did you want to buy something new?' asks Beth.

'No, and I can't afford to either. Particularly not the kind of something you wear to Benedict's, somewhere I'm never likely to set foot in again. What a waste that would be.'

Beth rolls her eyes. 'Well, you've answered your question then,' she says. 'Try the green one on again, I think it's a nicer colour.'

I rummage under the pile of clothing on the bed and pull out a green velvet skirt that's worked its way to the bottom. I love this skirt; I've worn it loads and it still doesn't look its age, but it's not really right, a bit too bohemian for Benedict's. I pull the shift dress I'm currently wearing over my head in one swift motion and toss it at Beth.

I check my watch. 'Okay, skirt. What next?'

She wrinkles her nose. 'I think you should wear the top that matches. It looks lovely.'

'But aren't the flowers a bit big? Fussy? Inelegant?'

Beth laughs. 'All of those things. But it still suits you.'

I hold up the top in question and subject it to further scrutiny. It's exactly the same colour as the skirt, with a fitted bodice and tiny velvet covered buttons in a row down the front and one on each cuff. And patterned with large dark-pink roses. It sounds awful, but it isn't. It's vibrant, the colours rich and sumptuous, but possibly something more suited to a student than a thirty-something-year-old shopkeeper.

'And wear it with your Mary Poppins boots.'

'Really?'

'Yes.'

'Okay.' I stare at Beth a moment before pushing my arms into the sleeves of the top and buttoning up the front. 'Are we done?'

She nods solemnly.

I take a deep breath. 'Now then, what do you think about my hair?' I turn back to the mirror. I've curled it and now it's… springy is the only word that comes to mind. It's shoulder-length, well, it was – now I have corkscrews somewhere round about my ears. I tuck the curls back behind them. Slightly better. I turn to Beth.

She cocks her head to one side. 'Not sure,' she says. 'Can you clip it back like that? Or… the curls will drop a bit anyway, won't they?'

I blooming well hope so.

Beth pushes the clothes off her lap and comes to stand behind me. She lifts the hair from the back of my neck and twists it up, holding it there so that I can see the effect in the mirror. 'Maybe if you pinned it up?'

But I don't really like my hair up. My face is too round, my cheeks are too chubby, I need my hair to soften everything. I pull a face and Beth lets go, the curls twanging back to their former position. I tug them behind my ears again and sigh.

Beth puts her arms around my neck, standing on tiptoes to peer over my shoulder. She grins at our reflection in the mirror. 'Mum, why did you leave this until tonight?'

That's easy. It's because I don't want to go, so I've been putting it off until the last possible minute. 'I don't know, I just seem to have been busy this week. Plus, of course, I haven't tried half this stuff on for ages, and somehow my memory of it has become a little distorted. I thought a lot of my stuff looked better than it did. I thought *I* looked better than I do.'

Beth drops her arms and squeezes me around the waist. 'You look gorgeous, Mum, and if Patrick can't see that then he's a—'

'Don't say it,' I warn, wondering which derogatory term she was going to go for.

'Okay, but you know it's true. Anyway, why do you need to make such a fuss about what you look like? You didn't when you met Cam. I mean, I know you put lipstick on and stuff, but you didn't dress up, not like this. You picked him up from the station in your jeans.'

I'd made light of her comment at the time, but now I can't get it out of my head. Because what Beth said is true. I hadn't made such an effort when I'd met Cam for the first time. Or rather I had, but not in the same way. I'd wanted to look my best, but I hadn't felt I should pretend to be sophisticated, or elegant, or any of the other things I'm not. And I certainly felt far more relaxed than I do right now.

Patrick is held up – some last-minute hitch at home – and is nearly half an hour late, so we only have time for a quick drink before dinner. Something I'm very grateful for. The pub he'd chosen is alongside the river and a popular spot. It's busy, even this early, and most folks are dressed casually, so I feel okay. Patrick is rather flustered when he arrives and, hidden under my coat as I am, he only gives my outfit a brief glance before bustling me out of the door.

The restaurant, however, is an entirely different matter.

It's calm, mostly white, hushed and serene. I'm relieved of my coat the moment we step through the door and there's nothing else for Patrick to look at, only me.

'That's a beautiful colour,' he says, subjecting me to another once-over. 'With your hair and eyes, I can quite see why you chose it.'

'Thank you,' I say, trying to have a furtive look at what other diners are wearing.

Patrick has chosen another suit. Pale grey this time. And although I'm not fully trained in suit recognition, I know enough to acknowledge that it's very on trend and expensive with it.

'Well, this is lovely,' I say, once we're seated. And it is, if you like the minimalist, barely-there style.

'Isn't it?' agrees Patrick. 'Wait until you taste the food. Have you ever been here before?'

I shake my head. 'No, I…' I trail off, reluctant to admit to my financial status. And love of baked beans.

'Well, I can recommend something if you're unsure what to have. Although it's all good.' He gives a self-congratulatory smile. 'I think I've tried everything over the years. My wife and I used to come here regularly as a treat after a hard-working week… although she's obviously decided that the best money can buy isn't quite good enough.'

My smile is nervous in reply. 'Oh dear,' I say. 'I'm sorry to hear that. My mum mentioned that, well, she told me you weren't together any more. Obviously, I mean we wouldn't be here otherwise, would we?'

'Quite,' he replies. 'The thing is, Abby, I can be honest with you, can't I? I'm finding it very hard to know what women want these days. I mean, I gave her everything she could possibly wish for. A beautiful home, filled with lovely things, and all the comforts too. But that didn't seem to be what she wanted after all, although it certainly was at the start. I'm quite sure I didn't hear any complaints then. But the thing is, I really don't think I'm cut out for the single life. I—' He breaks off as a waiter approaches and lays down a single white card in front of me.

'For madam… and for sir…' He passes Patrick the same menu, while holding aloft another. 'And the wine list?' He looks between us both, but before I even have a chance to open my mouth, Patrick claims it. He glances at it briefly.

'We'll have the burgundy,' he says, handing back the card.

'Thank you,' I call as the waiter withdraws, as swiftly and silently as he appeared. Patrick is studying the card in front of him.

'Sorry, you were saying?'

He looks up briefly, frowning.

'That you don't think you're cut out for the single life,' I prompt.

'Ah, yes. You see, the thing is, Abby, I work too hard. And my role is incredibly stressful. I usually have a huge number of projects on the go, and the constraints on my time are considerable. So, when I come home I like to know that my evening will be well-ordered and enjoyable.' He pauses. 'That makes sense, doesn't it?'

I nod. 'Perfectly,' I say calmly, while screaming inside. 'I wouldn't know what one of them was, unfortunately, but yes, sounds good to me.'

He frowns. 'I'm sorry?'

'A well-ordered evening,' I repeat. 'Mine are always a little bit scattered. Ad hoc might be a good way to describe them.' I grin at my hopefully witty comment, but my face falls when I see it's missed the mark.

'I see, so you'd probably like there to be an improvement then?'

'No, actually,' I reply. 'I quite like my life. I wish we had a little more money and more security for the future, but everything else is great. I really love my job and the flat is perfectly big enough for Beth and me. It's a bit draughty, a bit… like Bagpuss, baggy and a bit loose at the seams.'

Patrick's eyebrows shoot up.

'Never mind. It's an old building, and so nothing's shiny and new but I love it really. It's quirky and full of character.'

He nods. 'I see.' He looks down at his menu again. 'I can recommend the steak tartare,' he adds.

I ignore him.

'But you're on your own, just you and your little girl?' he asks after a moment.

'She's hardly a little girl any more, they grow up quite quick these days, but yes, there's just the two of us. I left her dad when she was three.'

'I imagine that makes your position rather difficult,' he replies. 'So, what is it that you want, Abby? From a relationship, I mean.'

Isn't it a little soon to be discussing this kind of thing? Shouldn't we start with something a little less direct, like, what's your favourite kind of potato, roast or mash? But Patrick is clearly waiting for an answer.

I think for a moment. 'Probably friendship, most of all, and then take it from there, I guess. Ultimately someone who shares the same ideals as me, someone I can journey through my life with. Kind, caring…' I trail off.

'Ah, a romantic then,' declares Patrick. 'Although I guess that hasn't been going so well though, has it? Mum mentioned you'd been on your own for some time now.'

My cheeks are beginning to glow. 'Through choice,' I reply. 'There's Beth to think of as well. But, actually… there was someone recently.' I really don't want to talk about Cam, but neither do I want to sit and listen to Patrick's disparaging comments about my love life. He's a fine one to talk. 'We met through the shop, as it happens. He was a mail-order customer originally. We used to email one another and kind of struck up a friendship from there.'

'I see, so one of those online romances.' He tips his head to one side. 'Of course, I've thought about that too, those apps you can get, but I'm not really sure how well you can get to know a person that way.'

'Actually, I thought Cam and I got to know one another really quite well.'

He scratches the end of his chin. 'Open to abuse though, I would have thought.'

'Well, he didn't turn out to be a fifty-four-year-old axe murderer if that's what you mean.'

'Oh, so you went ahead and met him? That's interesting.'

'I did, yes, last summer.'

I can see him mentally counting off the months in his head. He gives a small, somewhat smug smile. 'And yet you're not together, so there must have been something that didn't turn out the way you'd planned.'

'Yes, he died,' I say bluntly, face scarlet. But I don't care, I want to shut Patrick up, with his all-knowing, all-seeing ways.

'Oh… that's rather unfortunate,' he replies, giving the menu another glance. 'So now you're young, free and single again.' He looks up, eyes roving the dining room for the waiter.

I stare at him in amazement. How can he be so callous? Disregarding someone's death in four words. 'Rather unfortunate' is forgetting your list when you go shopping, not the end of something that lived and breathed, that shone with life. I stare at the white card in front of me, but there's nothing on it that I want.

Looking up, I smile. 'I get the feeling that you're altogether more sure of what you want from a relationship,' I say. 'So, go on then, tell me, Patrick. Are you looking for another wife?'

He considers the question seriously. 'Ultimately yes, that would be the end goal, and—'

'Well, good luck with that then,' I say getting to my feet. 'Oh, and enjoy your dinner. I hear the steak's tartare's very good.'

And then, head held high and knees shaking, I walk out, snatching my coat from the stand on the way.

The street outside is freezing, but I breathe in the calming cold, feeling it clear my senses. I pull on my coat, imagining the scene behind me and Patrick's haughty indignation. I've only taken about three steps when I feel a huge bubble of laughter welling up inside of me. Abby Prendergast, I tell myself, you have just had the luckiest escape. I suddenly feel light as the breeze, as if I'm flying. And with a loud explosive giggle, I run all the way home.

I close the shop door behind me and stand, leaning back against it for a moment, chest heaving. Everything is just as it should be. In all its baggy and a-bit-loose-at-the-seams glory. Exactly the way I like it.

I turn back to lock the door behind me once more and then, still smiling, I walk through the shop, blowing a kiss to Brown Bear as I go.

I can hear the sound of the television as I open the flat door. And there's a distinct smell of popcorn in the air. Just a regular Saturday night, and the thought widens my smile even further.

Slipping off my coat, I call a hello and set the kettle to boil on top of the stove. With any luck, I won't have missed too much of whichever film Beth and Debra are watching and, if I'm really lucky, there might even be some popcorn left. Time to put on my pyjamas.

I'm about to go through to the sitting room when two figures appear in the hallway.

Deb puts her hand over her heart. 'Oh, thank God it's you! We heard a noise and wondered what on earth it was.'

'Yep, only me,' I reply. 'I did shout hello.'

'But how come you're here?' she adds, quick to realise that I shouldn't be. 'Is everything all right?'

I smile at Beth. 'Oh yes, everything is fine,' I say. 'I decided to come home, that's all.'

Deb's mouth drops open. 'Why, what happened?'

'Well, Patrick was a complete…' I purse my lips. 'Evidently not my type. So, I decided to save us both the palaver and left.'

'Left?'

'Yes, got up and walked out.'

I can see Beth grinning at me from the corner of my eye.

'Abby, you didn't! The poor man.'

'That's hardly fair, Deb. He's far from poor and, besides, we hadn't got around to ordering so it's not like he's having to pay for me or anything. And he has such an inflated opinion of himself, I'm sure he'll have a lovely time.'

'I still can't believe you did that.'

'Me neither. Great, isn't it?'

Beth gives me a high five. 'Go, Mum!' she says, earning herself a disapproving glance from her aunt.

'Look, Deb, he was horrible, okay? And you know me, I'm not normally mean about someone, but, blimey, I can see why his wife left him.'

'But you must have only been there about five minutes.'

'I know, amazing, isn't it? I got all that and more in about three minutes. He doesn't want a relationship, or not the kind that other people might want, anyway. He turned his nose up at the suggestion that someone should be kind and caring. Called me romantic for wanting such a thing, only it wasn't a compliment, more like I'd suddenly contracted leprosy. What he actually wants is another wife, to make sure his evenings are ordered and enjoyable, his words. And that's because he has this mega-amazing job that means he works far harder than anyone else on the planet.'

Deb rolls her eyes. 'Well, now you're being melodramatic. I'm sure it wasn't as bad as that.'

'Were you there?' I ask, irritated now.

Beth sidles back into the lounge, sensing a confrontation looming.

'So, why, when I say it was awful, don't you believe me? Or at least give me the benefit of the doubt? It's almost as if you're saying that, given my position, I should be grateful for anything that comes along?'

'Abby, I didn't say that.'

'No, but yet you and Mum both seem to question my judgement. The man's a controlling, arrogant, self-centred scumbag and that should be enough. If it was evident to me within the first five minutes of meeting him that that he really isn't a very nice person, then why would staying make it any better? I've had enough miserable evenings, Deb, I don't need any more.'

Behind me, the kettle begins to whistle gently. I ignore it.

'I'm not saying that at all,' Deb replies. 'I get it, you didn't like him. But you didn't have to leave him sitting there, that's all I'm saying. I think it's a bit rude, especially as he was paying for dinner.'

'Which I didn't order, so no.'

She studies me for a moment as the noise from the kettle pitches up an octave. 'Not everyone is going to come up to Cam's standards, Abby, but if you don't let any of them at least have a chance then—'

'I was not comparing him to Cam, that's… that's…' I break off, unable to find the words, and then to my disgust, tears begin to well in my eyes.

'Oh, shit.' Deb comes forward to wrap her arms around me. 'I'm sorry, Abby, I didn't mean… Just ignore me. I let my mouth run away with me at times.' She gives me a quick squeeze. 'Of course you did the right thing in coming home. God, I'd hate to have to be part of the dating scene again. Imagine what I'd be like?' She gives a contrite smile, embarrassed by what she's said. 'Listen, I'll get out of your hair and you and Beth can watch the film together. You'll enjoy that. There are even some snacks left,' she wheedles.

I sigh. 'Why don't you stop too, Deb? Ian isn't expecting you back until later. Come and watch the film as well. It might be nice for you to have a girly night in, get away from the boys for one night.'

She hesitates, but then all too predictably, pulls a face. 'I'd better get back,' she says. 'But yeah, maybe we could do this another time.'

She picks up her bag from the kitchen table and ducks back into the living room.

'I'm going now, Beth, bye.'

I hear Beth's echoing goodbye and moments later, Deb's gone, leaving me standing in the kitchen as the kettle begins to scream.

Chapter 12

I lift my head from my keyboard as I hear a slow shuffle of feet outside the office door. It's twenty past nine but morning, for Beth at least, has just begun.

I'd got up early this morning, to tackle paperwork, but also to find the letter from the school I'd hidden. I need to find some time to talk to Beth today, before school resumes tomorrow. I've gone over and over the contents of the letter and I just can't see it. *Morose, sulky, uncommunicative.* Those were only some of the words her form tutor used, and that's not my Beth at all. I've looked for signs this week that anything was amiss, but she's been her usual self. Very pleased to be on half-term holiday, admittedly, but then she's always loved the school breaks, she's never bored. Like me, I guess, happy in her own company.

I quickly put aside the figures I've been going through so that I can join her for breakfast. Or in my case, *more* breakfast.

'Morning, sweetheart,' I say, entering the kitchen. I drop a kiss on the top of Beth's head as she pours herself a glass of orange juice from the fridge. 'Did you sleep okay?'

'Hmm,' she murmurs. 'Did you?'

'I did… woke up ravenous though. I only realised when I got up that I'd had no dinner last night.'

Beth's hand flies to her mouth. 'Oh no, you didn't, did you? And I ate most of the popcorn too, sorry.' She grins across at me as she sits down. 'Perhaps you should have stayed at the restaurant for something to eat at least.'

'No way, not a chance.' I grin back, taking a seat opposite her. 'Besides, seeing as it's the last day of the holiday, why don't I pop out for some croissants for breakfast?'

Beth's eyes flick downwards. 'It's okay, Mum, you don't have to do that. Besides, they're too expensive.' Her shoulders are also on a downward trajectory.

'Well, we don't do it very often. And I thought it would be nice to have a bit of a treat this morning. We've done nothing this week and I expect half your friends have been away, or out doing fun things, and you've been stuck here, helping your mum out in the shop.'

'But I like doing that.'

I smile. 'I know. But I sometimes think you might like to have a choice.'

Her finger traces a little bubble of condensation on the outside of her glass, but she doesn't reply.

'So then, croissant, is it?'

'Yes, please,' she replies. But she doesn't look quite as happy as I thought she would.

I'm halfway down the stairs before I realise that she's always quiet on the last day of any holiday; the thought of returning to school not a happy one when compared to being at home. In a way I hope it stays like that; that she always wants to be here with me. But I know that won't always be the case. I'm also very aware that it's quite possible that Beth knows I've received the letter from the school. That could well explain her quiet manner this morning. At least I can cross Patrick off her list of worries. And mine for that matter.

It's a bright morning and the town is beginning to get a little busier. There aren't many visitors here yet, but those that are, are already taking the opportunity of better weather for a leisurely Sunday morning stroll.

'Morning, Rumer,' I call, as I push open the door to her shop.

'Morning, lovely—' She stops. 'Blimey, things must be bad, I don't normally see you in here on a Sunday.'

'Last day of the school holiday,' I reply. 'A little treat is required.'

She gives me a sympathetic smile. 'Ah, say no more. Actually, Beth did look a bit down when I saw her the other day. Like she had the world on her shoulders. What can I get for you?'

My senses come to full alert. 'Just a couple of croissants, please. When was that?'

'Um…' Rumer stares down at the tongs in her hand. 'One day in the week. Wednesday, I think? She popped in for some cakes.'

'Oh yes, I remember.' It was the day that Patrick had been in to the shop to ask me out to dinner. But other than him putting a dent in the day, I don't remember there being anything else amiss. Beth had seemed her usual happy self. Head stuck in a book, but then… 'Did she say anything to you?' I ask.

'No, other than the usual time-of-day stuff. And she was fine when I was serving her, but it was busy when she arrived, and she had to wait. I looked up once or twice and she was staring into space.' She smiles. 'Not that there's anything unusual about that as such, especially not for someone's Beth's age. My Kieran is exactly the same. But she looked… the word "hopeless" springs to mind. Just staring out the window at the street outside with an odd expression on her face.'

I grimace, nodding. 'That makes sense. My mother had very kindly set me up on a date with the son of one of her friends. He'd popped into the shop before Beth came here. In fact, he was the reason *why* she came here and I think you might have given me my answer. I was a little bit worried how Beth would feel about me going out with him, particularly because our first encounter wasn't a roaring success. She must have been imagining all sorts of things.'

Rumer expertly drops two croissants into a paper bag and sets it down on the counter. 'Sorry, I didn't mean to dump this on you on top of everything else.'

I smile. 'No, it's okay, I'll have a chat to her when I get back. The date was last night; a bit of a disaster actually, so she's nothing to worry about on that score.' I hand over a five-pound note, only then realising what Rumer had said. 'What's everything else though?' I ask.

Rumer's eyes widen a little. 'The rates increase?'

I look at her in horror. 'Oh God, have they made it official then?'

She groans. 'Sorry, Abby, I thought you would have seen it. Me and my big mouth. It's not official as such, but it's looking that way.' She takes my money and hands over my change, before nodding. 'Hang on a sec,' she adds, disappearing into the small area at the back of her shop. She's holding a newspaper when she returns. 'This was leaked to the paper by an unknown source, although I've asked around and most people seem to think it's legit.'

Now that she's closer, I can see that it's a copy of the weekly news, folded in half so that one particular article is uppermost. I haven't got around to reading mine yet, it's still beneath the counter at the shop where I'd shoved it. I take it from her, the headline stark. And my heart rapidly sinks.

'But they can't do this, can they?' I ask, once I've finished reading.

She sighs. 'Apparently, they can. It's sneaky, but then that's about par for the course for the town council. They're going ahead with re-banding all the commercial areas, which is what Richard at the stationery shop was so concerned about, if you remember. And it seems as if he was right to be. They're not only going ahead with the re-banding, they're using it as an excuse to hike the business rates. Something about needing to provide more funding for infrastructure, whatever that is.'

I scan the article once more. 'From April… *this* April?'

'Yep. Start of the new financial year.'

'Shit.'

'Funnily enough, that's exactly what I thought.' She takes the paper bag back from the countertop and slides two more croissants inside. 'One each is not enough, is it? And my treat before you argue. While I still can.'

'Oh, Rumer…' I look back at her anxious face. 'What will you do?'

She shrugs. 'Not much I can do, is there? Do my sums very carefully, the same as everyone else. Beyond that, I really don't know at the moment. How about you?'

But I don't have an answer, I'm still trying to get my head around what this might mean.

'Richard is keen to start organising a few things,' adds Rumer. 'A petition and some kind of protest, I think. But I haven't spoken to him about it yet.'

'No, me neither.' I'd forgotten all about his letter, something I'm beginning to regret. 'Although we don't even know if the information is true yet,' I reply. 'The paper clearly says they can't confirm the details.'

'No, but the rates letters are due in about two weeks…' She trails off, not needing to say any more. We both know what's likely to happen.

I reach out to take the croissants. 'I'd better get back, Rumer, but thank you. And let me know if you hear anything else, won't you?'

She nods. 'And likewise.'

'Yes, of course. Keep smiling.'

Beth is still sitting at the kitchen table when I get back, although predictably a book has found its way into her hands. I'd already filled my coffee pot earlier and I set it on the stove to heat before joining her, placing the bag of croissants in front of us.

'As it is, straight out of the bag?' I ask her. 'Or warmed?'

She thinks for a moment, hesitant. 'Could I have it warmed?' she replies. 'With jam?'

'Aha! The full works. A brilliant idea. I've got some of that apricot jam you like too, shall we open a jar?'

She nods, pleased, but not as enthusiastic as she might have been. She gets up and takes the bag over to the oven while I disappear to the pantry.

'Oh…' I hear her say.

'Yes, Rumer slipped us an extra one each,' I reply. 'She thought we might be in need of them.' I rejoin her at the counter, jam in hand. 'And I agree with her. Actually, she mentioned that you'd seemed a bit down when you were there earlier in the week. The day when Patrick came in.'

Beth doesn't reply, but switches on the oven and pops the croissants onto a tray, sliding them inside.

'You don't have to worry about Patrick, you know,' I say gently. 'Or that Aunty Deb and I got a bit cross with one another.'

She looks up at me. 'I know. But it wasn't very nice, was it? Why does she always want to boss you around?'

I take two plates down from the cupboard on the wall and lay them out. 'She's a bit like Granny,' I reply. 'She wants what's best for me, but she doesn't always understand that what I want isn't the same as what she wants. We're different people, that's all.'

Beth thinks for a moment. 'But I don't get that,' she says. 'If they want you to be happy, why don't they listen to what you say?'

I give her a sideways glance. 'Good point. But they're only trying to help.'

She shakes her head. 'But it isn't just Granny, is it?' she says. 'Or Aunty Deb. Loads of people say it. They always want you to be a certain way, and I don't understand why you can't just be the way you want to be.'

Somehow I don't think we're talking about my mum and sister any longer. 'That's one of life's little mysteries,' I reply. 'And a question you'll probably have cause to ponder many times over the course of your lifetime. Can you get the butter out of the fridge, please?' I thank her as she passes it to me. 'But I wonder if it's because we can only really see things from our point of view, and never fully understand anyone else's. Therefore, we think our way is best. And then, logically, if our way *is* the best, we don't understand why other people aren't like us.'

Beth opens the oven door and hovers her hand over the top of the croissants, testing the heat. She closes it again and looks at me, frowning. 'But that doesn't make sense either,' she says. 'If everyone did the same as everyone else then we'd all be alike. What's the point in that? It would be awful.'

I smile, smoothing down her hair and tucking one strand of it behind her ears. 'It would. Which is why I always tell you that one of the most important things in life, and fun things, actually, is to find out who you are as a person, what you like and don't like and then keep adding to the list. It's that corny "life is a journey" thing,' I add, exaggerating my final words. 'But just because it's corny, that doesn't make it untrue. Not everyone understands that, even lots of adults. You're one of the clever ones.'

Beth had smiled at my words but now her face falls. 'Well, you're the only one who thinks so,' she replies, her expression glum.

'Which? Thinks you're clever, or thinks you should be yourself?'

'Both.' She turns off the oven and removes the tray with gloves, setting it on top of the hob.

I fetch the bread knife from the drawer and slice each of the croissants lengthways. 'Do you want to put your jam on, or shall I do it?'

'Can you? You always do it better than me.'

I slather on copious quantities of both butter and jam. This is not a day for half measures. I hand Beth her plate and watch as she sits down. The coffee pot has been burbling away happily for a little while and I pour myself a mug, before joining her.

There's a question to be asked here, but I don't want to spoil Beth's enjoyment of her breakfast and so I wait a few moments while we both devour the slightly warm and oozily sweet pastries. I'll need to run around the block several times after this lot but Rumer certainly does make exceedingly good croissants.

Beth's breakfast disappears rather faster than mine, and I watch as she runs a finger over some stray jam on her plate.

'Is everything okay? You know, at school and stuff?' I ask lightly.

She gives me a questioning look. And then rolls her eyes, having guessed, quite rightly, where this is going. 'Has Mr Cousens written to you?'

'He did.' I pause, taking in her expression. 'But I thought what he'd written was a load of rubbish. He used words like "sulky" and "uncommunicative" and I didn't think that sounded like my daughter at all. So, I wondered where he got those ideas from.'

Beth risks a peep at me from under her lashes. 'Because they think that's the way I am,' she says. Plural now, I notice.

'Whatever would have given them that idea?'

'Because I'm quiet, because I don't join in, because I don't want to be like all the other girls.'

I nod. 'Oh, I *see*. Why, what are they like?'

Beth leans forward. 'Awful,' she says. 'And silly. All they go on about are clothes and boys and stupid programmes on the telly.'

I know exactly what she means. And it's something that's always been a mystery to me too. My sister has accused me of being a snob in the past, saying I look down on her because she enjoys *Love Island* and pictures of fit firemen. Maybe I am, but it all seems so senseless to me, so boring and pointless. And that's another reason why Patrick and I were never going to work out. He doesn't read, something that I've built my whole life around. Given that one single piece of information alone, how could anyone ever think we would be compatible? I've spent my life feeling like a misfit, feeling like I didn't belong, because of the way I am. But Cam had changed all that. Cam hadn't needed things explaining, he… I bring the train of thought to a close.

The only difference between Beth and me is that, now I'm older, I've been able to carve out the life I want for myself and live it. With no interference from anyone. Beth doesn't have that luxury, at least not yet, and my heart goes out to her. She still has a lot of years in education ahead of her and that's a lot of time to feel on your own.

'What about Trudi?' I ask. Her best friend from primary school. 'How are things with her?'

'She's okay, I suppose, some of the time – when we're on our own. But when there's a whole of group of us, she pretends she's just like them. And worse, she thinks they like her, but they don't. I've heard them talking about her behind her back.'

Girls can be so cruel to one another.

'And you don't want to be like that either?'

'No, I don't, they're stupid.' Her voice raises.

'Well, I guess you have two choices. You can carry on as you are, true to yourself, or you can pretend to be like everyone else just to get along with them.'

'But which one is right?'

I sigh. 'That's a very difficult question. The trouble with pretending to be like everyone else is that if you do it for long enough, you can end up believing that's who you really are. Then one day, you wake up wondering what happened to you. Plus, the friendships you make under those circumstances aren't real ones. You can get on well enough, and enjoy their company, go out with them loads, all of that. But they'll never be the kind of friends who are there for you no matter what. The kind who understand you and like you for who you really are.'

People like Cam, I think.

'But of course the opposite is also true. If you decide you don't want to be like everyone else, then that might feel like a better choice, but it might also mean you're on your own much more than the others are, or you don't have as many friends, and that can be hard too.'

'Is that what you did?'

I smile. Busted. 'I did. I decided that in the big wide world there were bound to be other people like me so all I had to do was wait and someday I would find them. And I was right. But it's a very difficult choice to make and no one else can make it for you.'

'I don't want to be like them, Mum, but…' She stops, as if uncertain whether she wants to confess any more. Her finger is still running around her plate, tracing a circle. 'Anyway, I don't see what's wrong with being me. Am I really that awful?'

Her mouth is drawn into a pout, but I know that tears aren't very far behind. It tugs sharply on my heartstrings. Being eleven is such a horrible age, and I remember it keenly; the desperation to fit in, to look pretty, to be popular, coupled with the anxiety of a body doing things you wish it wouldn't and the realisation that relationships are no longer as simple as they were at primary school. But I'm immensely proud of Beth for wearing what she wants to and refusing to give up the things she loves simply because they aren't considered 'cool'. I was lucky though, I'd had my best friend, Helen, throughout my school years. The two of us were inseparable, and together we shielded each other from everything outside of our comfort zones. Even though that changed when I was eighteen, I was old enough, mostly, to weather the storm.

'No, you're not awful at all. Beth, you are one of the brightest, funniest and most special people I know. You have this spark about you that anyone with any sense can see. Don't let that go out, just to become like everyone else.'

'But you're gonna say that, you're my mum.'

'Perhaps. But I also know that plenty of other people think it too.'

She bites her lip. 'Was Cam one of those people, do you think? Only when he was here, he said he'd really liked my dungarees. Do you think he was just saying that?'

'No, I don't. I might not have known him for that long, but he never lied. He always said what he thought.' I think back to the discussions we had, on such a wide range of topics; how much like a breath of fresh air this was. 'But I also think that maybe the difference is that he was an adult. And he'd worked out what he did and didn't like. Which is not the case for the girls at school. They're not old enough yet to have experienced all the things which will allow them to make those judgements, and so they make fun of anyone that isn't like them. Simply because they don't know any better. Does that make sense?'

Beth scratches the end of her nose. 'I think so. Is that why they tease me?'

Tease… or bully?

'I expect so. What sort of things do they say?'

'That I'm a weirdo, and think I'm so clever because I'm always reading.'

I look at her carefully. 'Is that all they do, Beth?'

Her head drops.

'Who is it?' I ask. 'The girls in your class?'

'Partly,' she says. 'But it started with the girls in the drama group, making fun of me because I was too young to join in, and not good enough, even though I reckoned I was. The one girl said I was up myself, and she has a sister in my year so that's how everyone knows now. She started talking about how I was boring and dumb and now everyone believes her.'

'Well, I'm guessing that the girls in the drama group are jealous because you're a much better singer than they are. They're used to getting all the big parts in the shows, and everyone telling them how wonderful they are. I expect they feel threatened.'

It's easy enough to work out their motives, but that still doesn't make it any better for Beth. 'So, what kind of things do they do?'

'Ignore me, mostly, but one or two of them push me in the corridors, that kind of thing. Kick my schoolbag, or hide it.'

Which is why Beth has had a few marks on her weekly card recently for not being prepared for lessons. Things are beginning to make a lot more sense.

'So, what do we do about all this?' I ask her. 'I can talk to Mr Cousens, if you like?'

She stares down at her plate. 'Won't that make it worse? If the girls get into trouble, I mean.'

'Beth, if they've done something wrong, they deserve to get into trouble. But I can explain how worried you are to Mr Cousens. He doesn't necessarily need to talk to the girls, not yet anyway. He just needs to make sure that the teachers know what's going on, so they can keep an eye on things.'

'S'pose.'

I pop the last piece of croissant in my mouth and copy Beth's movement, chasing the remnants of jam and flaky pastry around my plate with my finger.

'Right then,' I say. 'That's enough talk about horrible girls and school. It's our last day, so what shall we do?' I'm desperately trying to think of something that Beth would really like. 'We could go to Norwich, if you want?'

Her face lights up, but then falls. 'It's a bit late for that though, isn't it?'

'It's not even half past ten yet. If you get a move on, we can be there for half twelve, and have the whole afternoon there. The market, the bookstalls, lunch at that place by the river, a walk, bit of shopping, whatever you like. And there's no rush back, is there? You've done all your homework – as long as we're back in time for a shower and hair wash.'

Beth jumps to her feet. 'I'll go and get dressed,' she says.

Chapter 13

March

Gwen takes one look at me as I come through the shop door and puts down the pile of books she has in her arms. 'One cup of very restorative tea coming up,' she says, disappearing into the back room.

For once I'm glad the place is empty as I have a feeling what I'm about to say isn't the kind of thing I'd want book browsers to hear. I slip off my coat and hang it up by the stairs before making straight for the shelf where I'd left Brown Bear a couple of weeks ago.

'I'm counting on you,' I say. 'You're supposed to be bringing hope.' Surveying the shop for another place to put him, I decide to give Mr Ridley's chair a go. At least if he's there, someone might pick him up and give him a cuddle, even Mr Ridley himself. Perhaps that will help.

There's a box of books on the counter that Gwen is in the middle of unpacking, but she slides them off and onto the floor. 'Those can wait,' she says, before disappearing again, reappearing a moment later with a mug and a carton of milk. 'Does this smell weird to you?' she says, thrusting the carton under my nose.

I shake my head. 'It shouldn't do, it's fresh this morning.'

She shrugs. 'Okay, just me then.' She directs my attention to a box of Jaffa Cakes under the counter. 'I bought those on the way in,' she says, handing me my tea before disappearing once more with the milk. 'And don't argue,' she adds, rejoining me. 'I had a feeling you might need them. Don't forget the school and I have had dealings before.'

Gwen used to work in the office there for a while before she joined me.

'So, come on then,' she adds, folding her arms. 'What did Mr Cousens say?'

I take a deep breath. The school is a fifteen-minute walk away, which means that I've had plenty of time to build up a good head of steam on my way back.

'Jumped up little—' I break off. I promised myself I wouldn't swear. 'Honestly, you'd think he was doing me a massive favour by seeing me at all. Never mind the fact that he's kept me waiting two weeks for an appointment.'

'But he was the one who wrote to you!'

'Exactly,' I reply. 'And yet Mr Cousens clearly believes that his time is far more valuable than anyone else's.' I take a sip of tea. 'He was surprised I'd wanted to see him, saying that his letter was only a courtesy to keep me informed of certain things. He'd tried to ring me first apparently before sending it, but couldn't get hold of me. I never had any missed calls though.' I give her a pointed look.

'Well, I hope he listened to what you had to say.'

'Barely. He seemed bemused that I was taking things so seriously, that he didn't think it was an urgent problem.'

'Not urgent?' Gwen looks disgusted.

'I did inform him of all the things which have happened during the last two weeks, but I could tell he thought I was overreacting. I couldn't make him understand that when it's something which involves your own child, you do consider it urgent.'

'But he has kids of his own, doesn't he?'

'Yes, but presumably ones who don't get bullied at school,' I reply. 'And I swear he looked at me as if he could completely understand why Beth is having problems.'

'None of that,' admonishes Gwen. 'What else did he say?'

'That as far as he was aware there were no specific problems. During the last pastoral staff meeting, several of the teachers had commented that Beth is very quiet, that was all. And was frequently on her own, looked upset, that kind of thing.'

'So, didn't he acknowledge that what people have seen isn't her normal behaviour, and that there are very clear reasons for it?'

'He just repeated that he wasn't aware of anything, but that he would "ask" around. He obviously wasn't going to admit to there being a problem, even when I pointed out that simply because he isn't aware of it, it doesn't mean it's not going on.'

Gwen pulls a face. 'Ouch,' she says.

'Well, he deserved it. Condescending so-and-so. Going on about how Year Seven pupils often find the transition between primary and secondary school hard, *some more than others*. So, I mentioned that Beth had tried to become involved in things she enjoyed, like the drama club, for example, and the show, but that she'd been discouraged from doing so. His answer was that the show in particular is viewed as a reward for the older year groups, those leading up to their GCSEs. As such, while there isn't a written rule to this effect, what it means in practice is that pupils from Year Seven aren't usually encouraged to take active roles.'

'Brilliant,' Gwen replies. 'So, it's Beth's problem, not theirs?'

'Pretty much, yes.'

'Have a Jaffa Cake,' says Gwen. 'Have several.'

'What really annoys me is how worried Beth was that my talking to Mr Cousens would get the girls into trouble, and the possible backlash she might receive as a result. When, in fact, now what's happened is that she's been labelled a troublemaker, while I'm a neurotic mother. Perhaps I am, I don't know.'

'You're not,' says Gwen firmly, giving me her no-nonsense look. 'You're a mother, and a damned good one. You're supposed to care about the welfare of your child. Don't ever feel guilty about that.'

'Thing is, Gwen, I can't help but wonder if it isn't all my fault. I was exactly the same when I was her age. I much preferred to have my head in a book than talking to other people.'

'There's nothing wrong with that. Okay, so people skills are important too, but it isn't as if Beth falls down in that regard. And neither do you, you run a shop for goodness' sake. Beth's just choosy about who she talks to. But when she does, she's articulate, has an exceptional vocabulary for someone her age and she's interesting too, *because* she reads. She's far more clued-up on the world and its goings on than most eleven-year-olds.'

I smile at Gwen, knowing she feels as indignant as I do. 'I know. But I don't really set a good example, do I? I hardly go out. I can count my friends on one hand. I have a failed marriage behind me and am welcoming spinsterhood at an alarming rate of knots. It worries me that this is all Beth has to look forward to as well.'

Gwen plants her hands on her hips, brow furrowed. 'Do you want to restate that sentence the way it actually is?' she asks, her eyebrows now arched in the way that I have always been envious of. One slightly higher than the other, a perfect point at its peak. 'In that you have several very good friends, who would move heaven and earth for you if you needed them to, instead of the opposite, which is a bunch of shallow acquaintances who would disappear at the first sign of trouble. In that you were smart enough to walk away from a manipulative relationship for the sake of yourself and your daughter. In that you are an independent, intelligent young woman who makes her own choices about life and doesn't need a man on her arm to validate who she is.'

A bubble of laughter escapes from behind the half-eaten Jaffa Cake still in my mouth. 'And that is why I love you, Gwen,' I say. 'Don't stop there.'

She laughs too. 'It's true!'

'You've been on the positive reframing course, more like,' I reply, but my smile is warm. Gwen has always been able to make me laugh. 'Beth has a lot of school years ahead of her though and, as we both know, that's not an environment where it's good to be an individual. And it's a long time to be unhappy or feel alone. She mentioned that Trudi seems rather ambivalent as well and they've been friends for so long, it would be awful if that were to end. I don't know what I would have done without Helen by my side when I was younger.'

'This was your friend who died?' asks Gwen.

I nod. 'Hmm, when I was eighteen. We grew up together and weathered everything that life threw at us. Oh God, listen to me, as if we had even had a life when we were eighteen. But that's what it felt like, it was just me and her against the world. I was devastated when she died, and for a long while I blamed myself about that too.'

'Why, what happened?'

'Her family had a house in Portugal and the summer before we were supposed to go to uni, they invited me out there with them. But I was getting over glandular fever so couldn't go. And then when they were out walking one day, a route they often used to take up into the hills, Helen slipped on a rock and fell, hitting her head. It was a freak accident, no more, but she died.'

'But you weren't even there,' replies Gwen. 'How could you be to blame?'

'For exactly that reason,' I reply. 'In my head I thought that if I had been there, I would have been beside her and the accident would never have happened.'

'You can't know that,' says Gwen, gently.

I smile. 'I know, daft, isn't it?'

'Human.' She rubs my arm, and I can see a thought catch hold of her. 'So that's why… You've said before how you only ended up with James because you were an easy target. That's why, isn't it? That's what you meant.'

'I'd never felt so alone,' I say. 'So, when James came along, and he was funny and charming and kind and caring, I fell for it hook, line and sinker. And even when he began to turn it on and off, making me jump through hoops for the teeniest scrap of affection, I didn't see it for the manipulation it was. It was like a drug, and I'd do anything to be in his good books. It took me a long while – too long – to realise that the price I was paying was simply too high.'

Gwen stares at me, eyes slightly narrowed. 'But none of that means the same will be true for Beth. And, in case you were thinking it, neither was it the case with Cam. That was the real deal, Abby.' Her face falls. 'But I think you know that too, sorry.'

'I think that might be why his death has hit me so hard,' I reply, straightening myself up. 'And I know that my past is no indication of Beth's future, but it's there all the same, staring me in the face. I have to be braver with my life, for her sake.'

Gwen takes a Jaffa Cake and then resolutely screws up the packet, pushing it back into the box. 'The fact that you know this means you are already halfway there. Besides, there's plenty of time yet to be brave. You don't have to do it all at once. Meanwhile, try not to worry about school and Mr Cousens' list of excuses.'

'Okay,' I reply, looking at my watch. 'Right, there're a couple of hours to go before Beth gets back from school. Will you be okay down here for a bit, while I go and deal with today's orders?'

She nods. 'I'll get the rest of that box unpacked. You go, and I'll bring up any others.'

I'd forgotten that the office is still a complete mess. I was in the middle of packaging books when I'd had to leave to keep my appointment at the school, but although it means that there's rather more to do than I'd first thought, at least it will keep me busy and my mind occupied. I click on my emails and refresh my memory of where I'd got to.

I've made a good start by the time Gwen appears with an armful of books and several letters balanced on top. She deposits them with a beaming smile and hurries back downstairs, leaving me groaning at her retreating back. But I mustn't complain: these are all orders, and orders mean money. I've already clocked the letter from the council among the pile of post. I dump them on my desk, steadfastly turning away and pick up the first of the books from the pile, smoothing out the delivery note that Gwen has tucked inside it.

The routine and rhythm of attending to each order is so ingrained, it's soothing. It's a combination of updating our computerised ordering and accounts system, together with the manual aspects of packaging the orders, printing out the postage slip, and my favourite part, writing a personal message on a postcard which I had specially designed. We're a small business and I'm proud we can do things in a small-business way.

I'm almost two-thirds of the way down today's pile before I pluck up enough courage to open the letter that sits mocking me on the desk. And even then, I open the others first, pleased to find several more orders among them. But I can't put it off any longer and, settling myself in my chair, I slide a finger under the self-seal on the back of the envelope.

It's even worse than I feared and my imagination had already painted a pretty bleak picture. I've obviously done the worst-case scenario sums, and the hike in business rates is only just affordable, as long as custom remains as it has been and with a following wind. But there are no guarantees, and it leaves me with no wriggle room whatsoever. Any variation in this and we're sunk. And with it, any thoughts I had about the security of my future. And Beth's.

I lay the letter back down on the desk. And then cover it with another. I've lain awake enough times trying to think of a solution to know that one isn't going to come to me now.

I pick up the next book from the pile and plough on. I want to get these finished before Beth gets home. It's Friday night, and that means chippy tea and no work.

It's gone half past three by the time I finish and I'm surprised to see how late it is. Beth is probably downstairs, nattering. She often does that on a Friday, when she has the promise of the weekend ahead of her and is therefore far more relaxed than on school days.

Except that when I emerge beside Gwen at the counter, Beth is nowhere to be seen. Gwen is serving a customer, so I collect her mug and take it through to wash, ready for when Beth appears. It's quite likely that she's saved up a bit of her dinner money from the week and is currently buying something involving chocolate from the newsagents. She knows I know she does this, but then, given the opportunity, I'd probably do the same.

Gwen turns the moment I leave the kitchen, enquiry on her face. 'How bad is it?' she asks.

My heart sinks. Gwen will have seen the council's letter and she talks to other shopkeepers as much as I do. She's very well aware of the council's proposals. It isn't fair to keep the information from her, however much I want to shield her from its impact because this affects her as well, very much so. She has every right to ask.

'About as bad as I feared.' I sigh. 'No, actually, it's worse.'

Gwen nods. 'Bastards,' she says succinctly. 'How can this be good for any of the businesses here? It's all fine and dandy wanting to raise extra funds for new pavements and car parks and fancy signs and stuff, but what good is that when half the shops will be shut? It's the worst kind of short-sighted behaviour.' She growls. 'It makes my blood boil.'

She's absolutely right of course, and I know her anger doesn't stem from concern over her own welfare, but rather mine.

'Why do these kinds of letters always arrive on a Friday so that you have the whole weekend to stew on them?? That just seems like spite.'

'They do it so that you can't ring anyone to speak about it,' replies Gwen with bile. 'They all finish early on a Friday at the council, don't they? It's the first rule of delivering bad news – the government do it all the time. Only ever release it on a Friday night.'

I blow out a puff of air and stare out the window down the street. 'The trouble is that people don't seem to want to buy books any more, Gwen. And that saddens me more than anything.' I give her a weak smile. 'Never mind, we'll think of something,' I add. 'I'm not dead in the water yet.'

'Well, so long as you think about you and Beth first. Never mind me, I can sort myself out.'

'Thanks, Gwen.' I hold her look for a moment, the warmth of our friendship passing between us. I know that she doesn't need to work here, she only does so because she enjoys it, but she also knows I'll do anything to keep her here too. I catch sight of the clock, frowning. 'Beth's late,' I remark. 'Later even than her usual late can be.'

But as I pull my phone from my pocket to check for messages, I see her figure come hurtling around the corner of the street. She's dishevelled, muddy and very upset. The door crashes open and she rushes through to the kitchen, barely containing her sobs. A line of water drips onto the floor behind her as she passes.

I look at Gwen. 'What the…?'

I arrive in the doorway to see her dumping her school bag in the sink, and even from here, I can see how sodden it is.

'Beth, what on earth's happened?' I open my arms as she throws herself into them, tears shaking her shoulders.

It's some minutes before she can speak.

I hold her away from me slightly to get a better look at her. The hem of her coat is wet and covered in mud, as are her shoes, her tights and her hands. A splodge of something dark clings to the side of her face.

'Have you hurt yourself?' I ask. My first though is that she's fallen somehow. But she shakes her head violently.

'I told them not to, Mum, but they wouldn't listen. Just kept jeering at me, laughing about my "precious books".' The sarcastic way she says these last two words lets me know that she's repeating something that's been said to her. And I feel anger stir.

'And I only got it back because a lady who was walking her dog helped me get it out.'

I flash a look between her and the sink. 'Your school bag?'

She nods. 'They threw it in the river, but I wasn't even doing anything, Mum, just walking!'

'Who threw it, Beth?'

'The girls, all of them. Well, Emily threw it, but all the rest of them were there, laughing at me, egging her on to do it. Only Emily's so pathetic, she couldn't throw it very far and so it landed in the reeds at the edge of the water. The lady helped me fish it out, then she yelled at them to go away, and walked me to the top of the High Street.'

Gwen has come to stand in the doorway, a murderous look on her face.

'But where was Trudi?' I ask, belatedly realising that she goes straight to her dance class after school on a Friday. So, Beth will have been walking home alone. I pull her back towards me, cradling her head and stroking the back of her hair. 'You don't need to worry about your bag, sweetheart. That can all be replaced. I'm just glad that you're okay.'

She sniffs. 'But my books...' And I know she doesn't mean her school books, but rather the ones she's been reading. 'Never mind, we can buy new ones.'

Gwen comes forward and wraps her arms around both of us, and we stay that way for several moments.

'I'm sorry, Mum,' says Beth eventually, her words still hiccuping between tears.

'It's not your fault,' I hush. 'It's not your fault.'

It's almost closing time before I come back down the stairs, having taken Beth up to the flat and made her a drink and buttered her some hot toast. I threw her uniform in the wash while she went to have a shower, and it was only when I was sure she was okay that I ventured back down to the shop.

Gwen gets instantly to her feet.

'She's okay,' I say in response to her unasked question. 'But Mr Cousens is going to be far from okay when I've finished with him, come Monday.'

Gwen nods. 'I've emptied her school bag and done the best I could with everything in it.' She pauses. 'But I took some photos first. I thought it would be good to have them.'

'Thanks, Gwen,' I say, touched by her solidarity. 'I'd like to see them argue against bullying now.'

She sighs. 'It's been a bit of a day, hasn't it? One way or another.'

'I can't argue with that,' I reply, giving her a weak smile. 'Makes you wonder why everything has to be so rubbish sometimes, doesn't it?'

'Hmm.' She collects the keys from under the counter and goes to lock the front door. 'Well, once we're done here, I recommend that you and Beth lock yourselves away from all the nastiness in the world, put on your PJs, paint your toenails and snuggle up on the sofa.'

'That sounds like a fine idea.' I pull my phone from my pocket and out of habit, click on my emails. I could do with something to cheer me up, and without even thinking about it, I open the folder holding Cam's emails.

It's such a beautiful time on the island, at least I think so. A lot of folks probably don't even notice the difference, so maybe it's simply that I'm outside a lot, but the air has this beautiful lightness about it. I don't mean the colour of it, just a slight warmth, a relaxing... that probably makes no sense at all. But I swear I'm not the only one that notices; the birds and animals do too. I was sitting out by the lighthouse today, watching a clutch of guillemots wheeling about the sky, riding the thermals. They were doing it for no other reason than because they can, just happy to be alive. And that's what the air feels like to me today, full of possibility, full of promise.

His words hover in the air in front of me, soothing and calming. I can picture it all so clearly. I look up as Gwen comes back towards the desk.

'Right. Well, I know one thing I'm going to do tonight,' I say.

'Oh, what's that?' she asks, frowning a little at the determined look that must be on my face.

'Book a holiday,' I reply.

Chapter 14

April

I've never understood people who say they don't like long train journeys. Even as a child, I loved them. The excitement of the station, the bustle of people, the thrill of all those lives interconnecting. Who were these people? Where were they going? Trains were romantic, they spoke of far-off adventure, exotic travel and experiences never before dreamed of. And once you'd got past all that, even if it didn't quite live up to your expectations, then you also got the chance to read, uninterrupted, for *hours*.

Apart from my grandparents who owned the shop before I did, I was the only one who read in our family. And now Beth, of course. It's as if it skipped a generation. I don't think my parents could ever understand my desire to forgo other entertainments for the opportunity to read instead. They were always nagging me to put my book down and join in, or would force me outside to get some fresh air. But on a train, or any other type of activity that took considerable time, they were never more thrilled at my ability to keep myself entertained for hours on end. My sister might cry and rant with frustration at how bored she was, but they never heard that from me. And I savoured those opportunities, even though they were few and far between.

Now, as Beth and I stand in my bedroom surveying our assortment
of bags and cases, the biggest question on our lips is whether we have
enough books. It's almost a seven-hour journey to get to Glasgow and
the onward leg from there will double that time. But on this occasion,
it's not just a corny expression, it really is as much about the journey
as the destination.

I still can't quite believe we're doing this. Two weeks ago, when I
impetuously booked this holiday, it had felt like the only course of
action open to me. I wanted to get Beth and myself as far away from
our current reality as I possibly could, and in terms of geography, I had
definitely succeeded. But it wasn't only the miles I wanted under our
belts, but the chance for us to breathe a different air, to be somewhere
there were different priorities, where lives were lived according to
different rules. Today, though, the sheer practicalities of getting us
and our luggage to the other end of the country and some seems like
a mission impossible.

As a single parent with a shop to run and a constant eye on the
budget, our holidays have usually amounted to nothing more extrava-
gant than a few days away in a caravan or camping. Certainly, never
anything as far or exciting as a remote Scottish island that, until I'd
started talking to Cam, neither of us had heard of before. But Beth's
as desperate to be away as I am.

She hasn't been involved in any other incidents in quite the same
league as the throwing of her school bag in the river, but in a way it's
been far more insidious. A constant stream of what's considered low-
level bullying now accompanies each of her days at school. Jostling in
the corridor, or comments made about her that she can't quite hear.
Sly looks, pointing fingers and laughter that erupts as she walks past
are only a few of the things she has to put up with. In the space of a

few short weeks, it's turned my daughter from a happy-go-lucky soul into a withdrawn and watchful shadow of herself.

So, above all, apart from the glorious scenery and the wildlife, and the wild and free air, what I'm looking forward to most is some space, not just around us, but in my head too. The chance to slow down, to think, to gain some perspective and some distance from our most pressing problems and decide in which directions our lives should go. Or not, of course. Maybe the best solution will be to simply stay as we are, but right now, it feels as if everything is being forced into a smaller and smaller channel, compressed and unable to breathe.

I've thought long and hard about whether I should let anyone know that we're coming to Kinlossay. But who would I tell? And what would I say? It could all end up being horribly awkward and that's the last thing I want. No one on the island will even know who I am, and I think it's better that way. I've been close to tears twice already this morning, not out of grief, although that's always there, pencilling in my days in various shades of grey, but because of the poignancy of going to the place where Cam lived. Maybe it isn't the most sensible thing to do, but he's like a ghost at the moment, one I can't exorcise, and I think this might be the only way to finally lay his memory to rest and move on.

I look around the room, mentally double-checking we have everything we need. Far too much, probably, but the journey there is going to require almost as much as the holiday itself.

'Right then, are you ready?'

I grin at Beth and she grins back, picking up her rucksack and slinging it over one shoulder. And then we're dragging suitcases down the stairs and out into the shop, where a departure committee are waiting to see us off.

Gwen is there, of course, and her husband, Rhys, holding her suitcase so that she can move in for a week while we move out. There's Lottie too, thrilled at the prospect of earning some money over the Easter break from uni, and my mother, who disapproves of our destination even though she hasn't said as much. Lastly is Mr Ridley, holding Brown Bear in his arms, and I'm touched that he's joined everyone to say goodbye. He'll go back to his seat once we've gone, and probably won't say another word, but it's the thought that counts.

We're almost out the door when Gwen comes rushing forward, throwing her arms around me for one last hug. Quick and tight, she pulls away, and there's a glint in her eye that could be a tear or could be the light catching it. But there's an odd look on her face too, like she's about to say something, but doesn't quite know whether she should.

'I'll text you,' she says, smiling.

She's already made me agree not to keep in touch. I'm allowed one message to let her know we've arrived safe and sound and then no more until we're on our way home. She's determined that I'm not to worry about anything. The shop will be in good hands and she doesn't want me to give the place another thought while we're away. I've told her that the phone signal on the island is patchy and the Wi-Fi weak at best, but she still made me promise. And now here she is, telling me she'll text me. I smile back, knowing that it's only because she wants this holiday to work for us as much as I do.

The sunshine is vague as we wheel our suitcases through the streets, but it's there, glinting on the windows and the pale, sandy-coloured stone of the buildings we pass, and it feels like a good omen somehow.

London would normally be greeted with great excitement, but today it's just a quick pitstop on our journey. There's only time to marvel at the grandeur of St Pancras station and take a quick look in one or two very glamorous shops before we board another train to Glasgow. It's the longest leg of our journey and although we chat for a while, content to gaze at the moving scenery, the conversation dries up as we wind our way north. In unspoken accord we both remove a book from our bags and settle down to read. And the miles pass.

By the time we reach Glasgow, we're exhausted, not just weary from the passage of time, but weary of being seated for hours on end. And, as we step from the train, I feel as if I will never be able to stand up straight again. But we are here, almost there, and the feeling is indescribable.

My heart is in my mouth as we descend from the ferry to the quayside the next day. We're back on dry land. This is Kinlossay. A tiny island in the Inner Hebrides and the place where Cam lived.

I've never felt so far from home, and what had felt like an exciting adventure when we left, now feels overwhelming and foolhardy. I'm very relieved to see that everything looks exactly as I remember from the countless images I'd googled of the island. The low, single-storey stone building that is the ferry terminal. The car park, dotted with utility vehicles and almost empty, and the single-track road that leads away almost in a straight line. And, on either side, green as far as the eye can see.

Beth wheels her suitcase up beside me, looking very grateful to be back on firm ground, and squints up at the sky. There seems to be an awful lot of it and one half is the brightest blue, as if split by some unseeing hand, and the feel of the sun on our faces is like no other. It feels as if we've arrived on a very, very distant land indeed. There is noise all around us, other people, vehicles and mechanical noises as things are unloaded from the ferry, but the silence here runs deeper than anything I've felt before. As Beth turns and stares up the road ahead of us, I swear I see her shoulders relax for the first time in weeks and my heart lifts.

A waving arm attracts my attention and as I peer closer, I see it belongs to a young woman standing beside a Land Rover at the edge of the car park. She walks towards us with a wide and welcoming smile.

'You must be Abby?' she says as soon as she's close enough for us to hear. 'I'm Fiona, it's so good to see you.' It's almost as if I'm a friend she hasn't seen in years and the gentle lilt of her accent is like a soothing balm.

She looks about my age, although she's considerably taller and slimmer than I am, with bright-red hair tamed into one large thick plait, the tip of which sits on her shoulder. Her deep-blue eyes are wide and friendly and the laughter lines that surround them are the only ones on an otherwise flawless skin that glows with vitality. Beside her I feel grey and lumpen.

'And this must be your daughter?' she adds, smiling.

'Yes, Beth,' I supply.

'So, it's lovely to meet you too. You'll have to come and say hello to my Shona once you're settled, I reckon you're about the same age.' She looks down at our cases, indicating the Land Rover behind her. 'Do you want to hop in, and I'll put these in the back?' Before I can protest, she picks up a case in each hand like they're no more weight than a bag of shopping.

I flash a grin at Beth and open the door for her.

'I wasn't expecting to be picked up,' I say as Fiona climbs into the cab. 'This is very kind of you.'

'Well, what kind of a welcome would it be otherwise? It's not far to the cottage, I'll grant you, but it must have taken you the best part of two days to get here. It doesn't seem right that you should have to walk the final length.' She starts the engine. 'So, did you have a good trip?' she asks.

'Yes, just long,' I reply. 'I feel like we've had a holiday already.'

'Aye, well, we'll soon get you settled. You'll be tired, I expect, but the air here will perk you up in no time. There's even time for a walk before supper if you feel like it.'

I nod, smiling across at her. It will be good to get my leg muscles working again. I've been sitting down so long, it feels like they're permanently stuck in a bent position.

She pulls out of the car park, gravel showering from under her tyres, and I turn my attention to the view from the window. I've seen pictures of this, but it feels ancient, permanent somehow, as if nothing will ever change it. And I find that oddly reassuring, as if it's dependable. And there's no denying its wild beauty.

We pass a couple of whitewashed cottages, and a group of buildings which Fiona explains are the island's stores. She laughs. They're pretty much everything, apparently. From there, the road continues in an almost straight line, and we can't have gone more than two hundred metres before she pulls up beside another whitewashed cottage, nestled into a dip behind a low bank carpeted in pink flowers. A bright-blue door sits snuggly between two windows, each hung underneath with a trough of what look like geraniums from this distance. Beth is out of the car almost before it's stopped moving.

'Mum, look!' she exclaims, already heading down the bank into the front garden. 'It's so pretty.'

Fiona catches my eye as she pulls on the handbrake. 'I think someone's going to have a lovely holiday,' she says.

Oh God, I hope so.

She picks up a bunch of keys from a shelf beneath the dash and hands them to me. 'Why don't you go and let yourselves in while I get your bags?'

I climb down from the cab and join Beth in the garden, jangling the keys at her. 'Do you want to do the honours?' I ask, pleased when I see her face light up. She doesn't need to be asked twice and I follow her down the path to the front door, the scent of something intensely fragrant in the garden following us as we go.

We step down into the main living room, small but perfectly formed. And so warm and welcoming, it makes our flat with its high ceilings and airy spaces feel positively cathedral-like. But this feels safe and leaves me longing for a cosy evening in front of the log burner.

Fiona arrives behind us a moment later, again with both cases at once. 'Now, I'll pop these through into the kitchen until you're ready for them, and then I'll get out of your way. You'll want to explore by yourselves, I know. But it's all very straightforward, I don't think you'll have any bother. But if you do, you only need ask.'

These last few words are delivered through the door, but she reappears a second later with another bright smile on her face. 'Right then, logs are in the lean-to, just outside the back door. We're getting pretty warm here now during the day, but you might find you need the fire of a night, and beyond is the shed where we keep the bikes. It's one of the best ways to see the whole island. I've put instructions for everything in the kitchen and left you the opening times of the shop, and what you can order and so on. They close at five thirty tonight, so you've a wee bit of time before then, but you'll find a few essentials to get you going. Oh, and there's a map for you on the table too, together with some leaflets for things to do if you're into that kind of thing...' She breaks off, staring over my left shoulder as if what she needs to say next is printed on the wall behind me. 'There's spare bedding in the wardrobe of the smaller room, but if there's anything else you need, just shout.'

'Thank you, I'm sure it's all... you seem to have thought of everything,' I reply, still looking around me as I take in the small details of the room. 'And it was very kind of you to give us a lift up here, I hadn't realised everything was so close, we honestly could have walked here.'

'Aye, you could have, but it's no bother, and I wanted to be sure you had everything you need.'

'Thanks. Well, I'm sure we'll see you soon.'

She laughs. 'Aye, that you will. It's a small island.'

As I walk Fiona to the door, I can already hear Beth's feet running up the stairs. I find her in the smaller of the two bedrooms. She has both arms leaning on the window sill, her nose pushed up against the glass. As a floorboard creaks beneath my weight, she turns, her eyes shining, and beckons me forward with a finger.

'Oh, Mum, come and look!'

But I can already see a strip of azure through the glass, and as I walk towards her, it grows in size until I can see the whole sweep of the bay with its arc of golden sand. Between the cottage and the beach is a swathe of green grass, and everywhere, tufts of pink flowers. It's thrift, the whole island must be covered with it.

Beth leans into me, for a moment quiet, just drinking in the view, but then she turns and throws her arms around me.

'Thank you so much for bringing us here,' she says. 'This place is amazing. Look,' she adds, taking my hand. 'Come and see your room.'

I follow her along the landing, where another window is set low in the wall, affording the same panoramic view, albeit at the height of our kneecaps. But the walls of this cottage are incredibly thick and in the deep recess the window creates are a padded seat and cushion.

There's just enough room to sit. And all the time in the world to drink in the view.

The second bedroom is bigger, not by much, but that hardly matters when there's a round window in the ceiling above the bed, like a porthole. By day, it shines a ray of light down onto the beautiful embroidered eiderdown, but by night, you'll be able to lie back and look at the stars or, if you're lucky, even watch the moon as she crosses the sky.

I sink down on the edge of the bed, and then overcome with a sudden burst of happiness, fling myself backwards, arms and legs outstretched like a starfish. Beth giggles and joins me and for a moment we lay there, heads touching, grinning up at the ceiling.

I could quite possibly sink into a long and blissful sleep, but she pulls at my arm.

'Come on, I want to see the rest of it.'

It doesn't take long. Downstairs, there is just the living room, the kitchen and bathroom, but it's all absolutely charming. The beams in the living room are hung with fairy lights, and I imagine that with the log burner glowing at night, the light in here will be magical. By day, with its simple whitewashed walls, it's a bright and unfussy space, but incredibly cosy too. A huge vase of flowers sits on a low coffee table, flanked on either side by a squishy sofa piled with cushions and throws.

In the kitchen, a table for two has been positioned in front of another window overlooking the bay, and smack bang in the centre of this is a cellophane-wrapped basket of some size, with a little card attached. I hand it to Beth to open.

'Oh, it's from the shop!' she exclaims. 'And it's addressed to us. It says, *Dear Abby and Beth, we hope you have a lovely holiday*. That's so sweet!'

I pick up the basket and begin to unwrap it. 'Fiona said there were a few essentials to get us going. Let's see what we've got, shall we? Something smells good.'

I peel away the top layer of tissue paper, releasing more of the distinctive aroma. Nestled below is a round loaf of bread with a beautiful golden crust and underneath that is a bag holding four croissants. I exchange a look with Beth, knowing that these aren't going to last very long at all. What follows next is the most wonderful assortment of goodies: a jar of local island honey, some scones, a thick bar of chocolate, shortbread and a box of tea. Plus, a bottle of fresh apple juice and some grapes.

'Well, if these are classed as essentials, I could quite get used to this.' I pull off two grapes from the bunch and hand one to Beth, popping the other straight in my mouth. It bursts on my tongue as I bite into it.

Further inspection of the kitchen reveals some milk, butter, bacon and eggs in the fridge and a tin in the cupboard holds a fat slab of fruit cake. Breakfast and afternoon tea here are going to be seriously good. There's also the promised stash of leaflets, as well as menus from the hotel, details of the shop's delivery service and a map of the island with all the notable beaches and viewpoints marked.

I glance over at the cases still sitting on the floor by the table. I'd been about to suggest that we unpack first before deciding what to do, but I'm suddenly gripped by an urge to be outside, to feel the wind in my hair and what's left of the day's sun on my face. The cases won't be going anywhere, after all.

'Shall we go and explore?' I say. 'We could walk down to the shop and see where the hotel is too, if you like, or even go for a ride.'

Beth pulls a face. 'Can we walk?' she replies. 'I'd like to go for a ride, but maybe tomorrow? I don't think I can bear sitting down on anything else today.'

I grin and pick up my bag from the table where I'd left it. 'Legs it is then,' I say.

We reach the shop about five minutes later and I feel even more guilty that Fiona came to pick us up when it takes so little time to walk here. But then I guess that's all part of the island welcome, and it certainly feels that way. Bright smiles are offered by everyone we meet and I'm surprised by how bustling a place it is. Granted they are obviously in the middle of receiving all the deliveries off the ferry, but there are customers aplenty as well as staff.

It's a bright and airy space, and very evidently the hub of the community. There's an area for tourist information, plus a noticeboard covered with announcements and invitations to various events. There might not be a huge number of people living here but they certainly know how to keep themselves busy. And entertained.

The central area is packed with shelves offering a wide variety of cupboard staples, household goods and a certain amount of hardware. But to one end is a beautifully displayed selection of delicatessen and bakery goods and it's here that Beth and I linger longest.

The discussion over what to have for tea doesn't take long. Beth is feeling as jaded as I am after two days travelling and comfort food is what's required. So, we settle on buying some gorgeous cheeses, another loaf and a selection of picnic-type finger foods that we can munch on with very little effort required on my part.

After another few minutes browsing, we carry our selection across to the till, where a woman is busy pricing up some more jars of the honey. She looks up as soon as she sees me approach, a warm smile on her face.

'Did you find everything you were looking for?' she asks.

I nod, returning her smile of greeting. 'And a lot more besides,' I reply. 'This is one of those "came in for two things leave with ten" situations.'

'Ah well, can't say as I'm going to stop you, it's too good for business.' She laughs. 'But ask if there's ever anything you can't find,' she adds. 'Supply can be a wee bit erratic at times, but it may be that we haven't got around to putting it out yet. When the ferry comes in, it's all hands to the deck.'

'I can imagine. Thanks, though, these will be great for now.'

She takes my basket from me. 'Will we see you at the ceilidh tomorrow night?'

The question is directed more at Beth than at me, and she turns to give me a puzzled look, unsure how to reply.

The woman laughs. 'Don't worry if you've never heard of it. It's something we islanders do from the minute we're born, but we forget that not everyone is as lucky as us.' It might be a bit of what the Irish would call blarney, an exaggeration put on as show for the visitors, but if that's the case, she's doing a good job.

She nods at Beth. 'What it's supposed to be is dancing, and singing, and a bit of storytelling too, but although there's plenty of talent on the island, there's also a fair few of us who have two left feet, so things don't always go according to plan. But it's always a hoot, I can promise you that.'

Beth ripples with excitement at the mention of singing, and as much as my natural instinct is to shy away from big social gatherings, I know that she would really enjoy it. And it would be good for her too.

Besides, there are only one hundred and thirty-five people on the island, of all ages, plus a few visitors. How many people are likely to be there?

'It sounds like it could be huge fun, doesn't it? What time is it on?' I ask.

'From seven, until people run out of energy, but you can come any time you like. It's up at the hotel, in the big room.'

'And do we need tickets?'

She smiles. 'No, just yourselves. There's food and a bar, but it costs nothing to come along.'

'Okay then, that sounds like a plan,' I reply, fishing in my bag for my purse. 'I wanted to say thank you as well, for the welcome basket we found at the cottage we're staying in. I gather it came from here?'

'Well, it's our pleasure. There are some wonderful producers on the island, and we like to support them as best we can. You're in Samphire, aren't you?'

I give her a puzzled look. Not at her words as such, but more that… She interrupts me, chuckling.

'Don't worry, I'm no a mind reader. But you get to know who's coming and who's going around here and Fiona mentioned she'd got a new lady coming today, with a wee girl as well.' She smiles at Beth. 'Although not too wee, as I can see now.'

'Ah well, that explains it.' I indicate the things we're buying, still on the counter. 'Everything looks so wonderful, I have a feeling we're going to be eating rather a lot while we're here.'

'Well, we can deliver too. Just let us know what you want and Dougie will pop it up for you. It's no bother.' She begins to tally up our shopping.

'Actually… This is going to sound really silly, but we'd planned to go for a walk before dinner, only I got a bit carried away when we came in. Could I possibly leave these things here for an hour or so, so I don't have to carry them? I'll make sure I come back before you're closed.'

'Of course.' And almost before she says it, I know she's going to finish her sentence with *it's no bother*. I'm beginning to love this place more and more by the second.

Once we've paid and been given directions to the hotel (ridiculously easy), we head back outside, turning in the opposite direction from the cottage.

'Can we go to the ceilidh, Mum?' asks Beth, as we walk across the car park. I hold her back for a moment as a van sweeps around on the forecourt and comes to a halt.

'Would I be able to keep you away?' I reply, giving her a teasing smile. 'But it does sound like good fun. Besides, I don't think you can come on holiday to Scotland without attending one. I think there's probably a law against it.'

She nudges me playfully. 'Mu-um,' she groans.

The van door opens ahead of us, and I ready a smile and a greeting for whoever climbs out. But, as he straightens up, his face turning towards mine, everything comes to a very sudden stop.

Chapter 15

I stare at the man in front of me. A man who shouldn't be here. A man who shouldn't be *anywhere*. My heart is a traitor, leaping wildly in hope when I know it should not, taking me somewhere I don't want to go. Dredging up feelings I've fought so hard to move on from. Cam is dead, I remind myself. Cam is… standing in front of me.

I meet his panicked eyes. Watch as he rakes a hand through his dark hair.

'I can explain…'

But he can't. There's nothing he could say that will possibly make this any better. He lied to me.

And then I stop, eyes widening even further as I force my brain to make sense of it all. A sliver of fear curls around the back of my neck. There is something terribly wrong about all of this, and I have a sudden urge to get both Beth and me away from here.

'Mum, wait!' Beth is standing in the middle of the car park, staring with horror at Cam, then back at me.

But I don't give her the chance to say any more. Instead, I grab hold of her arm to pull her along behind me. She drags at my jacket, trying to turn around to see Cam, and I can't begin to imagine what her head is making of this. The holiday that I'd planned for us both as a retreat from the real world and all its problems has just become a nightmare.

'Abby, please!' Cam's voice is a plaintive cry from behind me. 'Let me talk to you… Abby!' There's a loud expletive which makes me wince. 'Look, I'm not Cam, okay? I'm…' He trails off as I continue to put distance between us. 'Abby, it's Alfie. I'm Alfie. We spoke before… his friend.' His voice is resigned. Flat. Beaten.

I whirl around, scarcely understanding what I'm hearing. 'Alfie? But how can you be Alfie? You're Cam, you're… dead,' I finish lamely.

He stands there: jeans, a checked shirt, sleeves rolled up with arms dangling by his sides as if he no longer has any use for them. But his face is stricken. He takes two steps towards me, but I instinctively wrap my arms around Beth. That he isn't Cam doesn't make this better, it… And the full import of what he's said hits me. Did Cam even exist at all?

It's all been lies, all of it. The emails, the jokes, the laughter. The confidences, the endearments, the friendship, the love. All of it. And I've been played all along. Played like a fool.

He's still looking at me, an imploring expression on his face, but he makes no move to close the distance between us. He's struggling to speak, he knows he has to say something, but he's not quick enough to come up with anything on the fly. And I see the realisation hit home. He turns on his heel and climbs back inside the van, starting it up and gunning the engine as he pulls away with a roar. And the van's distinctive livery registers somewhere in my brain. Kinlossay Island Distillery. Cam had mentioned it once. No, not Cam, Alfie…

I swallow, feeling my pulse begin to slow a little as I watch the van gaining speed away from us.

'Mum, who's Alfie?'

Beth is staring at me with such a look of hurt bewilderment on her face. And it's my fault. How could I have done this to her? I've put us both in danger, because I don't even know who Alfie is. Is he

Cam… or someone else? But I already know the answer. He's exactly what Gwen said he was when she heard that someone had emailed me from Cam's account.

'It'll be some weirdo,' she'd said.

He'd made the whole thing up. Cam didn't exist at all. The whole thing has been some complicated cat and mouse game.

I shake my head. But how can it be? I'm more confused than ever, but whatever is going on, none of it is right.

I give Beth's shoulders a squeeze, pulling her to me. 'It's okay, sweetheart,' I say. 'Alfie's just a… Well, I thought he was a friend of Cam's, but…' I'm not sure what to say, I don't want to frighten her.

'But that man was Cam,' she insists. 'The man who came to see us, the one who liked my dungarees, the one who…' She looks up at me. 'But Mum, he *died*. You told me he died.'

'I know, sweetheart, he did die. That's what *I* was told. I think there's been a bit of a mix-up somewhere.'

'But I don't understand.'

'No, me neither.' I give her an encouraging smile. 'I'm sure there's a perfectly good explanation for it all.'

I look up the road. The van is no longer in sight, but that doesn't mean we're safe, not at all. I try to think quickly, trying to work out our options. We can't go back to the cottage where we'll be on our own; somewhere Alfie could find us all too easily. No, we need people around us, so we're safe, until I can work out what this is all about. What kind of sick trick he's pulled on us.

The shop is behind us, but we can't stay here either, and the only other place close by is the hotel. Granted it's in the same direction that the van took, but there are few roads on this island, there isn't a lot of choice. And from what I remember, it isn't too far past the ferry terminal. We could be there in minutes.

'How about we go up to the hotel, like we'd planned?' I say. 'We can have a drink and look at the map while we're there, maybe work out a plan of everything we'd like to do this week.' I'm doing what countless mothers have done before me; trying to pretend that everything is okay because Beth looks as if she might be about to cry. 'And seeing as it's our first night here, how about we have a look at the menu too and see if there's anything we fancy for dinner?'

'But we've just bought some things to have tonight.'

I force myself to smile. 'There's always tomorrow,' I say, wondering what on earth we're going to do then. As everyone keeps telling me, this is a small island. And remote. And in the middle of nowhere. And the only way off it is by ferry. Which won't be back again for three days.

Reluctantly, Beth agrees, and we set off back along the road we drove up only recently. It's a beautiful afternoon and I keep up a steady stream of chatter as we walk, not too quickly, but with purpose all the same. We pass a couple of other people walking towards the shop and the other side of the ferry terminal a man passes us on a bike, giving a cheery wave. The road beyond is quiet, but it's still a relief to see a large white building come into view as we round the corner. I'm even more reassured to see a number of cars parked outside. People. That's what we need.

I hurry us through the gardens only dimly aware of the glorious array of colour that surrounds us. The hotel door is propped open, another tub of bright flowers flanking the entrance on either side. Inside, all is calm and peaceful. The ceiling towers above us, timber framing criss-crossing the space, and sunlight floods through tall windows on either side, its warm and gentle colours comforting. I can feel my blood pressure begin to lower.

Our feet make little sound as we cross the wooden floor, but as I look left and right, wondering which way to go, I catch sight of a tall woman coming through another doorway. She raises a hand in greeting and, as she comes closer, I can see that it's Fiona. I hadn't expected to see her quite so soon.

'Hello again,' she says as she reaches us, her sunny smile instantly calming. 'Welcome to MacDonald's.'

'Oh…' The word is out of my mouth before I even realise. 'Sorry…' I force a smile. 'I hadn't realised that you worked here as well. When I booked the holiday, it…'

She reassures me with another sunny smile. 'Don't worry,' she says. 'We catch a lot of folk out. We're such a small island, we just have the one website – it makes life so much easier. You'll have followed the link to holiday accommodation and whether that's the hotel, the lodge, or the holiday cottages, it's all us.'

I nod, still trying to untangle the knots in my head. 'I see, yes, that makes sense.' Except I still feel there's something I haven't fully grasped yet. 'Um, we were wondering if we could have a drink,' I add. 'And maybe have a look at your dinner menu too.' I flash a reassuring smile at Beth.

'Sure,' she says, indicating the room she walked through. 'Come through to the lounge, or the conservatory and gardens are open at the back if you'd rather be outside?' She takes in my expression as I struggle to make a decision. 'Is everything okay?'

I'm about to reply when a girl with the brightest red hair I think I've ever seen comes in. Extraordinarily pretty, she suddenly stops when she sees us, and would have done an about-turn, had Fiona not raised her hand to halt her.

'Shona, come and say hello,' she says, beckoning. 'These are our new visitors in Samphire.' She turns back to me. 'Shona helped me get the place ready for you this morning,' she adds. 'She picked all the flowers.'

'Which are beautiful,' I say. 'You did a very good job.'

'And this is Beth,' says Fiona. 'Who I think must be about your age?'

'I'm twelve,' says Shona, without a hint of shyness. 'I like your jeans.'

Beth squirms beside me, looking down at her denim-clad legs, which have embroidered flowers down the side. 'Thanks,' she says. 'They're from Topshop.'

Shona flashes her mum a look, who pulls a face. 'We don't have one of those near here, and Shona is forever after "real" clothes,' she explains. 'But I think Maureen might be able to manage something similar,' she says to her daughter. 'We could ask her if you like, they are very pretty.'

Shona's eyes light up. 'Do you think she would?' She smiles at Beth. 'That would be brilliant. Can I go and feed the pups now?' she asks.

Fiona checks her watch. 'Aye, make a start and I'll get one of the lads to come and give you a hand in a bit. Just mind you don't let them out yet. You know what happened last time.'

Shona nods and is halfway back to the door when she suddenly turns. 'Would you like to come and see them?' she asks Beth. 'There're eight puppies altogether, five girls and three boys, although the boys are the naughty ones, of course. You could help me if you wanted, only I need someone to hold them while I open the gate.'

Beth gives me a questioning look. 'Can I?' It's always been her dream to own a dog. 'What sort are they?'

'Sheepdogs,' replies Shona. 'Only they look like big balls of fluff.'

I wave Beth away, watching her go with a smile on my face.

'Are you sure you don't mind?' asks Fiona. 'Shona's not backwards in coming forwards when it comes to girls her age. She's always desperate for new playmates, but say if it's not something your daughter wants to do. I know it can be hard to say no sometimes.'

'Not at all. Beth will love it, although I'm not sure I'll hear the last of it. We live in a flat above a shop, so a dog's not really an option. But she's always wanted one.' I pause a moment. 'And it will be good for her too,' I add. 'She can be a bit shy sometimes with people she doesn't know. She's very quiet, like her mother.'

Fiona sighs. 'I sometimes think I might like to be quiet, but I never quite get the chance.' Her face creases into a smile. 'Och, I'm only joking, mind. Life can be a bit busy here some days, but there's no many folks can go and stand on the edge of the world at the end of the day. I wouldn't swap it for anything.'

'You like it here then?' I ask.

'Aye, love it. It's not for everyone, mind. Sometimes it can be frustrating, when the weather's bad, and when things take an age to get done. I think the children miss having lots of friends – school can be a difficult thing for them to get used to as well – but to my mind the pluses far outweigh the minuses. We maybe do things differently here, but that doesn't mean they're not good ways. I only have to visit the mainland for a little while to be reminded how much I long to be home.' She stares into the distance. 'I think maybe that's what it is really,' she says. 'That sense of being somewhere that's so familiar to you, with people who know everything about you, it's comforting in a way. True, it can be a pain in the bum sometimes, but mostly, I'm glad of it. I never have to pretend to be something I'm not, and there's a lot to be said for that.'

I think about the truth of her words for a moment, realising it's this very thing that has been on both my and Beth's minds of late.

'Anyways, would you like to come and sit through here, and I'll get you a drink? What would you like?' she says, mistaking my silence for a desire to be 'quiet'.

I eye the soft comfort of the lounge she's referring to. It looks incredibly inviting. 'Some tea would be lovely, thank you.'

'Coming right up.' There's a moment when I think she's about to say something else, but then she gives a mild tut before moving away, as if chiding herself for dallying. She makes it as far as the door, where she turns back. 'I probably shouldn't be asking you this and you can tell me to mind my own business, but when you came in here... Well, you looked like Morag does when she gets bad news, sort of scattered, like you're trying to think of too many things at once. And you were going to answer, I think, but then Shona came in and...' She trails off, looking embarrassed to have mentioned it.

I'm not sure what to say. My first instinct is to bat away her concern, but that might not be the most helpful thing under the circumstances. I'm safe here but I can't stay here forever. Also, I don't want her to think there's anything wrong with our accommodation either, not when everyone has been so welcoming.

'I'm fine,' I reply. 'Really. I just bumped into someone I wasn't expecting to. It was a bit of a surprise.'

'One of the visitors, is it?' She shakes her head. 'You wouldn't think it, would you? You come all this way, miles from home, and you meet someone you know. Och, well, it's true what they say, it's a small world right enough.'

'Yes, but...' How can I possibly explain? 'It wasn't anyone I know from home, but rather...' I need to tread carefully, everybody knows everybody here. 'This might sound a little odd, but do you know a man called Cam? Cameron Innes? I thought I saw him but...'

I wasn't quite sure how I expected her to react, but her eyes grow impossibly wide.

'You can't have just seen him,' she says. 'Have you?' Her voice is a whisper.

'I really don't know.' I shake my head. 'I don't know what to think, I'm so confused.'

Fiona frowns first of all before a succession of emotions cross her face. The last is compassion. She stretches out a hand towards me. 'I'm so sorry, Abby, but it couldn't have been Cam, I'm afraid he died just before Christmas.' She's about to say something else, but then her eyes widen even further and her fingers touch her lips. 'No, you knew that, didn't you? Oh my God, you're *Abby*! You're Cam's Abby, aren't you?' She flings her arms around me, pulling me into the tightest hug. 'I can't believe you're here. It *is* you, isn't it?'

Her words are muffled against my shoulder but I manage a nod as a wave of relief courses through me. Cam is real… *was* real, and the love I shared with him was real too. I can feel Fiona's body shaking with emotion and when she pulls away, her eyes are shiny with tears. She stands there, looking at me, still holding my arms and sniffing.

Cam was real. It's all I can think. But with the realisation comes a sudden reawakening of grief. My lip begins to tremble and I feel the first tingle of my own tears. I've found someone who knew Cam, who knows what he was like, someone who still feels the pain of what it's like to have lost him. At last someone with whom I can share my grief, someone who understands.

I pull her back into a hug. We're both crying openly now, our tears turning to laughter as we part again, wiping our eyes and staring at each other, revelling in what we see, what we know.

'Come, come and sit down,' Fiona urges, pulling me into the room she'd originally indicated. 'Can I get you some tea? Oh, I was already supposed to be doing that, wasn't I? Or maybe you'd like something stronger?' She smiles. 'I could do with a whisky, actually.' And then finally, 'I don't know what to say.'

I sniff, helplessly, still crying. 'No, me neither. But, yes, a drink would be lovely. Anything – no – tea, please. Is that okay?'

There's a series of rapid nods. 'Don't move, will you? I need to tell Morag and Gillie.' She moves off at speed, shouting the name 'Andrew' as she goes.

My head is spinning. There's a connection here somewhere that I'm still not seeing. The name Morag… But my thoughts go no further as a woman appears at the doorway. She's slim, wearing jeans and a navy-blue fisherman's-type jumper, grey hair tumbling onto her shoulders. And her face… feels like one I've known all my life.

She's drinking me in, her eyes roving my face, my hair, like she can't get enough of me. And she's smiling, but there's recognition too, of my own raw emotion as her expression changes again. Her arms stretch out as she walks towards me, uncertain now.

'Is it really you?' she asks. 'Are you really here?' And then, as she stands in front of me, the warmth of a welcoming smile. 'My darling, Abby,' she says. 'Thank you so much.' She takes my face in her hands and kisses my forehead tenderly. She smells of flowers and something so familiar, my tears come again.

She takes my hand and pulls me to sit down on one of the enormous sofas that grace the room. 'Thank you,' she says again. 'It's so lovely to finally meet you. We always hoped that one day we would. We didn't know, you see… Cam, he… Well, none of that matters now that you're here. I can't quite believe it.'

I wipe at my eyes again, not knowing how to begin. There's so much to say. 'You're Cam's mum,' I manage, almost a question, but rapidly turning to certainty, although no one has explained it. And I squeeze her hands in reply.

The room suddenly fills with people. Fiona reappears, a man by her side, even taller than her, with very little hair but a burgeoning ginger beard and beside him someone much older, and shorter, with a round face to match his belly and a silky-eared spaniel by his side. A dog I'd know anywhere.

I get to my feet, suddenly shy in front of Cam's father. It can only be him.

He comes forward. 'Lassie…' he says, a slight tremble in his voice. 'Well, look at you! And come all this way to see us? I never thought it somehow.' His arms open wide. 'Call me Gillie, everyone does.' He hugs like a bear and I can feel the warmth of him through his shirt. 'And this is Gin.'

'Yes, yes, I know. Cam used to talk about her all the time, she's…' I bend to meet the dog's ecstatic welcome as she tries desperately to lick my face.

'*Gin…*' warns Morag. 'Leave the poor girl alone. She doesn't want your stinky breath all over her.' She pats the sofa. 'Come and sit down, lass, so we can talk to you. Gin, *here*!'

The dog and I both sit as requested, Gin pressing into my side, although the wild gleam in her eye lets me know that she'd be in my lap with the slightest invitation.

'I'll bring the tea,' says Fiona before dashing off again.

And then we sit, Morag and I on the sofa, Gillie and the other man in armchairs opposite, all looking at one another, not knowing who should go first.

The tall man leans forward. 'I'm Andrew,' he says. 'Fiona's husband.' And he shakes my hand and then laughs at the strangeness of both the action and the situation. 'This must be very confusing for you, all of us suddenly appearing.'

He's right, I'm struggling to make head nor tail of anything. I nod. 'And you run the hotel with Fiona?'

Andrew smiles. 'Aye. And with her folks, although they're semi-retired, and off just now, gallivanting around the Mediterranean on a cruise. A big wedding anniversary,' he adds, by way of explanation. 'So, Gillie and Morag have been drafted in to help for a bit.'

I turn in their direction. 'Oh, I see.' I want to ask more – they're Cam's mum and dad, I want to know everything there is to know about them – and him. But I'm not sure if I should.

'Will we wait until Fiona gets back?' Morag says as if reading my mind. 'Or she'll only be cross to have missed anything.'

'Aye,' says Gillie, settling back in his chair.

An expectant hush falls. So much so that when Fiona does reappear, carrying an enormous tray, she stops dead in front of us. 'What?' she says.

Morag gets up to take the tray from her, and places it down on the coffee table that sits between the arrangement of seating. The tray is laden with a huge teapot, cups and saucers, milk, sugar, a plate of shortbread, and a round cake, several inches high. 'Go get yourself a chair, dear,' she says.

Fiona is already dragging one across from another seating group. 'I've told Beth where we are,' she says. 'But she and Shona are getting on like a house on fire. They'll be a while feeding all the pups anyway, but I've left some squash and cake for them in the kitchen too.' She smiles the reassuring smile of a mother who knows how important these things are. And then she too sits down and looks at me.

'The poor girl,' says Morag. 'Stop looking at her like she's an exhibition in the museum. She'll run away and never want to talk to us again.' She settles the cups and saucers on the tray and hefts the teapot. 'You'll take tea though, Abby?'

I nod, eyeing the shortbread, suddenly desperate for something sweet.

'So, you've some questions for us, I expect,' she continues. 'And maybe you should go first, because I think we might know a wee bit more about you than you do about us.'

'Okay,' I reply, nervous now, not wanting to say the wrong thing. I swallow, licking my lips slightly. 'Thank you all, this is so lovely. I really didn't expect, well, any of this. I just thought... My daughter and I needed a holiday, you see and...' I break off again, assailed by thoughts of what brought us here. 'I wanted to leave the world behind, and so here seemed the perfect place to come. And the more I thought about it, the more I... Well, I realised that I wanted to see where Cam lived, that perhaps it might help.'

Grief renews itself among us. It's there in the air, a shared emotion, heavy and so familiar.

'I don't... Sorry, this might sound very rude, but I don't even know how he died.'

There's a sharp intake of breath from beside me, faint, and Morag tries to hide it, but it's there all the same. 'You poor child,' she says. She clears her throat. 'Gillie, perhaps you had better...'

Gillie looks fondly at his wife as she finishes pouring the tea, and nods gently.

'It was the cancer,' he says. 'A brain tumour. Cam had been ill for a while and we... we hoped, obviously, that things would improve, but they didn't. He'd had a few operations, but the last... Cam said it made him feel different and he didn't want another. We could understand that. The surgeon told us it might not make a difference anyway, that the tumour had tangled itself in too much of Cam. They probably couldn't remove it all and leaving it, any part of it, well, it wouldn't help.' He looks down for a moment, smiling as he remembers a beloved son. 'And so that was that. Cam decided that he just wanted to live, properly, with whatever time he had left to him.'

He gives Morag a look that reveals the pain they share.

'It was a hard thing to come to terms with. When it's your child, you'd do anything to keep them with you that little bit longer, but we agreed, we had to. It was Cam's wish. And so life carried on, as best it could, and one of the things which helped enormously was you.' He gives me a wry smile. 'Not that we knew very much about you, to start with, anyhow. Cam mentioned you once or twice but it wasn't until, well after, that we found out what had been going on, how close you'd become. But even if we didn't know it at the time, we could all see how different he was. The upswing in his mood for one, how he became happier, more settled, as if he had come to terms with things. And his ability to cope with his worsening symptoms improved dramatically. And so, for a short while at least, we got our old Cam back.'

I nod, but I can barely take it all in. That all the time we were sending messages back and forth, Cam was slowly dying. And I never knew.

'I expect you think that harsh of him,' Morag says as if reading my mind. She passes me a cup of tea. 'Because we know he didn't tell you about his illness. It was clear that he hadn't, and it caused…' She pauses a moment. 'A little upset when we found out. But I think that was what helped him, you see. You were a part of his world that hadn't been changed by the cancer. Something, possibly the only thing, that was untouched by it. And that meant such a lot to him, you reminded him of how he used to be.' She smiles, but there are tears glistening in her eyes. 'But his decision has also caused you considerable pain, we know that. And it's almost unforgivable, except that when it's your own child, you'll forgive them almost anything.'

Her look is full of anguish, torn by the love she has for Cam, and the understanding of the damage his final decision had wreaked. But there's hope there too, that I might also find a way to forgive him.

I don't know what to think. I've had four months to get used to the idea that Cam has gone from my world, the one person who I had harboured a hope to share it with. And in all that time, I'd thought on far too many occasions about how he had died. An accident most likely, I had assumed. After all, he was young, he hadn't mentioned any health problems. I'd met him and he'd been fine… My thoughts grind to a halt. No, that's wrong.

'It's too much to hope for, I know,' continues Morag. 'But perhaps, in time, when you understand how much happiness you brought him, you might not think too badly of him. You were his first proper girlfriend. Hard to believe, isn't it? But it was true. Not that there hadn't been other girls, but Cam grew up with everyone here and well, none of them was ever his soul mate. Not like you. I just don't think he expected to fall in love.'

My teacup rattles on its saucer, and I seat it on my knee, clamping hold of it for dear life.

Morag's hand settles over mine. 'Is there anything we can do? Anything we can tell you?'

I shake my head. My tears are only being held at bay by the tiniest of margins. And I suddenly long to be away from everyone, with their sympathetic looks and warm smiles. But I don't want to be rude. I study the veins on the back of Morag's hand in an effort to keep from crying.

A throat clears, once and then again. It's Fiona. 'I think perhaps...' She places her cup back down on the tray. 'That Abby might like a little time to herself,' she says. 'I imagine all this is rather a lot to take in, and we are rather crowding the poor girl.'

I look up gratefully, catching her eye before glancing away again.

'Why don't we let her finish her tea in peace and then meet up again on another day, when Abby is ready?'

Morag's hand gently withdraws and Gillie gets to his feet. 'Aye, there's a lot of sense in that, Fiona, thank you. We've no right to assume, and the lass is here on holiday, after all, and with her wee girl.'

I look up, smiling at his kindly face. 'I'm a bit worried about Beth,' I admit. It's true, but it also lets me off the hook a little. 'But I would like to talk some more, maybe tomorrow. It's been a long day and...'

There's a flurry of movement as everyone else stands, replacing cups, Andrew swiping a piece of shortbread. But they understand, I can see the apology on their faces. Slight embarrassment too.

'Will we leave it with you, Fiona?' asks Morag.

'Yes,' says Gillie on her behalf. 'I think that's best. But Abby, well, just so's you know, it's been so lovely meeting you. And I can quite see why Cam... Anyway, you let us know if there's anything you need, anything we can do. Right then.' He holds out his arm for Morag and leads her away.

Andrew clears his throat. 'I'll be off now too. I'll pop and see how the girls are getting on, shall I?'

I wait until he's left the room, looking back and smiling at Fiona. 'Thank you,' I say. 'It's not that I didn't want to talk, just—'

'You've no need to explain, Abby, really. I'm sorry, I should have thought before fetching them all in here, it's just that...' She blows air out from her cheeks. 'This has been such a hard time for all of us.

I don't think any of us knows how to be.' She gives a sheepish smile. 'And grief doesn't come with a manual, does it? It would be so much easier if it did. But, well, whatever happens, we're all really glad that you're here.' She passes a hand across her face as if to catch a stray hair. 'I know this has all come as a huge shock to you, but try not to think too badly of Cam, he…' But she can't finish and instead she indicates the tray of things on the table. 'Please do help yourself, and shout if you'd like anything else, won't you?' And then she too is walking back across the room.

I'm wondering whether to say anything about Alfie, whether to voice the thing that's still in my head, the thing that needs some thinking about. It's as if I've got all the pieces of the puzzle but somehow can't see how they all fit together.

I hadn't reckoned on Fiona's perspicacity, however. She turns at the last moment.

'Sorry,' she says, taking a few steps back into the room. 'Earlier, when you mentioned that you'd seen Cam, I took it that you'd seen a ghost. Stupid, but it was the first thing that came into my head. It was the shock of hearing you say his name. And yet you also said it was someone you knew, from here on the island.'

A ripple of panic runs through me. I had feared that Cam wasn't real, that he never existed and yet his wonderful family is absolute proof that Cam was exactly who I thought he was. At least in the beginning. But Fiona is only too aware that I shouldn't know anyone on the island, so how do I explain how I know Alfie when I still don't understand myself?

'No, I…' I give a weak smile. 'I got it wrong too. I think coming here… Perhaps it's had more of an impact on me than I thought.' I'm having to think way faster than my brain can keep up with. 'It wasn't

Cam at all, obviously, but turned out to be his friend, Alfie. Cam mentioned him a few times in his emails to me, and we bumped into him outside the shop. I probably made a complete fool of myself.'

She smiles. 'I doubt that. Anyway, Alfie won't mind, he'll have been thrilled to meet you. It was he who told us all about you, we wouldn't have known if it wasn't for him.' She pauses. 'I'm not sure how you'd muddle them up though, one blond, one very dark. They might be cousins, but they look nothing alike.'

I stare at her, trying to work out what her words mean. And then suddenly the fog clears. 'Hang on, did you say they were cousins? So that would mean…'

'Aye, Alfie's my brother.'

I swallow, brain now moving at lightning speed. Of course he is, I already knew that. Cam had made mention of Alfie's sister in his emails, helping her at Halloween, and that in return, Alfie would help run the bar for her on Christmas Eve. But if he and Cam were cousins then…

'And Morag's my aunt,' adds Fiona, smiling.

Panic is making my heart fluttery. Oh dear God, I came so close. So close to telling her that Alfie had been pretending to be Cam. Fiona is Alfie's sister, and Morag is not only his aunt, but Cam's mother, and they are such wonderful, kind people. How can I possibly tell them what Alfie has done? It would break their hearts.

Chapter 16

Dinner was lovely. At least it looked lovely, and Beth seemed to really enjoy hers, but I don't remember how it tasted. I only managed to stay at the hotel long enough to eat our meal out of sheer willpower. I couldn't let Fiona and Andrew down, nor could I refuse. It was their gift to us, they said, a welcome to the island, and a thank-you as well. Besides, it wasn't them who had done anything wrong.

As it was, I had to try to explain things to Beth, who was still confused but basically under the impression that Cam was alive and well. Fortunately for me, she was also still revelling in the excitement of not only making a new friend, but a friend whose dog has just had puppies, so my glib explanation and promise to tell her more about it later had got me off the hook, for now at least. Besides, I couldn't tell her very much more. I still don't understand it myself.

But now, back at the cottage, all I want is to get to bed. I've barely slept the last couple of days and the long journey is beginning to catch up with me. Beth, too, who's now taken herself up to the window seat on the landing upstairs and is propped on the cushions, her head resting against the wall. There's a book in her hand, but she's not reading. Instead, she's gazing out at the slowly fading view, as the sun descends the sky. It's a quite beautiful evening.

'I think an early night might be called for,' I say, joining her to perch on the edge of the seat. 'I don't know about you, but I'm worn out.'

Beth smiles. 'I was watching a man walking his dog,' she replies. 'But there isn't anyone else on the beach, only him. I was thinking how different it is from home.'

'It's certainly that. But then we are a very long way away. And living in the middle of a city is bound to be busier and noisier, it would be odd if it wasn't.' I still find it surprising that the city often comes to life as I'm thinking of turning in for the night. I had worried that Beth might find things a little too slow here, but I don't think that's going to be the case.

'So, the beach tomorrow, is it?' I say.

She nods. 'The one that Fiona told us about. I'm going to take my sketchbook with me, I think.'

'Good idea. And we'll take a picnic, of course.' And then I look at her in horror.

Beth's hand goes to her mouth; she's just realised as well. 'We never picked up our shopping!' she says.

I roll my eyes at her. 'We'll have to go and say sorry in the morning,' I reply. 'We can always go early, there will still be time to make up a picnic afterwards.' I get to my feet. 'Shall I go and make us a drink? Then I think it might be bedtime.'

Beth yawns and nods. 'Would it be all right if I had a bath first?' she asks.

I smile. 'Just don't take hours and hours, I know what you're like.' I drop a kiss on top of her head, before going back downstairs. I might sit with a cup of tea myself for half an hour or so before making Beth her drink.

As I cross the lounge, I notice that a piece of paper has been slipped under the front door. I eye it warily. In all likelihood it's from Alfie, and I have no desire to read whatever he has to say. But it's lying there, imploring me to pick it up, and that makes me even more cross. I shall put it in the bin, where at least I won't have to look at it.

Except as I get closer, I see that my name is written on the front, or rather the formal version of it – Miss Prendergast. That doesn't seem the way Alfie would address me, whatever the circumstances. I pick it up, pausing for a moment. I don't have to read it. I can check who it's from and relegate it to the rubbish if needs be.

But when I open the note, I can see straight away that it isn't from Alfie. It only comprises three lines:

I thought I'd bring your shopping up to save you the trip.

Hope that's okay,

Dougie (I've left it in the shed)

What a lovely thing to do. I've never even met the man. I head back into the kitchen, unlocking the door and waiting for my eyes to become accustomed to the rapidly falling light before venturing outside. The shed is a low, squat affair, old stone and a corrugated-tin roof, joined to the house by a slabbed path. And presumably open. I did look for a key to it earlier on the bunch that Fiona had given us, but there didn't seem to be one.

The air outside is still and fragrant as I make my way down the path, and the silence deep and enfolding. This time of year, the nights stay light until about eight o'clock or so, but once darkness has fallen, I've a feeling it's absolute.

The shed door opens easily and I spot our bag of groceries inside. There's no window but I can make out the shapes of the bikes that Fiona mentioned, plus a few other things besides. It will be worth having a proper look in the daylight before we set off for the beach tomorrow. Beth might be eleven, and I might be thirty-two, but we can still enjoy building sandcastles and digging holes. A bucket and spade could come in very handy.

Behind me the kitchen doorway is a bright silhouette against the night, and I make towards it, a sudden shiver prickling my senses. An owl hoots off in the distance and it's a relief to step back inside the house, where I can smile at my foolishness. Placing the bag down on the table inside, I pick up the keys and return to close and lock the back door for the evening. Just beyond the pool of light cast by the kitchen doorway is the dark outline of a figure standing in the garden.

I stifle an involuntary cry, reaching for the door as the figure comes forward.

'Abby, please don't! I'm sorry, I didn't want to make you jump, but...' Alfie raises his hands in a helpless gesture. 'I was walking the dog and I saw you come home. I've been standing in the lane for a while, wondering whether I should knock, so when I saw you come outside, I...' And now that he mentions it, I can see the darker shadow of a dog, sniffing the bushes.

'Stay where you are, Alfie,' I warn, folding my arms across my body. 'I don't know what you're doing here, but just go away. I don't want to talk to you.' My voice is low, but it carries clearly across the space between us. I'm suddenly very conscious of Beth inside.

'Abby, please…' His voice is ragged. 'Jesus, I'm not going to hurt you. Why would I do that?'

'Oh, I don't know,' I hiss. 'Perhaps the same reason why you pretended to be your best friend.'

He sighs with frustration. 'Look, I know you've seen Fiona. I had eight missed calls off her while I was at work. And once I got home, I could barely get her off the phone. And then Morag called in, and what Fiona hadn't managed to tell me, Morag more than filled in. I know they told you what happened, how Cam died, all of it. And so you've probably guessed how I come into things. I just want to talk to you, Abby, please. Let me explain.'

'And why should I do that?'

'Because you want to know the answers, that's why.'

He looks at me, one side of his face in deep shadow the other pale in the grey light. But he's right, and he knows he is: I do want answers.

He gestures towards the still-open doorway. 'Can I at least come in?'

But I step into the garden and pull the door to behind me. 'No, Beth is in the house, or had you forgotten that? Someone else who thinks you're Cam, who hasn't a clue who Alfie is.' I dash a hand at my face as something flutters into it. 'All right then, go on, explain. Tell me who you are. I know you're Fiona's brother and Cam's cousin, but you told me you were his friend. *He* told me you were his friend, but that's not the word I'd use. More like…' I trail off when I can't think of a bad enough adjective to describe him. 'Snake…' I say at last, knowing how pathetic it sounds. 'But who actually are you?' I put out a hand. 'No, don't tell me.'

I turn back as if to go inside and then change my mind, stalking across the distance between us. 'You bastard,' I hurl into his face. 'Have you any idea how it feels? When all the times I emailed Cam, all the times I thought about him, *still* think about him, which is a lot by the way. All of those times, the face I see is yours. I fell in love with someone and I don't even know what he looks like!' I jab my finger in his chest. 'And that's *your* fault. You did that. And what's worse is that it wasn't just a one-off, was it? The weekend you came to visit. No, I've seen pictures before, photos he'd sent. But not pictures of him, like I thought, pictures of you.' I break off as emotion comes perilously close to the surface. 'It's like I've lost him all over again.' I stop as a thought comes to me. As I realise what all of this meant for our visit last summer, the blissful weekend we spent together. The things we said to one another, the things we did… And a wave of white-hot shame and embarrassment washes over me, leaving me speechless, immobile under Alfie's gaze.

He takes my silence for something else. 'Are you done yelling at me now?' he says. 'Are you going to let me explain?'

'Oh, I've *nowhere near* finished yet.'

We stare at each other, and if looks could kill, Alfie would be stone-cold dead. The thought stops me in my tracks.

'Was any of it true?' I ask. 'Or were you using Cam as a sob story to get to know me? How could you have done that to your friend? He was dying, for God's sake.'

'What? I wasn't selling you a sob story.' He rakes a hand through his hair. 'At what point did you ever know that Cam was unwell? I haven't used you at all. It wasn't like that.'

'Then why were you pretending to be him? That isn't normal, Alfie. That isn't what people do. Pretend to be someone and lie in order to get to meet them. There's a word for people like you. Jesus, you're the kind of person I warn my daughter about. Don't always believe people you see on the internet, I tell her, they're not always who they say they are. Well, I got that right, didn't I?'

And then I'm suddenly aware that Alfie's face is bright red. Even in the rapidly dimming light, I can see how angry he is. I back away slightly, realising how stupid my words have been. What danger I've put myself in.

'You think I did it without him knowing…' His mouth drops open. 'My God, that's sick. It wasn't like that at all.' And then to my horror, Alfie's gaze drops to the floor and he turns away, his shoulders heaving. He wraps his arms around himself and I've been there so many times myself, consumed by grief, that for a moment I want to reach out to him, to comfort him. Until I remember what he's done.

He turns back. 'So, what would you have done?' he yells, embarrassment at his tears making him angry. 'He was my best friend! We grew up together. I never knew a time when he wasn't around, so what was I supposed to do? He begged me, Abby. Begged me to help him. To help him have the one thing that made him feel normal – you. Who reminded him that whatever ravages the awful disease wrought, he was still the same person inside. Imagine how you would feel being constantly looked at with sad eyes, with pity, having people apologise whenever they talked of the future, knowing that you didn't have one. He just wanted to be normal. Christ, he never even told his parents the half of it. How could I refuse him that?'

His chest is heaving with the effort of getting his words out. And they're the same words I'd heard from Gillie earlier, more or less. And then I remembered what Fiona had said – try not to think too badly of Cam. He lied to me. He didn't tell me anything about his illness. I stare at Alfie. Was that right? Was Cam the one who had lied to me?

'But didn't you ever stop to think about what you were doing to me?' I whisper, emotion fighting my voice.

Alfie's eyes are locked on mine, and filled with tears he no longer tries to hide. But my family aren't given to outward shows of emotion and

I've only ever seen a man cry once before. So now, when faced with it, I don't know what to do. Should I be comforting him? I don't think I can.

'We argued about it, actually,' he says. 'I think it was one of the few times there were ever cross words between us. You have to believe me when I say that he was very much aware of how you would feel, as was I, but in a way, it was too late.' He pauses a moment. 'Because by then he was already in love with you. He couldn't bear to lose you, Abby, and I didn't know what else to do, so I agreed. I know it was wrong, and hindsight has shown me how wrong, but...'

I wait, knowing that he'll continue when he can.

'Maybe when you're faced with knowing you have so little time left to you, maybe you do become selfish. But you know what? I forgive him that, because he deserved so much more than his life gave him. He knew it would be hard on you, but when the end came...' He breaks off, unable to speak. 'It was worse than we ever imagined, but he was adamant that you weren't to know. Even at the end his parents didn't really... And I didn't know what to do. What to say to you.'

Tears spring into my eyes. 'Have you any idea how I felt when the emails suddenly stopped? I thought it was my fault. That I'd done something to upset him.'

Alfie hangs his head.

'And then, when there'd never been any indication that something was wrong, I had to scout about trying to find a way to contact him, ringing the number for the hotel because it was the only one I could find, only to be told by someone I don't even know, that he had died.'

'I know, I should have kept writing. I just couldn't, Abby. Not because I didn't want to, but because that last week was like nothing on earth.' He stares at me a moment, unsure what to share with me and what not.

'So, it was you then, writing his emails?'

He shakes his head, compassion flooding his face. 'No, not at first, not for a long while. But when Cam's condition deteriorated, he lost his coordination, and so he would tell me what to say and I would type it for him. But later when his speech… I just carried on writing, Abby, it wasn't hard. By the end he could barely speak, and when he did it was to ask if I'd messaged you. Or to see if you'd replied. And I would sit on his bed and read your words to him, over and over.'

I put out my hand. 'Stop. Please, Alfie. I can't hear any more of this.' The tears are streaming down my face now.

'I tried to write to you so many times but I just couldn't. I watched my friend die, and even when I saw him at his very worst, I still didn't believe he'd actually go. Stupid, isn't it? I still thought there'd be a tomorrow. And then there wasn't.'

His words hang in the air and it suddenly feels ridiculous to be standing out here in the gloom, talking about something so profound as life and death. But I don't know how to change things. I don't know how to make any of this right. What's happened has gone too deep.

'So why *did* you write to me? Because even then you weren't honest with me. You told me that Morag had wanted some photos from Cam's laptop, and you happened to check his emails. Yet you knew all about them, you'd been writing them for goodness' sake.' I look away.

'Because I miss him too,' he says, simply, his words bringing us right back to the present. 'And I wish more than anything that he was still here. That things had a point to them, that I'm not simply going through the motions. I didn't check his email account after he died, not until that one day, when I messaged you. And I only did so because I couldn't bear the way I was feeling. I thought that reading your emails would at least allow me to pretend that things were like they used to be. So, when I saw you'd still been emailing him, I knew that you felt exactly the same way. I thought that perhaps we could carry on, that...' He runs a hand over his face, inhaling a deep breath. 'It doesn't matter. What are you going to do? About all of this?'

'I have no idea,' I say, a bitter note creeping into my voice. 'You know, you're not the only one with problems, Alfie, struggling to cope. Beth and I came here to get away from our life back home, just for a while. From a shop that I don't think I can afford to keep going any longer, from my grief, which rises up and drags me down to the depths again when I'm not looking, from my daughter's classmates, who have been making her life a misery, from a world that wants us to be something we're not. That's what this holiday was for. A chance to breathe again, to come out from under the weight of all that threatened to swamp us. And you, you've made that impossible.'

'Please don't tell them,' he begs. 'Cam's mum and dad, I mean. They don't know that we've met, none of them do. They don't know that you thought I was Cam.'

'I may not have to tell them,' I reply. 'Fiona's as astute as they come. And if you don't tell her, then I think she'll work it out anyway.'

I start as a wary voice comes from behind me.

'Mum, who are you talking to?'

I turn to see Beth silhouetted in the kitchen doorway, tousled hair, dressed in her pyjamas, cosy from her bath. I'm about to reply, to shepherd her back inside, when Alfie comes forward, smiling.

'Hi, Beth. I was taking Nipper here for a last walk before bedtime,' he says, the dog rushing forward at the sound of her name.

Beth bends down, her arms outstretched.

'I thought you were Cam, before, when I saw you. But you're not, are you?'

He shakes his head gently. 'No, I'm not. My name's Alfie and I was Cam's best friend.'

She looks up at him from where she's petting the dog, but her eyes narrow. 'But you came to visit us. And you didn't say your name was Alfie then. You told us you were Cam. My mum thought you were Cam.'

Alfie drops his head. 'I know. And I'm sorry. That's what I've been trying to explain. It doesn't make it right, but Cam asked me to do it. He wasn't well, you see, and he wanted to meet your mum, and you. Only he couldn't come himself so...' He clears his throat. 'I came instead.'

Beth doesn't say anything for quite some time, but then she stands up, releasing her grip on the dog. 'Okay,' she says. 'But that was a really mean thing to do.' She turns and walks back inside. But not before I see the glint of tears in the corner of her eye.

I'm left looking at Alfie, seeing the pain on his face, seeing how sorry he is. But it's not enough. I walk back towards the door, turning when I'm aware that he's following. 'No,' I say, my hand on his chest. 'I'd like you leave now,' I add. 'And I don't want to see you for the rest of the week. Is that understood?'

And then I close the door in his face, turning the key against both him and the darkness outside.

Chapter 17

I don't sleep. How can I? Instead I lie there, looking up at the night sky through the porthole window in the ceiling above my bed, letting memories flood in. Trying to make sense of them now they've been altered almost beyond recognition. Beside me, Beth seems calm. She's asleep at least, pulling free from my arm to lie on her side, curled towards me. It took a while for her to stop crying after Alfie left, but perhaps that's a good thing. She's been keeping everything bottled up inside for weeks now. Maybe this might have given her the release she needed; I hope so.

The light comes in a gentle pale dawn, around seven o'clock, and with it, rain. But both are soothing, and the next time I look at the clock it's half past nine, so I must have fallen asleep after all. Beth is just beginning to stir.

An hour later we're sitting at the table in the kitchen, staring out the window at the drippy day outside. It doesn't feel at all the way I wanted our holiday to be, and the beach is certainly not going to be an option. I look across at Beth's morose face. She looks tired too, but disappointed more than anything. I get to my feet.

'Right then,' I say. 'The first rule of holiday is that you have to have an enormous greedy breakfast. And we have eggs and cheese and bacon, and bread and biscuits and grapes and…' I check our supplies.

'Croissants, better not forget those, and honey and cake and sausage rolls and ham and tomatoes and a jar of olives. I reckon that should do it, don't you?'

Beth smiles. 'Mum,' she tuts, 'what are you like?'

'About to be very full indeed. Now, what are you going to have? Croissants, obviously, but what else?'

She thinks for a moment. 'I can't decide… No, wait, can I have a boiled egg and some toast as well?'

'Coming right up. I think I'll have some cheese and tomato on toast and then croissants and honey for pudding.'

'Can you have pudding for breakfast?'

'I don't see why not,' I reply, crossing to the cooker. 'And then when we've eaten the lot, what do you reckon we should do? I don't think the beach is going to work today but there are still loads of other things.'

She looks at me, a careful expression on her face. I can tell she's wondering whether to say the thing that's on her mind, and mine.

'It's okay, Mum,' she says. 'We don't have to ignore what happened yesterday. I know you're cross, and sad too. So was I. But we can still have a good holiday, can't we? Otherwise, it's all a bit rubbish.'

I smile, struck once again at the marvellous resilience my daughter displays. Just one of the many reasons why I love her so much. 'Of course we can. In fact, we must make sure we do. We've come a very long way only to have a rubbish time. The trouble is that this *is* a very small place, and we may well bump into Alfie again at some point, I can't promise that we won't.'

'I know,' she replies. 'But we liked him when we met him before, didn't we? And I've been thinking. It wasn't a very nice thing he did, but perhaps he was trying to be a good friend. I think he must miss

Cam as much as you do. And people do silly things sometimes, you're always telling me that. So maybe it won't be that bad, after all.'

I sometimes wish I could still see the world with the eyes of an eleven-year-old, but she has a point. Even if I can't bring myself to be quite so philosophical about it yet.

'Okay then,' I say. 'Cam's family seem very nice, and the island's beautiful. There's the ceilidh tonight, and puppies to visit. I think it's going to be a lovely week.' I pull a face as I look out the window. 'Even if it is raining.'

Beth's mood lifts almost immediately. I'm still tired, feeling washed out and a little misplaced, but she's right, we have to make the most of this, or what's the point? At least that's what I tell myself. Our chatter resumes at its normal level and half an hour later, as we tuck into plates of delicious food, I do begin to feel a little more like my usual self.

It's still wet out by the time we're ready and so we decide to ride down to the hotel rather than walk. There's a place that makes chocolate on the other side of the island, and today would seem to be perfect for a visit. I don't think we'll have any difficulty finding it but asking for directions isn't the only reason I suggest we pop into the hotel; I also want to thank Fiona for her hospitality yesterday, and the considerable tact she showed. I didn't really get a chance during our meal. In fact, I hardly saw her at all during the evening; I've a feeling she was giving us some space.

But there's no one in reception when we arrive and a quick check on the lounge confirms there's no one there either, except for a couple of guests. I'm about to suggest that we make our way to the chocolatier anyway, when there's a shout from an open doorway to our left and the strident sound of dropped crockery. With a quick glance at one another, Beth and I follow the direction of the noise.

We walk into a large room, halfway up which on the right-hand side is a set of double doors open to the garden. A tray lays on the floor, just inside, surrounded by broken crockery, although three cups still nestle inside each other, miraculously whole.

Almost immediately another shout goes up and a black-and-white puppy hurtles into the room, followed by Alfie, swearing loudly. Fiona is close on his heels, carrying a dustpan and brush. She stops when she sees us.

'Oh, morning!' She darts an exasperated look at the puppy, who is still giving Alfie the runaround, and comes over. 'We're having a little fun, as you can see. One of Maureen's lads came to "help" this morning and left the gate open to their pen. *Again…* Houdini here thinks it's a riot to run around, tripping folks up and generally getting in everyone's way.'

'Is that really his name?' asks Beth.

Fiona smiles. 'No, but it should be. That one's Milo. At least I think it is.'

Beth takes a couple of steps into the room, sinking to her knees with her hand outstretched. 'Milo,' she calls. 'Here, boy.'

The puppy streaks past her, skids to a halt on the polished wood floor and then takes off again, running back the way he came. Except that when he gets halfway, he suddenly stops, sniffs the air and then calmly trots over to Beth's waiting hand. Fiona stares, clearly astonished, as Beth fondles the dog's ears before picking him up, holding the bundle of fluff close to her chest. Alfie is by her side in an instant, a solicitous arm helping her to stand.

'Well, would you look at that!' Fiona says.

The puppy lies snuggled in Beth's embrace, looking nothing like the wild animal of a few moments earlier. Beside her, Alfie stands, panting slightly. He nods in greeting.

'Oh, Abby, this is Alfie, my brother. Although I think you've met?'

A ripple of panic runs through me until I realise what she's referring to. I smile as naturally as I can. 'Oh, yes, we did, just briefly the other day. When I thought I'd seen a ghost…' I meet his eyes, seeing the same glint of panic in them. 'Sorry about that, I was… We'd been travelling a long time, I think I must have been more tired than I realised.' I'm gabbling. 'I'm Abby,' I finish, with a half-smile, which is all I can muster.

He holds out his hand. 'Yes, Abby. I've heard so much about you.' No need to say from who then, obviously. No need to make reference to Cam at all.

I stare at his fingers, remembering the last time I'd held them, almost a year ago. I lift my hand to take his, just as he takes my arm, pulling me in to kiss my cheeks.

'It's so lovely to meet you.'

'And this is Beth, Abby's daughter,' adds Fiona. 'And champion dog whisperer, obviously.' She smiles at us both as if there's absolutely nothing amiss.

Alfie dips his head. 'Hi, Beth.'

This is excruciating. I'm sure my face must be scarlet, and I cannot think of a single thing to say.

Alfie pats the dog's head. 'Shall we go and put this rascal away? Before he does any more damage.' And before I can stop them, Beth follows Alfie out of the room. I'm left looking helplessly at Fiona. She pats my arm.

'Don't worry,' she says, leaning slightly towards me. 'Alfie's been warned to be on his best behaviour.'

I raise my eyebrows.

'He won't mention Cam unless you want him to,' she adds. 'We all know how hard this is for you.'

I smile a thank-you. 'Here, let me help you,' I reply, indicating the crockery still on the floor. 'It's hard on you too,' I add. 'But that was one of the reasons why we called in this morning. I wanted to thank you, for yesterday, for giving me a bit of space. You never really know how you're going to react, do you? And I think being here has hit me harder than I thought it was going to.'

Fiona rights the tray and begins to collect the broken crockery. 'Everyone understands, Abby. We all cope differently, and I think in many ways Alfie has found it hardest. He and Cam were such good friends. Plus, of course, if it wasn't for him, we wouldn't have known so much about you, or quite how close you and Cam had become. I think he feels that puts him under some kind of pressure. Now that you're here, I mean.' She gives me a rather direct look.

'No, no pressure,' I reply. 'Oh, he mustn't feel that.'

'And he feels a little guilty too.'

'Oh?' I say, picking up a cup handle and placing it on the tray.

'Because it was him who found your emails, the ones to Cam. He let us read some and…' She clears her throat a little. 'We stopped as soon as we realised how private they were, but I think he feels bad about the fact that we saw them at all, as if it was his fault. But honestly, Abby, the rest of us are clueless when it comes to technology, and Morag was only after some pictures of Cam. They were on his laptop, you see.'

I nod, remembering what Alfie had first told me. At least that bit was true.

'I can imagine that Morag and Gillie would be very keen to have photos,' I reply. 'It's okay, I understand.'

She smiles. 'Good. I'd hate you to think badly of us.' She sweeps up the last of the bits of china, adding the dustpan and brush to the tray. 'Let me go and get rid of these,' she says. 'And then I'll be with you.' She pauses a minute. 'Or come through, if you like, I'll make us a cuppa.'

I have no choice but to follow her; I have no idea where Beth has got to for one. A path leads from the double doors out into the garden, cleverly winding its way under an arched canopy so that we can walk without getting wet. It curves round slightly to the right and I can see that we must be heading for a room that lies behind the hotel's main lounge area. The gardens are beautiful, even in the rain.

We enter another small lobby with a room in front of us and another to our left, the door to which Fiona indicates as we pass. 'Our private rooms are through there, which is where the pups are. Taking over nearly the whole of the living room, I might add,' she says. 'And this is the hotel kitchen. It's a bit mad this morning, sorry.' She pushes her way through the door into a bright and airy space, full of the most amazing smells. Morag is standing at one of the sinks, peeling potatoes, while Andrew is busy stirring something at one of the huge ovens which sits in the middle of the room.

'Morning, dear,' Morag says, although it isn't clear whether she's speaking to Fiona or me. 'Did you sleep well?'

I falter a second, not sure whether to reply, but Fiona completely ignores the question and carries the tray through to another room at the back. Morag's clear blue eyes are turned in my direction.

'Oh, yes,' I lie. 'Thank you. The air here is so lovely, and all that travelling caught up with us rather. Beth and I both had early nights.'

'That's good. Will you have a cup of tea?' She lifts her hands from the sink, still dripping with water.

'Morag, I'll get it, don't worry,' says Fiona reappearing. 'Is Gillie still here?'

'No, he and Shona have gone to pick up the drinks, but they'll be back any moment, I'm sure.'

'Ceilidh night,' Fiona says to me by way of explanation. 'So, it's all hands to the pumps. Although this one is a bit bigger than usual. It's ceilidh and *curry* night, which is always a big hit with our visitors. Plus, the lot from the festival will be here, so we have to get it right.' She smiles at her husband. 'We're banking on Andrew's special spice mix to count in our favour.'

'Well, if they don't award it to us, I'll have something to say,' adds Morag darkly. 'It's our turn, apart from anything else.'

I give Fiona a puzzled look.

'The folk festival,' she says, crossing to a small sink in the corner to wash her hands. 'The islands take it in turns to host it. Although take it in turns is a rather loose description of what happens. There's an organising committee who choose the venue each year, supposedly on the basis of everyone having a go, but some of our neighbours seem to have been awarded it rather more often than they should,' she says. 'Although I imagine that's pure coincidence, and nothing to do with the chair of judges being resident on the particular island in question.' She rolls her eyes. 'It's mostly friendly rivalry, but to be fair, the festival brings a massive upsurge in visitors, they come from all over the world, so it's pretty important to us that we get to host it.'

'Oh, when is it?' I ask.

'Not until August,' replies Morag. 'But the judges are coming to us tonight, so although the ceilidh is a regular event, this one's a bit special.'

I look around me at the quiet but obvious industry.

'Then I should get out of your hair,' I say, smiling. 'Honestly, you don't need to worry about the tea, you've got enough to do.'

'Aye,' says Andrew. 'But you have to keep the cook fed and watered or else there's trouble.'

'Grab a seat,' says Fiona. 'Now will you take tea or coffee?'

And so that's how I find myself washing up twenty minutes later with no clue as to where Beth has got to. But that's okay, and I smile to myself at the sudden realisation of how easily we've been taken under this family's wing.

Andrew places a couple of plates beside the sink with a sheepish smile. He leans in so he can whisper in my ear, although when he does so his voice is as loud as normal. 'I probably shouldn't say this, but let Fiona take an inch…' He trails off, grinning.

'I heard that!' comes Fiona's reply from somewhere deep in the room, but it's good-natured. 'Abby and Beth are both free to leave at any time they like, but it's turned into a real dreich day outside. What else are they going to do when the weather is like this?'

I'm being teased, after all I did offer to do the washing up, and I'm about to reply when the door opens and Gillie and Shona come through, both carrying boxes.

'In the back, is it?' Gillie asks.

'Aye, please,' calls Fiona. 'And shout Alfie, he can give you a hand.'

'He's in the hall, Mum,' says Shona. 'He and Beth are stringing up the lights on the beams.'

'Oh, are they?'

Fiona and I both turn at the same time, our eyes meeting across the room. 'I'm sure she's not… I'll go and check,' she says, rushing from the room.

'Morning, Abby,' says Gillie as he walks past me. 'Sleep well, did you?'

'Yes,' I reply, grinning at his back. He doesn't seem in the least bit surprised to see me. I finish the plate I'm washing and dry my hands quickly on the towel beside me. 'Can I help?' I ask, as Gillie comes back my way, now empty-handed.

'That you can, lass, thank you. We've a truck full. Folks on this island can dance, can sing too, some of them, but boy, can they drink.'

I follow him out of the room, meeting Fiona on her way back in. 'It's all right,' she says to me. 'Beth's footing the ladder, that's all. Alfie's doing the scary stuff.' She carries on past me.

'Okay, thank you,' I call, feeling somewhat breathless at all the bustle. I thought the pace of life here was supposed to be slower.

At two o'clock, Fiona declares a halt in proceedings for a late lunch and even though I haven't been aware of it, somewhere along the line she's managed to make a pile of sandwiches and rustle up a huge cake.

A call goes out and seconds later, Alfie, Beth and Shona appear from where they've been setting up the hall, with Gillie following a moment later.

'Come through,' says Fiona, handing me a stack of plates and leading the way to their private accommodation. Beth and Shona immediately disappear to see the puppies, which are in the next room, and soon there's just the six of us standing in the centre of a large family room – part dining room, part sitting room – all looking rather awkwardly at one another.

'Och, for goodness' sake,' says Fiona, wafting her hands at everyone. 'Will you just sit down. It's not like you haven't been here before. It's only Abby that's new.' She makes a clicking sound with her tongue in exasperation. 'And I'm not standing on ceremony either, get on with you and eat.'

Andrew beams at her and begins to load a plate with food from the tray that Fiona has put down on the coffee table. And then Alfie and Morag do the same. Fiona catches my eye and grimaces ever so slightly.

'All apart from you, Abby,' she says. 'What can I get you?' She indicates an armchair set back slightly from the others. 'You might want to sit there,' she adds.

I sink gratefully into the seat, touched once again by her thoughtfulness despite the whirlwind pace of her day. Moments later, she thrusts a heaped plate at me and pulls up a footstool so that she can sit down herself.

'That's better,' she says, pausing as if to gather her breath before taking a huge bite of her sandwich.

'I hadn't realised you'd be so busy,' I remark.

'Aye, well, weekends are always busy during the holidays, with the ceilidhs and so on. They're mostly for the visitors at this time of year, but we make the most of it, the season doesn't last that long. Just as well we're not serving food in the hotel today, or we'd never cope.'

'Is it very quiet here in the winter?' I ask.

Fiona chews and swallows as a gentle smile comes over her face. 'That's when I love it the most,' she says. 'Don't get me wrong, I love what we do, but the island comes into its own in the winter, when it's just us. The islanders, I mean. The place relaxes, gets comfortable again.'

Her comment makes me laugh. 'But I thought you were pretty relaxed here as it is. Isn't that the point of coming to a remote Scottish island, for the peace and quiet?'

'I shall point out your use of the word *coming*... For our visitors it's absolutely the best thing. For the rest of us... Maybe we're like swans, all calm and serene on the surface, but underneath our legs are paddling like fury.' She stares out into the room for a moment. 'You must make sure you see the island, while you're here,' she says, dropping her voice. 'Don't let this lot monopolise you.' But then she grins. 'Or me, for that matter. I don't suppose you had plans to come and wash up for us today, did you?'

'No, but I don't mind. I can see how busy you all are. And it's nice for Beth. I was a little worried that she'd be bored here, so to find someone her age…' I take a bite of my sandwich, before I reveal any more.

'And what's waiting for you back at home?' Fiona asks. 'I think Alfie mentioned you have a shop. Is that right?'

'Yes, a second-hand bookshop. Beth and I live in the flat above. It's right bang in the middle of town in a beautiful old building. We love it.'

I'm suddenly aware that Alfie is sitting away to my left, his head turned at the sound of his name. Almost imperceptibly the sound in the room drops, as if everyone is listening. Or perhaps I'm imagining things.

'I remember,' replies Fiona. 'Isn't that how you and Cam got talking in the first place?'

I smile at the memory of that first email. Even then, Cam's personality shone through. 'Yes, he wanted a copy of a particular novel that I had in stock, one of my favourites, actually. He said it was just possible that I could save his soul and—' I break off, horrified at what I've just said. Repeating Cam's words, but not realising how poignant they would become. If only I *had* been able to save his soul.

But Fiona simply smiles. 'That sounds like Cam,' she replies. 'He was always very passionate where books were concerned. You'll know about the literary festival, of course?'

I shake my head, looking at the cast of Alfie's eyes, which is resolutely downward. 'No, I don't think so. Is that something that happens here?'

Fiona nods. 'Well, did do. We haven't had one for a couple of years. I'm surprised Cam didn't mention it. It was him, you see, he organised it and…' She doesn't need to say any more. She clears her throat.

'Anyway, I'm not the only one who thought he should have been a writer himself. But frustrated English teacher it was. He certainly had a way with words, though, as you obviously know.'

I flick another glance at Alfie but his head is still down. And I'm not imagining things, the sound in the room *has* fallen away. Morag shuffles her way along the sofa, until she's sitting almost next to my chair.

'Would you like to see some photos of him?' she asks.

There's a slight tut from my other side. 'Morag, what are you like?' says Fiona. 'Give the poor woman some breathing room.'

'What? I'm only asking. And Abby doesn't have to look at them now if she doesn't want to. She doesn't even have to look at them at all. Anyway, why did you go to the bother of fetching them out if you didn't want Abby to look at them?'

I pull my head back slightly as the two women talk across me.

'I thought she might like to, that's all. And if she does, I can leave them for her to look at any time,' counters Fiona. 'In fact, she can take them back to the cottage if she wants to.'

I lean forward. 'I'd love to see them,' I say, acutely aware that Alfie is now looking at me. 'I've seen some photos of him, of course, but not that many.'

Morag smiles, with a triumphant glance at Fiona. 'There now, I told you she would.' She pushes herself out of the sofa's depths and crosses to the kitchen counter, where a stack of books is piled. She cradles them all in her arms and carries them over.

'Some of these are from when he was a wee baby,' says Fiona, as Morag piles the photo albums up on the sofa. 'But…' And then she breaks off, giving Morag a telling look. 'How about we leave Abby to have a look on her own?' she adds, raising her voice so that it's clear to the whole room. 'We had best get back to work anyway.'

I look down at my plate and the food I've hardly eaten. Apart from Andrew, who has finished his sandwich, everyone else seems to be midway through their lunch too. Even so there's a round of collective nodding and within moments, Gillie and Andrew have both disappeared and Fiona and Morag are making ready to leave.

'Please, there's no need to leave on my account.'

'No, looking through photos is a thing best done in your own company,' says Morag. 'We can finish up in the kitchen. Alfie, will you see where the girls have got to? It's gone awfully quiet through there.'

And I realise as she says it that the excited chatter of girls playing with puppies has faded away. Alfie does an about-turn from the doorway and comes to stand in front of me.

'Sure,' he says. 'If I know Shona, she'll have dragged Beth off somewhere to help her rehearse.'

'Rehearse?' I ask.

'Aye, for the ceilidh. Shona's doing a star turn. But don't worry, Shona will look after her. I'll go and make sure they're okay though.'

'Thank you,' I say, as I reach across for one of the albums. I know he's still looking at me, the book of photos in my hand very real proof of his lies. But I'm not about to offer any reassurance that I'll keep his secret safe. These albums detail the life in pictures of a man who until very recently I thought I had got to know well. Now, I don't even know what he looked like.

'And see if you can get them to have something to eat,' calls Fiona at his retreating back.

Moments later, the room is quiet, the swirling eddies of movement settling around me until all is still. It's as if I'm holding my breath. I stare at the cover of the album in my hands and then, swallowing, heart beating a little faster, I open it.

Chapter 18

The hall looks incredible. Even though I'd had a hand in the preparation for tonight's event, I hadn't really taken in what I was seeing as I bustled about. It isn't really a hall, but the function room in the hotel. Long and open to the rafters, it could so easily look bare and draughty but, instead, with lights strung along the wooden beams and huge vases of flowers on the tables, it looks warm and welcoming. The rain stopped and a bustling wind blew away the clouds so now the afternoon sun floods through the windows along one side, burnishing the already golden wooden floor. The fresh smell of the garden wafts in through the double doors, which have been propped open, and I'm told we'll be glad of it once the dancing gets going; it can get rather warm, apparently.

There's just time for a short break before the ceilidh kicks off at seven. Beth and I have been at the hotel all afternoon, although I've hardly seen her. When I have, her face has been wreathed in smiles and I haven't thought to worry about her. Alfie might have been economical with the truth in some respects, but he was right about everybody here being like one big family. That much is evidently true.

I sat for a good hour earlier, looking through the photo albums. I hadn't been sure what to make of them. Because I had nothing to go on, no points of reference, so the pictures of Cam as a baby or a young child made no impression; I could have been looking at anybody. Even those taken more recently which showed people or places I recognised didn't connect with me in any way. I was curious, and it was lovely to see the closeness of the family, snapshots of island life and the community too, but I couldn't relate any of it to the man who had written to tell me about all of these things. It's almost as if he never existed.

Morag and Fiona were both solicitous when I'd eventually reappeared in the kitchen, fussing over me and making sure I was all right, but I didn't know what to say to them. How could I tell them that the photos of a beloved son and cousin meant nothing to me? It would break their hearts. Or at least the truth would. And that had made me angry. Furious that, although Alfie claimed he had acted out of the best of intentions, by taking Cam's face, he had stolen away from me the man I fell in love with. And I'm not sure I can ever forgive him for that.

But the thoughts in my head had been quickly pushed to one side when I realised how busy everyone still was. The cooking was still continuing apace, Andrew brewing up more huge pots of delicious-smelling curries, and Morag and Fiona baking cakes and sausage rolls, making sandwiches and dishes of coleslaw. Gillie had been dispatched to pick up the sound system and Alfie was busy ferrying chairs and tables into the hall and erecting the staging. The organisation ran like clockwork but there were still plenty of times when an extra pair of hands was welcomed, and I helped gladly. It seemed the least I could do.

At half past five, Beth and I had sloped off back to the cottage to have a break, a quick bath and get ourselves ready, and now at half past six we're back in the hotel, trying to be helpful while not getting in everyone's way.

An hour later, our first experience of a ceilidh is in full swing and I haven't stopped smiling since. Or been able to catch my breath.

There is an energy here that's infectious. It isn't just the relentless toe-tappingly catchy beat of the music, although I admit that has much to do with it, but from the islanders themselves. And what quickly becomes very apparent is how at ease everyone is. There's no self-conscious shuffling, or reluctance to join in; slightly inhibited dancing or shy conversations and wallflower impersonations. No one is at all worried what they look like, and it makes me wonder if this is an island thing, or a ceilidh thing.

There is such familiarity here among everyone, and although the visitors obviously come and go, you can see that it's rubbed off on them. I can't imagine going anywhere else and being so utterly abandoned. The parties I've been to in the past, not that many admittedly, have been excruciating things, neither knowing where to put yourself or what to say. Inhibitions worn like party frocks, garish and uncomfortable. Not here though.

It's about the sheer enjoyment of losing yourself in the music, in the rhythms and having fun, for no other reason than because you can. The fact that it's all of their own making makes it even more special. It's very much a case of what you bring to the party, you receive, and these are extremely generous and giving people.

I collapse on a welcome seat for a few moments, waiting for my head to stop spinning a little. I've been whirled around that many times, and although I haven't a clue about the steps, somehow even that doesn't seem to matter. There's always someone to lead and once you relax, it almost seems second nature, as if your body knows where to go, even if your head doesn't.

I look up as Morag lands beside me, not in the least bit out of breath, even though she's an accomplished dancer and seems to move much faster than everyone else. She laughs at my astonished expression as I blow out a puff of air.

'You'll get your wind soon,' she says. 'Probably around eleven. Then you'll think you can dance all night.'

'Eleven?' I say in horror. 'I'll never make it that far. Do people ever stop?' I look at the empty chairs around the room.

Morag laughs. 'Oh, aye, they do. You think people are moving fast now, you wait until the food gets brought in.' She gestures to where Beth and Shona are standing up near the stage. 'Your lassie looks as if she's having fun.'

'Oh, she is! She's loving it here.' I think carefully about my next words, but there's no reason not to confide in Morag. 'She's had a bit of a rough time at school lately, so I hoped this holiday would put some colour back into her cheeks, and it's certainly doing that.'

'Well, she'll naught go far wrong with Alfie looking after her; he's a good lad. He misses Cameron like crazy, of course, but he knows how much you two meant to him, he'll not let anything spoil your visit here.'

I hope the expression on my face doesn't give me away. 'Well, Beth is already a fan,' I say lightly. 'He made an instant hit with her the minute he said he liked her dungarees.'

Too late I realise what I've said. Beth isn't wearing her dungarees today. She has on the same jeans as yesterday, the ones that Shona so admired. I keep my face averted in Beth's direction, praying that Morag won't notice my slip.

'Plus of course he's musical so that helps,' I add, moving the conversation on. 'Beth doesn't come across many folk who are so openly encouraging of her in that direction.'

To my relief, Morag simply nods. 'You probably saw the photos earlier,' she says. 'Watching Alfie trying to teach Cameron to dance has to be one of the funniest things I've ever seen. I think Cam must have been the only man on the island who couldn't dance, bless him. And he was tone deaf too, just to add insult to injury. None of us could understand it; everyone else in the family was born singing and dancing, but not Cameron.' She smiles across at me. 'But I expect you know that, dear. I'm sure he must have told you.'

'Yes, of course,' I say, feeling a sudden heat bloom on the back of my neck. 'He joked about it too.'

I'm saved from having to say anything further by the appearance of Gillie in front of us, both arms outstretched as if in invitation, his legs still moving to the beat. I wave my hand, shaking my head. 'No, I can't!' I exclaim. 'Not just yet. Give me a minute more to get my breath back.'

Morag laughs. 'You young things have no stamina.' And she gets to her feet to join her husband.

But rather than sitting to get my breath back, I wander out into the garden instead, grateful for the soothing balm of delicious air outside. A bench sits a little distance away, alongside a tub of flowers whose scent fills the air, and I sit down, shoving my hands under my thighs.

I never realised that coming here would be so hard. That there would be so many reminders of Cam, or rather reminders of someone who I thought was Cam. I'd hoped this holiday would be somewhere I could lay his ghost to rest, but instead his spirit seems more restless than ever.

The most obvious thing would be to leave the island early, but I can't do that to Beth. I haven't seen her look so happy in a long while, in fact, not since last summer when she was enjoying the long school holiday, full of excitement at the prospect of joining a new school and all that would bring. Seeing her here this evening, it's as if none of the upset of the last few months has happened.

The welcome that's been extended to us by Cam's family has been so lovely, their friendship genuine and incredibly touching. But even though I'm grateful for it, it isn't making things any easier. And now I feel as if whatever I do will affect them too. And that's a huge responsibility.

I stare at my toes, scuffing at a pebble on the path until a soft noise to my left causes me to look up. Coming towards me is the last person I want to see.

'What?' I say. 'Come to check I haven't given your game away yet?'

Alfie looks as if he's been slapped, and I instantly feel ashamed. That is until I remember why I'm sitting out here.

'No,' he says pointedly. 'I wanted to say thank you, actually, for not saying anything earlier.'

I drop my head.

'Besides, I saw you leave the dance and thought I might come and say hello. I don't seem to have spoken to you much since you've been here.' He looks as if he's about to say something else but then changes his mind.

'Yes, well, there's a reason for that,' I reply. 'I think I asked you not to, if memory serves. So why are you here, Alfie?' I stare up at him from where he towers over me. 'Don't tell me, let me guess. You don't want people to think it's odd that I'm not talking to you. Because I should want to, shouldn't I? After all, you were Cam's best friend.'

He glares at me. 'That hadn't actually occurred to me, but now that you mention it...' He holds my gaze a second or two longer and then looks away sighing. 'You know, Abby, I understand why you're angry with me. I can see how it looks, only too clearly, but what saddens me the most is that you're so keen to be angry with me that you're throwing away the biggest opportunity you have not only to find out more about Cam, but what he thought about you. Because believe me, you were the world to him. And whether you want to believe it or not, that means something to those of us he left behind, and frankly, I thought it would mean more to you too. Please don't dishonour his memory by ignoring it.'

My breath catches in my throat. Is that what Alfie thinks I'm doing? Is that what everyone will think I'm doing? It's so unfair.

'You don't even realise the worst of what you've done, do you? Don't you dare tell me I'm dishonouring his memory, not when you've made me feel as if Cam never existed.'

He opens his mouth to speak and then closes it abruptly and I can see that my words have hit home. He thrusts his hands into his jean pockets and comes to perch on the other end of the bench, staring down at his feet.

The silence between us stretches out, incongruous amid the joyful music that spills out from the open doorway to the hall.

'So, how's business?' he asks eventually.

I lift my head. 'Really?' I say. 'You want to talk about the shop?'

'Well, why not? Talking about the past isn't helping, so I thought we should move into the present. If you and Cam were emailing one another that's what you'd be talking about. You'd be telling him about your day: where you'd moved Brown Bear to, what awful blind dates your mother has been trying to set you up with and in return, I'd tell you how the orchids up at the estate house are looking amazing, and how I wished you could see them. Or I'd mention that we've been working on a new gin recipe which even I might like, though I can't usually stand the stuff.'

'You'd tell me...?'

He nods gently and I see the reality of my conversations with Cam laid out before me. I drop my head again, picking at the seam on my jeans.

'Alfie, can we not? Do this, I mean. Pretend as if nothing's changed. Those conversations belonged to a different time. One where I thought I knew how things were. Now...' But I don't finish the sentence, I don't need to.

'You didn't answer my question,' he repeats. 'So how is business?'

I ignore him. I refuse to talk about this, here, with him.

'Only last night you mentioned something about the shop. You were worried that you might not be able to keep it going.'

I can feel his eyes boring into the side of my face.

'You know, you should call in and see Maureen at some point this week,' he continues. 'She orders her stock in from the mainland at the moment, but it's worth asking her where from. She might take some from you.'

And despite my determination not to, I look at him, puzzled. 'Maureen? From the shop? Why, is she a big reader too?'

Alfie smiles. 'Not so's you'd notice, but she does do incredibly well with the books, and not just in the summer either.'

I'm still blank, trying to make sense of his words. 'You mean, Maureen sells books?' I ask, casting my mind back to our time in the shop yesterday.

'Didn't you didn't spot them? In the room at the back.'

I hadn't noticed anything, but then there was stock piled everywhere, fresh off the ferry. I hadn't wanted to get in the way.

'And there's me thinking I was genetically disposed to hunt out books,' I reply. 'I'll have to have a look next time we're in there.'

Alfie's suggestion is interesting, but the logistics of getting stock from the shop to Maureen don't really make it a sensible proposition.

I would imagine she uses suppliers who are as close as possible on the mainland. She might even travel over on the ferry to collect them. And books are heavy; she probably also gets lots of donations from visitors who don't want to carry their books home with them when they leave.

Alfie gives an exasperated tut, this time mistaking my silence for something else. 'Abby, don't be so stubborn. When you told me about the shop yesterday, you told *me*. Not Cam, and not some combination of both of us either, but me. And now *I'm* asking you how things are, because whether you like it or not, it's been a shared topic of conversation between us in the past and because I'm interested. I know how much the shop means to you, and how much it would worry you if things weren't going well.'

I doubt that. No one in my family understands it, why should he? But Alfie isn't finished.

'I've explained to you what happened when Cam was ill, and what happened after he died. I'm not pretending it was the right thing to do but we've been through a lot together, you and I...' He grinds to a halt, swallowing. 'I thought we'd become friends.'

'And that's true, is it? You haven't misled me in any other way?'

'No, of course I haven't.'

I raise my eyebrows. 'And you're absolutely sure about that, are you? Because I've just seen you dancing, singing, playing your guitar. Just like in the photos of you and Cam I saw earlier this afternoon. Except that when I was talking to Morag a few minutes ago, she told me that Cam had two left feet and was tone deaf as well, probably the only islander who was, in fact. And yet, I distinctly remember having various conversations with Cam about Beth, about her singing, how she was so keen to be in the school play. And Cam replied saying how much he was looking forward to seeing her, and how important all those things were in his life. So, tell me, Alfie, what's the truth here? Was Cam as musical as he made out, or is his own mother telling me lies?'

His face is scarlet.

'And while we're at it, you are not my daughter's friend. When you and she were messing around in my kitchen last summer, she thought you were Cam. You know, the one who was supposedly musical. I think she just about gets that you pretended to be Cam, to help out a friend, but when she finds out about all the other lies you've told. No, I'm not going to let that happen so don't you dare try to get close to her as well.'

I stare at his flushed face, see the light dying from his eyes as he takes in what I've said. The fact that he has no answer for me.

'Yes, I thought so,' I say, getting to my feet. 'Excuse me.'

'Oh, for God's sake! Why does everything have to be about that?' His voice is almost a shout. 'For your information, one of the things I came to talk to you about just now is Beth. To thank you for letting me spend time with her this afternoon, and to tell you how talented I think she is.'

His words reverberate around me, stopping me in my tracks. 'Oh…'

'Abby, please. I understand why you're so angry at me. But I'm not a monster. And I'm actually very grateful to Beth too.' He rakes a hand through the thick hair that's fallen across his brow. 'And you know why? Because every other ceilidh I've helped out with, and believe me, there's been a few since Cam died, all I've seen is the hole where he used to be. Every time, except for this afternoon when I had the company of a funny, talented young girl who loves life as much as he did. And you know what, Abby? It's helped. It's filled the space where Cam should have been.'

He gets to his feet.

'Alfie, wait!'

But he doesn't stop and even though I try to take his arm to slow him down, he pulls away and I'm left staring at his back, my arms hanging helplessly by my sides.

It's a full ten minutes before I'm able to re-enter the hall, skirting the wall on my left and walking back through to the hotel reception. Fiona is making her way towards me, carrying a plate of food.

'Is everything all right?' she asks, concern showing on her face.

I brighten my expression. 'Yes, perfectly. This is great, isn't it?' I reply. I indicate a doorway to my left. 'I'm just popping to the loo,' I say. 'I'll be back in a minute.'

It's quiet inside the cloakroom, and empty, fortunately. I stand there for quite some time, staring at myself in the mirror. Wondering how I could have been so cruel. I can feel hot tears coming closer and closer, and I have to fight to push them away, sniffing and holding my head up high. I turn on a tap over the hand basin and let the warm water pour over my hands, soothing and calming. The soap is heavily scented and the feel of it silky-smooth.

I practise a smile in the mirror and, when I feel I've got myself back under control, I turn to leave, almost crashing into Fiona coming through the door.

'There you are!' she exclaims. 'Come on, or you'll miss it,' she says, grabbing hold of my arm.

'Miss what?'

But even as I ask the question, my ear, constantly tuned in the way only a mother's can be, has picked out something above the general noise and music coming from the hall. I stare at Fiona.

She nods. 'Come on.'

By the time I've made it to the open doorway, the hairs are standing up on the back of my neck. Up on the stage, apart from Alfie, and another man whose name I don't know, is Beth, singing in front of a crowd of people, most of them on their feet. Singing as I've never heard her before.

I can scarcely take it all in. But everywhere I look are happy, smiling faces, lost in the sound of her voice as it soars into the space around them. It's not a song I know. In fact, it's not even one I've heard before, and I can only imagine that it's one that Beth has just learned, but you'd never know it from her performance. She looks assured and confident, but more than anything, she looks *right where she should be*.

Her only accompaniment is Alfie, softly filling in some of the spaces with his guitar, but as I watch, the other man lifts what I can now see is a flute to his lips and begins to play. As he does so, there's a movement off to the side of the stage and I see Shona, slowly climbing the steps to cross the stage until she's standing beside Beth. The music dies gently away with Beth's voice and I see a look pass silently between the two girls. Beth is watching her, I realise. There's the tiniest of signals and then both girls start to sing in close harmony.

Beside me, Fiona's hand touches my arm. Her other hand is covering her mouth as she too stands in awe. 'I've never heard Shona sing like this before,' she says, turning to me with tears in her eyes. 'They're so good together.'

'They're incredible…' But I can't say any more. I'm listening as if I've never heard anyone ever sing before. Beth's voice suits the style of music perfectly, but she's found a new quality to it, which is still prickling the hairs at the back of my neck. It's lilting and lyrical, centuries-old and uniquely modern.

And the phrase fills my head once more, *She's right where she should be*.

Chapter 19

Given my conversation with Alfie in the garden, another sleepless night was no surprise, even though in part it was down to the excitement at hearing Beth sing. But although Monday dawned with a black pall of clouds hovering over the island, which gave way to squally bursts of rain the entire day, in truth both Beth and I were glad of it. Our exertions from the ceilidh and a very late night had well and truly caught up with us, and although Beth was still buzzing from her performance, without the aid of adrenaline rushing around her system, she collapsed in a lethargic heap.

This morning, though, it's as if we're on a completely different island. The sky is incredibly high, wide and the brightest blue, with only the faintest trace of wispy clouds on the horizon. The light had propelled us early from our beds and after another indulgent breakfast, we're getting ready to go to the beach. At last.

The island is famous for its incredible coastline and sweeping sandy vistas but, so we've been told by countless people, the photos don't do them justice. And, like many things, the best places to visit require a little effort to truly appreciate them. Here, that means walking. There's pretty much only the one road circumnavigating the island, and so much of its wild beauty is best explored on foot or, in our case, by bike and then on foot.

I'm packing a rucksack with provisions for the day when Beth appears in the kitchen, waving her phone around in the air.

I give her an amused look. 'The best signal's by the front door,' I tell her. I know because I stood there myself this morning, checking if Gwen had been in touch. 'What are you doing anyway? We're nearly ready to go.'

'Trying to download something,' she calls through the doorway. 'But it's taking an age.'

I give my watch a quick glance. There's no urgency to our timetable but we've been here two and a bit days already and seen nothing of the island yet and I'm keen to make the most of what's left of the week.

'Okay, but we said we'd get going as soon as we're ready,' I remind her. 'Can't it wait until later?'

But there's no reply from the other room.

I wander through to see Beth standing by the door, holding her phone out as if it's a Geiger counter. She stops, moves a couple of inches, stops again, and then holds steady.

'It won't be long, it's only a couple more songs.'

'Beth, we're going to be outside, on a beautiful day. The birds are singing, the wind will be rustling the trees, the waves will be washing the shoreline. You won't need your ears plugged with headphones, listening to music.'

She gives me an exasperated look. 'I'm not, Mum. They're songs Shona sent me. I need to learn them.'

I peer closer. 'What for?'

Another look. 'I just do.'

I pick up the book I'd been reading the night before. 'Have you put everything in the kitchen you want to take?' I ask, knowing there's no way I'm going to be able to stop Beth from singing now. Not that I'd want to.

She nods. 'Yes, just my book. It's on the table. And my water bottle.'

Fifteen minutes later we wheel the bikes out from the shed and get going, sailing past the shop and then the hotel. We carry on, heading north, aiming for a secluded spot that Fiona has recommended.

Within minutes the scenery begins to change. Surrounding the cottage all is wide-open vistas and hummocky hills, revealing nothing but sky above, but gradually as we cycle inland the first few trees begin to appear. After another mile or so the road narrows considerably and becomes bordered on both sides by thickets of trees offering glimpses of wild flowers in the meadows beyond. Here and there are larger fields, fat round bodies of sheep grazing peacefully under the sun.

We stop for a moment and wheel the bikes. There's so much to look at that even the speed of a bike seems too fast to garner it all. The island is definitely a place to be savoured slowly. A couple pass us, hand in hand, and although they smile, they're evidently wrapped up in each other. They're only young, and I can't help wondering whether they might be honeymooners. I can't think of a more romantic, away-from-it-all place. But then I also wonder when I stopped thinking of myself as young, and quickly turn the thought away.

Back on our bikes again, it isn't long before we flash past a small track on our left, the only one we've passed so far. Beth calls out to see if I've noticed it, and I nod, scanning the hedgerow for the gap and small wooden post that Fiona told us to look out for. Spotting it, we quickly bring the bikes to a halt and dismount, wheeling them to the side of the road. Just beyond the post is a field through which feet have laid a faint trail through the grasses that blow lazily in the breeze.

It had worried me that there didn't appear to be any bike locks in the shed at the cottage until Fiona had smiled, telling me we wouldn't need them. 'Just tuck the bikes behind a hedge whenever you need to. I promise you they'll still be there on your return.' Even so, I still make sure they're as hidden from the road as they can be, before hitching my pack a little higher on my back and setting off across the field. We pass through an area of woodland when we get to the other side before emerging into grassland, filled with wild flowers. Machair, they call it here, and it extends as far as the eye can see. It's so beautiful, tipped with points of colour, bright-red clover, delicate violet bells that seem to tinkle in the breeze, along with pinks and yellows, orange and deep purple.

It seems criminal to walk through it, but we tread lightly, pushing on slightly uphill now. After another mile or so the wide expanse of horizon becomes wider yet, teasingly waiting to deliver its promise of the sea. And then it does, in an arc of shimmering silver-blue that disappears into the distance.

Even Beth stands still in awe. And there we stay for several minutes, drinking in the sight of everything that lies around us. I'm hot, quite thirsty and slightly out of puff, but the reward for these slight inconveniences is something I don't think I will ever forget. Nor the way it makes me feel. As if a part of me has always been here, has come home.

With the sun on my skin, the warm thermals of the breeze lift my soul higher and higher. I have an almost overwhelming temptation to lie down, flat on my back, and stare at the sky. To feel impossibly small under an impossibly huge universe, but the feeling is suddenly replaced by the sheer excitement of discovering what comes next and so, in unspoken agreement, Beth and I walk on.

We crest the final tip of the rise and below us a wide arc of sand curves its way around a bay of bright-blue water, a tumult of the blackest rocks on either edge. It's only a tiny bay and totally deserted, almost as if it were waiting here, undiscovered, just for us. Our pace picks up as we make our way down to it, dropping through grassy tussocks in stages to the beach.

Beth breaks into a run, streaking out across the pale sand, arms held wide to either side. It's wonderful to see her so uninhibited, instead of holding herself in check as I've often seen her do. The contrast between how she looks here and how she had been looking at home – hunched and drawn – is stark.

She slows to a halt and stands for a moment, face upturned to the sky, and then she comes back to me, the happiest smile on her face.

'Can I go for a paddle?' she asks.

'We have all morning,' I say. 'You can do whatever you like.' It feels good to stop the clock for a while. 'And I know we said we'd go to the gardens this afternoon, but we don't have to.'

I shrug my rucksack from my back and place it on the sand.

She pulls a sad face. 'But you want to see them,' she replies.

'I do, but it's so lovely here. Let's see how we go, shall we? We don't have to decide now.'

I glance down at my shoes, wondering how quickly I can undo the laces, or failing that, just pull them off. Beth catches me looking and her face broadens into another grin. Her eyes twinkle as they meet mine.

'Race you?' she says, but I'm already trying to wrestle off one of my trainers. 'Mum, that's not fair!' she exclaims, but quickly kicks off her shoes, which land beside my bag.

By the time I'm on my way, she's already halfway down the beach, and reaches the edge of the bubbling surf long before I do.

A tiny squeal leaves my lips as the first waves break over my toes, freezing cold and exhilarating, but then it just feels delicious and I take Beth's hand to jump the rushing tide.

We walk together for a while, feet still tickled by the water, and I have a sudden urge to run as fast as I can along the shoreline. The sense of freedom here is profound and for a moment it makes me rather emotional. I don't recall ever feeling trapped in our flat or the tightly-knit streets where we live, but the awareness of space here is in such contrast that I wonder how I ever put up with it before. It's just different, I remind myself. After all, isn't that one of the reasons I chose to come here, so we could experience the landscape?

After a few minutes I turn back, leaving Beth to wander by herself, caught in the familiar pose of the beachcomber, eyes down, looking for treasure. I'm thirsty, but I also want to 'set up camp' – not that there's anyone else here – but so that I can feel I've claimed a space on this broad expanse of sand. I'm also very much looking forward to laying back to stare at the huge sky and perhaps feel the sun against my eyelids.

Beth joins me a few moments later, racing up beside me, to have some water, but also to claim her phone, fishing out the headphones that go with it from a little pocket inside the bag. She grins at me.

'I might sing a bit,' she says, almost as if she has to apologise for doing so. And I realise how inhibiting life in a flat might feel to her too. Where singing might be heard by anyone in the street below, or in the shop downstairs.

'You can sing a lot, if you want to,' I reply. 'I think it's only the seals who will hear you. Oh, and the mermaids, of course.'

'Do you think there are any here?' she asks, and then rolls her eyes. 'Seals, I mean.'

'Probably. But further round on the rocks, I would imagine. We can go and see later if you like?' There seems to be time enough to do everything here.

'Okay.' She smiles, already plugging in the headphones.

I watch her as she walks back towards the sea. Bare feet, cut-off jeans and a tee shirt, hair hanging down her back in a loose ponytail, whipped by the wind. And I think it might be the first time I've taken a good look at her in a long time. The kind of 'take-it-all-in' way that parents only ever get the chance to do once in a while, the rest of the time too caught up in the day-to-day life of school and homework and meals and bedtimes and hasty conversations. And what strikes me most about Beth now is how poised she is. Not just poised as in the way she walks and carries herself, but poised as in on the threshold, a young woman right on the edge of a new period in her life. And it suddenly seems incredibly important that we get it right.

Watching her sing the night before last had been an emotional revelation. Of course, I've heard her sing on many occasions before, but there's a difference between a school play, or an end-of-term concert to singing with musicians at a ceilidh in front of nearly a hundred people. And not simply singing with a band, but singing with such confidence, enjoyment and a new self-awareness. As if she's found a way of singing that has unlocked something inside of her.

I take another swig of water before shaking out the small blanket I'd brought from the cottage. I spread it on the sand and settle myself, book by my side and a piece of shortbread that had found its way into my rucksack too. I could become quite addicted to these.

After a few pages I realise there's very little point in trying to read. My attention keeps wandering to the world outside of my book, in which nothing is going on, but which also has the most incredible lure. And so the book falls to my lap and my legs straighten out in front of me and I tip my head to the sky.

Even the sudden noise behind me seems a part of the soundscape here, just the rustle of sand blown through the grasses, until a shadow falls slightly to one side of me. I turn, looking up.

'You're very brave,' I remark as Alfie steps onto the sand beside me. 'Or are you a glutton for punishment?'

He shrugs. 'It seems rude to be here and not say hello. Otherwise it would seem as if I was avoiding you, which I'm not.'

He holds my look for a moment and then to my amazement, plonks himself down on the blanket. I wish he hadn't, I can feel my cheeks growing scarlet.

'And before you ask, no, I haven't been following you, neither have I been looking for you. But you might recall from various emails that Cam and I often used to come to this spot at lunchtime.' He's right, Cam's description of this incredible beach is one of the reasons I wanted to come here. Or was it Alfie's description?

Alfie checks his watch. 'And it's most definitely lunchtime.'

As if to illustrate his point, he lifts an arm so I can see the small square box he carries in one hand. I hadn't even noticed it.

'Egg and cress?' he asks, peeling off the lid.

'God, no…' But I smile, I can't help myself. 'Thank you, anyway. I think it was beach holidays as a kid that put me off egg and cress. My grandparents had a beach hut in Bournemouth, so we had two weeks there every summer, and I distinctly remember eating crunchy sandwiches. Either because my grandma had left eggshell in it or from the sand, I could never work out, but it put me off for life.'

Alfie's smile is warm as he takes out a sandwich and bites off one corner. 'So, this wouldn't be the same grandparents who left you the shop then?'

'No, it was my paternal grandparents who had the bookshop. Those on my mother's side were definitely more for high days and holidays, we didn't see that much of them otherwise.'

Alfie nods, swallowing, as he stares down the beach towards the sea. 'Someone's enjoying herself,' he remarks, as he indicates Beth still wandering the shoreline. We can't hear her from where we're sitting, but it's evident she's still singing; pausing, waving her arms about, stopping every now and then as she delivers a longer or more powerful note. 'That was some performance the other night.'

His comment brings a renewed flush to my cheeks. 'Alfie... Can I say sorry before we get any further? You certainly didn't deserve the things I said to you and I'm not normally like that. I'm not quite sure what's got into me.'

'I seem to bring out the worst in you,' he replies, still watching Beth. 'Which is odd, because up until you came here, I would have said I brought out the best in you. It certainly seemed that way.'

I hang my head. 'Funnily enough, it felt that way to me too. And I am sorry, for what I said, what I accused you of.'

'And yet there was truth in it too,' he replies. 'I can't deny there wasn't. I *did* allude to Cam having talents that he clearly didn't have, but it was easier for me to talk about those things and—' He stops suddenly, as if unsure he should continue. He sticks his tongue in his cheek to fish out an errant chunk of his sandwich. 'And there's no point being anything other than honest. I did it because by then, I already knew that at some point I would meet you. I *wanted* to meet you.'

I narrow my eyes as the meaning of his words makes itself apparent. '*You* wanted to see me, or Cam did?'

He sighs. 'Both. By then, it was both.' He looks at me, his face full of remorse, but something else too. Something altogether more dangerous. He takes another quick bite of sandwich, leaving me to sit and stew over his words. After a moment, he points back to Beth. 'I meant what I said yesterday, you know. She is incredibly talented.'

I nod. 'Yes, I know. I've always known but somehow... somehow it's more evident here.'

'She's found her tribe,' replies Alfie. 'Maybe that's all it is.'

Which is exactly what I'm afraid of.

'It was a lovely thing you said though. And I never thanked you for it. Or for keeping an eye on her during the afternoon, helping her.'

Alfie brushes a hand across his lips. 'Well, like I said, she's not exactly hard work. It was a pleasure, and I got as much from it as she did. That wasn't a lie.'

'No, I believe you,' I say lightly, saddened that he now feels the need to justify everything he says to me.

I look down at the book on my lap, toying with a page. It's hard to know what to say from here.

'It must be difficult for you, for all of you,' I say. 'Seeing constant reminders of Cam everywhere you go.'

'True,' replies Alfie. 'But there are a lot of memories here too, good memories, ones I never want to lose. I think that would be the very worst thing – to forget.' He pauses a moment, wrinkles appearing around his eyes as if he's peering at something. His past perhaps. 'When Cam first died, I could hardly bear to be here. I know life moves on, but it seemed almost ridiculous to try when that was clearly impossible. Everything had changed, how could we pretend it hadn't? I thought seriously about leaving the island too. That perhaps I'd reached a crossroads and Cam's death was a sign, telling me it was time to spread my wings and find out what else there was in the big wide world.' He gives a rueful smile. 'I certainly wouldn't be the first islander to think that. We lose quite a few younger folk, who go off to find the bright lights of the big city.'

'But not you?'

He shakes his head, looking a little sad. 'No, not me. Just because it's out there, doesn't mean it's better.' He puts down his sandwich and scoops up a handful of sand, letting it trickle slowly through his fingers. 'In fact, I was sitting not far from where we are now when that particular revelation came to me. It was a couple of days before Christmas, and bitingly cold. My office back at the distillery was lovely and warm, we'd all enjoyed some festive drinks, but I had a sudden yearning to be here, to have the wind scour away everything in my head. And after a couple of minutes, even though a part of me felt desolate, I found a little spark of happiness was still there. It hasn't gone out, it's just burning on a rather lower setting now. And if I move on from here, where I have everyone and everything I love around me, I have a very great fear that it will go out forever.'

I study him for a moment. The way his hair curls over his brow, the strange grey-green of his eyes, and the little creases at the corner of his mouth that dimple when he smiles. I'd know them even without looking at them, I've studied his photos so much. Pictures I had thought were of a completely different man. That aside, however, I know his features well enough to see that, despite his words, Alfie looks anything but happy.

'So why the sad face?' I ask, knowing full well I'm playing devil's advocate.

Alfie rubs his chin. 'Ah, the sixty-four-million-dollar question.' For a second or two I don't think he's going to answer me, but then he sighs and looks directly at me. 'Because you're what made it so hard,' he says. 'Part of what made it so hard... With Cam, I mean.'

I frown. 'Sorry, I'm not sure I understand.'

'Do you know what some of Cam's last words were?' he asks. It's a rhetorical question, I know he's about to tell me. 'He wanted you to know how sorry he was, mainly I think for going and dying on you. But also, because Cam would never have left the island, Abby. And I know that weighed heavily on his mind.'

I'm confused for a second, wondering why Alfie is telling me this, and then it hits me, what he really means.

He gives me another smile. 'Cam wanted you to be with him, here, on the island.'

'Here?' I break off, thinking about his words. 'But that's ridiculous, Alfie. I have a life back home, I have...' But my words run dry.

'And he hated that he never got to say that to you. To ask you to come here, because he knew what time he had left was limited. Actually, he worried that you might not even have thought that far, about your future together. But *he* had, Abby, and he wanted you to know that. He was just sorry that he never had the chance to tell you.'

I think for a moment about something Fiona mentioned the other day. Something that surprised me. 'I never knew you had a literary festival here.'

Alfie gives me an odd look. 'Abby, we're islanders, we're a nation of storytellers. It's in our blood. You only have to listen to our music to know that, it's one of the most folkloric there is. It's all stories.'

'Then why didn't you tell me about it? You must have known how interested I would be.'

Alfie looks down and I see I don't need an answer. Of course I'd have been interested. Interested enough perhaps to come to the festival myself.

'There hasn't been one for the past two years,' he says eventually, his words seeping between his lips with a soft sighing sound. 'I keep thinking I should do something about it, but...'

I look at the fall of hair over his forehead. 'Was it popular?'

'Aye, it was. Very...' He breaks off to stare across the sand. 'It would have been last weekend, actually, always the first in April traditionally.'

I should say something, but I can't and a very poignant silence blooms between us.

Away in the distance Beth has spotted us. She gives a wave that Alfie returns, a broad smile on his face.

'Can I take you somewhere tonight?' he asks, his voice more urgent now.

'Tonight? Well...'

'I know Beth is having a movie night with Shona so... There's something I want you to see on the island, while you're here.'

'Okay...' I say slowly. 'Sounds mysterious.'

He holds my look but doesn't elaborate.

'You're not going to tell me, are you?'

He shakes his head. 'No. But I *would* like to show you.'

Beth is now halfway up the beach, running towards us. Alfie's face is lit with enquiry.

'Okay. Yes, where is it? Shall I meet you somewhere?'

He readies a smile for Beth. 'I'll pick you up at seven,' he says.

Chapter 20

Alfie doesn't stay long. Once Beth appears and says hello, he munches his way through his sandwiches, talking all the while, and then professes a need to get back to work. I've no doubts he does, but now that he's gone, it leaves me wondering what our conversation has really been about. The things which haven't actually been said but which have nonetheless threaded themselves through our words.

It's still relatively early, but our exercise and all this fresh air has made Beth and me hungry and so it seems the perfect time to break out our picnic too. For a while all is silent as we eat our food, until a sudden breeze blows a line of sand up onto the blanket and all over the slice of fruit cake I had momentarily placed there. I'd only put it down to take the lid off my water bottle. I groan, rolling my eyes at Beth, and looking pointedly at her share of the cake. She breaks off a piece and gives it to me.

'Shall we go for a walk in a bit?' I ask. 'Or are you happy staying here?'

Beth looks at her phone to check the time. 'Can we just sit for a little while? It's so nice here.'

And so that's exactly what we do, and I have to say I'm a little surprised. I had wondered if Beth would be bored on an island that is mostly just scenery, albeit as gorgeous as it is.

The weather at this time of year is mild, even in summer the temperature on the island isn't what you'd call hot, but this afternoon the sun is unseasonably warm and raises the temperature by enough to feel pleasant.

It's almost two o'clock before either of us stirs sufficiently to think about moving, and if we want to see the estate house and its garden, we ought to get going. It isn't far from the road where we left our bikes but we have to get to them first, and suddenly the thought of it seems too much; my body has acclimatised all too easily to the timeless feeling at the beach. Beth is lying on her stomach, knees bent up, bare feet waving in the air, with a book in front of her. She doesn't look much like she wants to go anywhere.

'Shall we do the house another day?' I suggest. 'It isn't going anywhere, is it?'

She cranks one shoulder round to look at me. 'I don't mind,' she replies. 'If you still want to go.'

I lift my eyes to the sky, seduced by the warmth and wide-open space. 'No, another day, I don't think I can move.'

Beth smiles and settles herself back down, digging her elbows deeper into the sand. Pulling a spare fleece from my rucksack, I lie down on the blanket, folding the fleece under my head for a pillow. And within seconds I know that I'm going to fall asleep, just as I know that before I do, I'm going to think about my conversation with Alfie.

I wake, coughing and spluttering, as a gust of wind showers my face with sand and I feel the grittiness of it on my lips as I wipe them. The vague wispy clouds of before have gone, replaced by much meaner-looking ones. And they would seem to be on the march.

Beth is already sitting up, blinking in surprise at the change in the weather and flapping the pages of her book to get rid of the grains of

sand that have blown there. She pulls a face at me, but it's evidently time
to leave and she gathers up her belongings without even being asked.

The sun is still shining, but our walk back across the machair is rather
much quicker than on the way out. Fortunately, Fiona's promise that
our bikes will remain where we left them holds true, but by the time
we reach them we're both hot and rather out of breath. The heavens
haven't opened yet, but a bank of black clouds directly above our heads
would suggest it's imminent.

Five minutes later, we're pedalling like fury along the road, trying to
outrun the rain which has finally caught us up. Fat drops slice through
the tree canopy above to slide down our necks and run off our knees.
And the gentle downward slope of our journey to the beach, scarcely
noticeable on the way, has now turned into a mammoth long, slow
hill that is making my leg muscles burn. I wave at Beth.

'There's a little tearoom at the top of the hill,' I yell across the space
between us. 'Let's stop and see if the rain will blow over.'

She readily agrees and we pick up our pace even more, before the
rain becomes the deluge it's threatening.

The tearoom is quiet as we burst through the door, laughing and
rubbing at our wet limbs. But the noise of our arrival also ensures that
we don't go unnoticed and a woman appears through a doorway to
greet us almost immediately. She clucks at the sight of our dishevelled
appearance.

'Come in! Come and sit down. Will I get you a towel as well as
some tea?' Her laugh is warm and bright as she shepherds us to a table
by the window. She points to another, nearer the middle of the room.
'Or would you rather sit somewhere you don't have to look at the rain?
Goodness, it's coming down in torrents.'

I assure her that the window seat is fine. 'I think we got here just in time,' I add.

'Aye, you'd have been soaked through if you'd gone much further. It'll pass though, it's often like that here. We always say to our visitors if you don't like the weather, just wait five minutes.' She gives us another crinkly smile and I wonder how many times a day she finds herself saying that.

She plucks two cards from a stand on the table and lays one before Beth, passing the other to me. 'Now, can I get you something to drink while you decide if you'd like anything else?'

I look down at the card, full of tempting things, both savoury and sweet. 'Tea for me, please.' I look at Beth.

'And a banana milkshake, please,' she adds, as I knew she would.

The woman nods. 'And just to let you know, our cakes of the day are a strawberry shortcake, an orange and honey cake, and a chocolate cream gateau.'

'What shall we have?' I ask Beth, once the waitress has disappeared. 'Just cake or a snack? Or something a bit more substantial?'

Beth chews her lip. 'Chocolate cake, or maybe the strawberry thing. Oh…' She peers closer at the card. 'They have scones as well. The ones that come with jam and cream.'

I nod. I've been eyeing them up myself. We might be in Scotland, but it would seem the cream tea is a thing here too. We're still deliberating when the waitress reappears with our drinks.

'Have you decided?' I ask Beth, momentarily distracted by the rear of the card, which lists another selection of tempting savouries. I tap my finger against one of them. 'Or we can have an early tea if you like, and then you won't be in such a rush to get to Shona's.'

Beth looks a little reticent. 'Would you mind if I had tea at theirs? Only she offered and Fiona is cooking anyway, or rather, Andrew is, for the restaurant, so Fiona said it was no problem.'

'Okay,' I say lightly, surprised by how much this bothers me. 'Just cake it is then.' I smile up at the waitress. 'I'm going to go for the strawberry shortcake in that case.' She makes a scribble on her notepad. 'Beth?'

'The chocolate cake, please.'

I stare out the window. The rain is already slowing, but it's brought the lush green plants outside to life. The garden is in such marked contrast to the open, more rugged space of the coast that it doesn't seem possible for two extremes to be so close.

Beth lays a finger against her arm to remove a ladybird that has settled there, relocating it onto the leaf of a huge potted fern that stands beside our table.

'Won't it be brilliant if the folk festival does come here?' she says as she watches it crawl away. 'Everyone says it's going to.'

'Well, Fiona says she's optimistic,' I reply. 'The feedback from Sunday seemed good. I would imagine it's quite a big thing here.'

'It is, Shona says it's magic. People come from all the other islands, and even further away. Sometimes she even gets to stay up all night because groups of people go back to the hotel or the other holiday cottages and carry on singing.'

'It sounds exhausting,' I comment, smiling. I've never stayed up all night for anything. Or anyone, for that matter.

'Yeah, but it doesn't matter because it's the school holidays. We're going to practise again later anyway cause even if the festival doesn't come here, Shona's family always go, wherever it is. And I don't know half the songs yet.'

I nod, feeling a little flicker of unease. 'It's very nice that Shona's teaching you,' I say cautiously.

And then I see it, the confused look on Beth's face; confirmation of my fear. I'm going to have to nip this in the bud.

'Beth, I'm so happy that you've made friends with Shona, and the singing, well, you know how amazing that was. But you do know that we won't be here in August, don't you?' I say as gently as I can.

I'm hoping against hope that I've got it wrong, but the way her face crumples is proof that I haven't.

'But I thought we'd come back.' She looks utterly heartbroken. 'I thought you'd want to.'

'Oh, Beth, it isn't that easy. There's the cost for one. But the shop too. I can't take time off whenever I want to. And you can't have time off school either.'

'But it would be in the holidays.'

I ignore her comment. 'I'd love for you to take part, I really would. But…' I break off, thinking. I don't want her to get upset here, but neither do I want her to keep harbouring the delusion it's going to happen.

'I tell you what, let's have a chat about it later. I can have a think and see what's possible. You've haven't told Shona you'll be here, have you?'

She drops her head. 'Why do you think she's teaching me the songs, Mum? She's going to hate me now.' And immediately I can see all her old insecurities come rushing back.

'No, she won't, she'll understand. But, sweetheart, you really shouldn't have promised without asking me first.'

'But I didn't think I had to. I'm sorry, Mum, but I thought you'd want to come back to see everyone.' She looks contrite, but emotion is lending anger to her words too.

I choose my words carefully. 'They're lovely people, Beth, and it's nice to be friendly but we're just on holiday. I'm not sure they'd really want us to keep in touch. Imagine if everyone who stayed in the hotel did that?'

'But we're not just anyone, are we? And there's Alfie too, he—'

'He what, Beth?'

'Well, I thought you liked him,' she replies, sulkily. 'You liked him last summer.'

'Beth, that was different. I thought he was someone else.'

'But he wasn't, was he? He was just Alfie, like he's always been.'

I frown, struggling with her words for a moment. 'Look, I do like Alfie, I like them all, but that doesn't necessarily mean I would come here just to visit them.' I pause a moment, but however hard this is, I have to say it. 'Beth, things might be different if Cam was alive, but he isn't and…' I'm not sure what else to say.

'Well, I wish we could live here.' She stares out the window in defiance.

My heart sinks. 'Oh, Beth… I know it's easy to feel that way when you're on holiday, because you don't have any cares or worries, and everything seems wonderful. But when you live in a place, it's very different. When the shine has gone from everything. The reality is that if you lived here you'd be far away from your family, your friends, everything that's familiar to you.'

'Yes, but nothing that I want.'

I search her face. I'd so love to give her the answer she wants but I know how impossible that is. Things seem so simple when you're her age, but talking about it now isn't going to accomplish anything.

A door swings open behind us.

'Here we go, ladies. One strawberry shortcake and one chocolate cake.' The waitress carefully unloads her tray, smiling all the while. 'There now, would you look at that? The sun's coming out again.'

She's right, it is, but the room still feels gloomy.

She straightens, looking at me expectantly. 'Can I get you anything else?' she asks.

I smile. 'No, thanks, this is all perfect.'

'Lovely.' She pauses. Turns slightly. Pauses again. 'I heard you singing on Sunday,' she says, smiling down at Beth for all the world as if she's a favourite grandchild. 'You have such a beautiful voice.' She smiles at me, the proud mother. 'You looked like you were having a whale of a time.'

Beth doesn't know what to say, particularly given the conversation we've had. She squirms with embarrassment but manages a thank-you.

'And I wanted to say how sorry we all are for your loss,' she adds, looking at me. 'I've known Cameron since he was knee-high to a grass-hopper. It doesn't seem right, does it? Not for someone so young, and with his whole life ahead of him.' She gives me a fond look. 'But I know how much comfort you've brought to the family. It's been such a difficult time, for poor Alfie especially.' She clucks her tongue. 'It's a sad business and no mistake, but... You'll give him my love anyway, won't you?'

I stare at her, bewildered. She seems to know exactly who I am, yet I'd swear I've never set eyes on her before.

'Sorry,' she says, tucking the tray underneath her arm. 'I forgot. You have no idea who I am, do you?' She shakes her head, amused. 'We all know who you are, but... Anyway, I'm Catriona, but you must call me Trina, everyone does. I'm Morag's friend. Our boys used to play together when they were nowt but wee laddies. Alfie too, more often than not. Always in and out of each other's houses, we were.' She gives me and Beth a bright smile. 'Well, I'll leave you to enjoy your cakes.' And a moment later, she's gone in a flurry of embarrassment for having said too much.

I look at Beth but we're both robbed of words, and I pick up my cake fork resolutely, grateful for the distraction.

We ride back to the cottage in virtual silence.

Chapter 21

Once we're back at the cottage, it doesn't seem very long at all before Shona calls to collect Beth. But despite encouragement to have a lovely time, she's still a little subdued as she waves goodbye and I feel awful that our earlier conversation has pulled down her mood so much, but they were things that had to be said. And now I'm left biding my time restlessly until it's my turn to go out.

Alfie is prompt, drawing up outside the cottage in his van at a minute to seven. The sky is now clear and it's a beautiful evening, but I still walk down the path to meet him with very mixed feelings. Try as I might, I cannot seem to think of him as the person whose company I enjoyed when he visited Cambridge. It's as if we've become strangers over the last few days.

His smile is welcoming as I climb into the passenger seat, the sun glinting off the stubble on his chin, and catching the strange lightness to his eyes. He looks pleased to see *me* at any rate.

I pull the van door closed and reach for my seatbelt, mentally reproaching myself for my mood.

'Hi,' I say cheerily, turning back round to face him. 'So, where are we going then?'

But Alfie's only reply is to lay a finger alongside his nose. 'It's not far,' he says.

He wasn't kidding. We literally drive for a couple of minutes before he turns off the road onto a rough track to the right. We're following the coast, although the sea is hidden by the rising land, which stretches away up a hill, green and undulating, and I can't see anything of note.

'I thought you should see this place before you go,' says Alfie. 'Because I don't think anyone else will show it to you.' He looks curiously close to tears. I give him another puzzled look, but he evades my glance, instead pointing ahead. 'But it's important that you see it.'

The track crests the rise and there in front of us is another strip of machair, lit up by the golden evening sun, and quite beautiful. But it isn't that which brings my hand to my mouth in surprise. Where the meadowland ends is a tiny crescent of beach, and beyond is the sea, no longer the silvery blue of the daytime, but instead striped with fiery reds and orange, which lie along its surface like ribbons. The sun is still above the horizon, hanging low in the sky, the last of its rays casting light and shadow onto everything in its path. In the distance I can see the long outcropping of black rock which reaches into the sea, and beyond it, catching the light, the lighthouse with its red and white stripes. Closer to me, and much smaller, are three jags of rock which stretch out from the shore, each slightly smaller than the last.

I've pictured this scene in my head over and over, wishing I could stand and look at it for real. Except now that I am, I almost can't bear it. And then my attention switches to the low-lying, whitewashed cottage that sits in a small dip away to our right. And as if any further proof were needed, the first thing I notice is the bright green of the door and windowsills. I know exactly where we are: this is Cam's house.

I'm about to climb from the car when Alfie's hand lands on my arm. 'I hope you like it,' he says.

I'm about to reply, when the warmth of his hand disappears, and he turns abruptly to open his door.

My lip trembles as I stand and look at the house, and I swallow hard, gulping at air that no longer seems to fill my lungs. My vision blurs as tears pool and overflow, but I let them come. Holding them back seems as pointless as trying to hold back the tide. Wordlessly, Alfie slides his fingers into mine and I feel the weight of his emotion, as if it's written across his skin. This is the view that Cam looked out on every day and I'm here, standing where he would have stood, breathing the air that he would have breathed. And I can feel it wrapping its arms around me, warm and comforting. The rightness of it seeping through me.

'I wondered if you would hate me even more if I brought you here,' says Alfie, a nostalgic sadness in his eyes.

'Oh, Alfie… I don't hate you. Please, don't ever think that.' But I can't say any more. My head is a jumble of emotions.

'I thought it was somewhere you ought to see. Cam wanted you to see it. He wished…' But he's unable to continue. 'There are so many beautiful places on this little island, but I happen to think this is one of the most special,' he says. 'The light here, especially of an evening. Well, you can see, I don't have to tell you.'

And this was Cam's reward. At the end of the day. When his teaching was done, when his lessons had been prepared, and when his books had been marked, this was where he would come. He would sit out here, and let the day seep out of him, with just a drink and something to read for company. Most likely something he had ordered from me.

I nod. 'Thank you,' I say. It's not enough, but it's all I can manage.

Gently, Alfie withdraws his hand. I hadn't even realised I was still holding it. 'Would you like to go inside?' he asks.

My eyes widen. 'Can we?' But then I stop. 'Oh God, I don't know if I can.' I take a hesitant step. And stop. But then take another. Cam had always wanted me to see this. I can't leave now or I will forever wonder what it was like, inside the home that had been his. 'Are we even allowed inside? Doesn't anyone else live here now?'

Alfie shakes his head. 'No, we can stay as long as you like.'

My legs feel like jelly as I stumble over the rough grass to the cottage. It's almost identical to Samphire, but twice as long, with a chimney at one end and another in the middle. The bright-green paintwork outside giving it a cheery appearance.

'It's open,' says Alfie. 'You can go in.'

I look at him, his clear grey eyes are searching mine.

'Will you come with me?' I ask. 'I don't think I can go on my own.'

'Whenever you're ready,' he replies.

I don't know what I expected, but the cottage is empty, stripped of all its possessions apart from a stack of boxes in one corner. Yet I don't need to see Cam's things to know that they're here. I can still see them, imprinted on my memory from his emails.

'We cleared it out early in the year, Fiona and I. Morag thought it was best to do it sooner rather than later and I think she was probably right.'

I nod, looking around me, walking into what I know was Cam's living room and crossing to the window. I gaze out at the view, staring for quite a few moments until I realise that something isn't right. I move into the next room and do the same, turning around after a few seconds to let my eyes wander, before rejoining Alfie.

'This is the living room, isn't it?' I say, indicating the fireplace and the two thick beams which cross above our heads. 'In which case his desk should have been in this window. But it can't be. He always said that when he looked up from typing, he could see the three rocks that stretch out into the sea, almost touching as if they were holding hands. But from here, they're too far apart, not touching at all. It's only if you look at them from the window in the other room that they appear that way.'

Alfie gives a gentle nod. 'His desk used to be in here, you're right, but as Cam's condition worsened, we moved his bedroom down here, through into the other room. There's no heating upstairs, you see. There doesn't really need to be because the heat from the fire warms the rooms up there a little. So, at night, when you're tucked up in bed, it's fine. But as Cam got weaker, he found it too cold and so we moved him through there so he could still see the view. We moved the desk as well.'

I look back at the window. I'd had no idea.

'So that was where you sat too, when you…?'

He nods. 'And for the last month I stayed here, sleeping on the sofa. The last week I did virtually nothing but sit through there, just talking or reading.' He breaks off. 'Rambling mostly. Chatting about anything and everything so Cam could hear my voice, reading passages from his favourite books. I don't think he really took in much, but then he knew some of his books practically off by heart anyway.' He hesitates momentarily before running a hand through his hair, buying himself a little time. 'That's what's in the boxes,' he adds.

I turn to look where he points.

'His books,' says Alfie, answering my next question. 'Everything else we sorted through, took away, but those… It didn't seem right to get rid of them, and I think I…' He gives me an odd look. 'I think in my head I'd always hoped that you might come here one day, so I kept them for you. I told Morag I'd sort them out, I just haven't quite got around to it yet.' He suddenly smiles, self-deprecating, rueful. 'What am I like? I thought you might like to help me, actually.'

'Oh…' I press my lips together, staring at the lid of the topmost box, flaps which aren't sealed, the books within only inches from view. But I don't think I could. Not now.

'No, of course not,' says Alfie. 'Crazy idea.' He gives another smile, one designed to mask the pain.

His words seem to hang in the air, reminding me that there is so much to this story that I don't know. So much that this room has seen.

'That must have been incredibly hard for you,' I say. 'I can't imagine what those last few weeks, days, must have been like. I'm sorry I didn't know. Perhaps if I had done it might have been easier. I could have…' But what could I possibly have done or said that would have made things any easier for Cam? Or for Alfie, who had borne all this alone. And as I look at him, I remember something he said before, about Cam's parents.

I turn and look at the spot in the room where I imagine the sofa would have been, the one that Alfie had slept on during Cam's last few weeks, and I'm beginning to wonder how far Cam's deceptions went.

'You said before that his parents didn't know. But what didn't they know, Alfie? Surely Morag and Gillie must have been here, seen what Cam was like?'

And I can see at once that Alfie understands how much I've worked out. He looks relieved, if anything. Perhaps because he can finally put down the burden he's been carrying.

He sighs. 'Yes, of course they were. They came to see Cam every day. The rest of the family too. But Cam always made sure they texted first so that I could get him ready, hide all trace that I'd been staying here. To make it look like things were, if not okay, then better than they were at least. And he could pretend that his pain levels were fine, for a little while at least.'

Suddenly it hits me how much Alfie had done for Cam. How much he had shielded his family from hurt and suffering, keeping alive the memory of the Cam they knew of old, not the shadowy image of himself he had become. Something he had also done for me.

I look around the room once more, seeing it in a completely different light, the light of truth.

'Why did you bring me here?' I ask.

Alfie looks surprised. 'Cam wanted me to,' he replies. 'Like I said, he always hoped that you might—' He stops abruptly.

I raise my eyebrows. 'Might what, Alfie?'

He looks like a fish caught on a line. In pain and desperate to be free.

'The thing is, Abby, this house, it belongs to the Island Estate, like most houses here, which is why it's still empty. It won't ever go on the open market and there's not really that many folks on the island who would... Anyway, it's available. You could have it if you wanted.'

My mouth drops open. It's the last thing I expected him to say, and the thought hovers in the air. An invitation. But to what?

'Alfie,' I say as gently as I can. 'I can't do that. It's just a...' I fish for the right word. 'Fantasy,' I say after a moment. 'That's all this is. A nice thought, a lovely thought, but a fantasy just the same.'

'Why is it?' he challenges.

'Because I have a home, a business, my family, all elsewhere. Things I can't just drop to move hundreds of miles away. And there's Beth too; her school, her friends. We have a life already, but it's not here, Alfie, I'm sorry.'

I can hardly bear to look at him, thoughts are crashing about my head. Had he really thought...? But his eyes are glued to mine.

'How many people have you ever been in love with, Abby?'

I turn my head away. Not many. Not even that. Only one in fact.

'Did you ever really love Cam?' he asks, eyes flashing with anger, mistaking my silence.

'You know I did! And for your information, yes, he's the only person I've *ever* loved. Not even Beth's father, not really. Happy now?'

'But even though you say you loved him, you never thought you had a future together? You never dreamed what that future might look like?'

'No, I… Don't look at me like that. Of course I hoped that we would have a future, but I hadn't really thought about how it would look. I daren't, because I knew how difficult it would be.'

'Well then, let me tell you that Cam did think about it. He thought about it all the time. And this was his dream, Abby. His dream of what that future would look like. But how could he possibly have told you about it when he knew he didn't have a future at all?'

I look away, I can't bear to see the judgement in his eyes. 'You know, you say these things, Alfie. You say them and you make them sound wonderful. But now, thanks to you, half the time I don't feel like I even knew Cam, not really. You tell me that this is what he wanted for us, but how do I know what you say is true?'

Alfie gives me a long look. 'Okay, well how about I give you a more tangible example then? No hypotheticals, something you can actually think about. What if it were me saying those things? Me asking you to come and live here?'

'You?' I stare at him. But that would mean… I'm so confused. Everything is so mixed up: Cam, Alfie, this place. I can't tell what's real and what's made up any more.

I shake my head. 'Stop playing games with me, Alfie. Tell me why you really brought me here.'

He walks to the window, staring out at the perfect view, and I can see the glow of the evening sun on his face. He doesn't even turn as he begins to speak.

'Because I want you to be here, okay? I want you somewhere I can see you every day, and talk to you every day and… Jesus, Abby, it's really very simple.' He spins around and drags his eyes up to mine. 'When Cam first began to email you, it *was* him emailing, him talking to you, but even then he knew what was happening to him. He knew the time he had left was dwindling day by day and he would have given up long before if it hadn't been for you. He knew it was wrong, Abby, but he was on a lot of drugs by then, and you were one of them.'

He heaves in a breath. 'So right from early on, he told me what he wanted. Which was to see you, to visit your little shop, to peep into the life you had because he knew that you could never do that to his. So, yes, when he became unable to email himself, I took over for him. He would tell me what to say, or we would decide between us. But somewhere along the line, it became more of me and less of Cam, and then one day it stopped being Cam, and it was just me. I had to keep going, for him, don't you see? And if he realised what was happening then he never mentioned it, he—'

'And what *was* happening, Alfie?'

He swallows, his voice ragged. 'I began to fall in love with you too. I fell in love with you… I *am* in love with you.'

My heart is hammering so hard, I can barely get my words out. 'You don't know me.'

'Abby, I do. I know your favourite colour is autumn, I know your favourite food is cheese on toast, or honeyed cashew nuts if you're in the mood for something sweet. I know you don't have a favourite book because it wouldn't be fair on all the others, and I know that you love the ocean but hate swimming. That your eyes are flecked with gold in sunlight but at night are almost black. I know that you're one of the kindest, most honest people I know and I love that you hate dating and think you're awkward and have never been in love with anyone else, because all this, all of it, you, are perfect.'

Tears are running down my face.

'And I know you loved Cam, Abby – when it was just you and him – but then the line between what was me and what was him became blurred and, even though you didn't know what had happened, I hoped that meant you loved me too. Well, now you do know everything, and I have to understand how you feel. If you feel anything for me at all. And if you don't, then please tell me now and I'll leave you be. I'll go back to doing what I did before your words poured hope and sunshine into my days. But you need to tell me how you feel, Abby. You need to tell me now.'

My mouth opens and closes, but no words come out. But if they could, what would they be? I look at Alfie. I see his face, his features, every curve so familiar. The pattern of his speech, the way he holds his head to one side when he's listening to you. The fact that he takes one sugar in his coffee and that, above all, he will move heaven and earth for the people he loves.

It could be so easy…

'It isn't that easy, Alfie. I have Beth to think about, the shop, which is more than simply books and a business. It's my home too. When my grandad left it to me, he gave Beth and I a chance, hope that we could finally have a future away from her father. I dread to think what might have become of us without it. It's the last thing I have left to remember him and the person I was able to become because of him.'

'Abby, you don't need the shop to do that, your memories of him live inside you. You've allowed the shop to become your cage, because it suited you to ensure the status quo was always kept, preserving your grandfather's memory and honouring his gift to you. It gave you the perfect opportunity to stay. I'm giving you the perfect opportunity to leave.'

Chapter 22

I must have slept because when I wake it's early, but undeniably morning. For a few seconds there's nothing beyond the comfortable arrangement of heavy limbs in the cosy bed, but then the thoughts start, taking up where they had left off the night before. I push the covers to one side. There's no way I can outrun my thoughts so it's seems as if I have no option but to run through them one more time. And if I'm going to do this, I at least need a cup of tea.

The room along the landing is quiet and I tiptoe down the stairs, avoiding the third step from the top that creaks alarmingly when trodden on. Minutes later, my morning cuppa is made and, impulsively, I shrug on my jacket over my pyjamas and, mug in hand, slip out into the quiet, still space that is the morning.

As dawn breaks, the first gleam of silver begins to work its way across the sea. Soon its surface will turn the colour of the sky and the silver will turn to brightest gold. I shiver. It's cool, but it isn't that which sets the goose pimples rising on my arms.

I could do this every day. I could greet every morning through nuance of sea and sky, not chimneys and roof tops. But it isn't that easy. It isn't. My jaw is clenched hard and I open my mouth, stretching it wide to try to relax the muscles, consciously letting them go with my thoughts. I'm on holiday, I remind myself. I'm watching the dawn, on a beautiful morning, on a beautiful island, but that's all this is. And I should try to enjoy what's left of the week. Except that this doesn't feel like any holiday I've ever been on.

I've gone backwards and forwards, every which way through what Alfie had said to me last night. And the story he told is heartbreaking. I'd had no idea that he'd had such a heavy burden to bear, and the truth of it is that I'm not sure it was fair of Cam to place that upon him. But then I've never been in that situation. Faced with it, what would I do? Was it love that kept him from revealing the truth to his family and to me? Or was it selfishness to even ask Alfie to help him hide it? If it was then Cam had been forgiven, so whichever way you look at it, it paints Alfie in a good light. But it's there that my thoughts come to a juddering halt each time. Because he still lied to me. He had met me under false pretences and never given me an inkling that there was anything wrong. He had raised me up, and then he'd let me fall. And there's no getting away from that fact.

But the thing I'm finding almost as hard to reconcile as the revelations about Cam's house, and Alfie's feelings for me, is what he'd said about the shop, and my grandad. Was Alfie right? Had I latched onto a relationship with Cam simply because the chances of its long-term survival were slim? Had I set myself up to fail because it suited me to? Believing the shop to be my harbour, my shelter, my port in a storm, and never slipping my moorings to discover if the world beyond the harbour walls was as dangerous as I led myself to believe.

Maybe I have, but I can't ignore my heritage either. We have a history in the town, the shop has a history, and I've always been immensely proud to be carrying on the family name. There's Gwen to consider too, and now, very importantly, the battle against the proposed rates' increase. It's a battle which all the other shopkeepers will be taking on, fighting for their livelihoods. Surely I have an obligation to stay and fight alongside them, to combine my strength with theirs?

And there's also the very real question of what I would have if I came here. Somewhere to live perhaps, but no means of supporting myself, or Beth for that matter. I'd have to sell the shop and even though it's not in the best of condition it would still bring in a pretty penny. Pennies which wouldn't last long with nothing to replace them. We'd be miles away from everything familiar and safe, away from people we loved and what if things didn't work out? I'd have to return and start all over again.

I sip my tea, letting my eyes drift over the landscape as it's pulled from its shadowy cloak by the sun, rising higher and higher with every minute. But worry over the shop is one of the reasons I came here too, I mustn't forget that. And the truth of it is that whether I stay or go, I have a battle ahead of me. As does Beth. And what about the things Alfie offered me? If I said yes, would I be running from my past? Or have I been given the push I need? Will I be grasping the chance of a brilliant new start? Or simply clutching at straws? I turn my face to the sky, but neither the sun, nor the birds have an answer for me.

Breakfast is a rather subdued affair. Beth wasn't late in coming home last night but she looks tired, and preoccupied, her answers to my questions about her evening verging on monosyllabic.

'So, did you and Shona manage to practise some of the songs you'd been learning?'

'A bit,' she says, but doesn't elaborate, her eyes drifting past mine. She gets up to put her plate in the sink. 'But there's not really any point, is there?'

And so I do what I hate myself for, put on the 'jolly hockey sticks' voice that fools neither of us and chivvy us both along, bustling us out of the door half an hour later. We're finally going to the estate gardens today, and I intend to make the most of our remaining time on the island. There isn't much of it left.

'Abby, would you have a minute? There's something I'd like to show you.'

I turn around to see Maureen beaming at me from across the aisle of the shop. I almost look around to see who she's talking to. Even though she's used my name it's the way she speaks to me that seems odd, as if I'm a neighbour, or someone far more familiar to her.

I return her smile. 'Sure, I was just…' I indicate the bag of apples and other provisions I'm holding.

'I'll take them, Mum,' says Beth, coming forward. 'Shall I choose us some other things for lunch?'

Maureen's smile is steady and I look between them. 'Yes, good idea. Thanks, love.'

I hand over the packages and give Maureen a small nod. I have a horrible feeling I know where's she's taking me. It isn't that I don't want to visit the bookshop, just that I have such conflicted feelings about it. Under normal circumstances I'd be there like a bee round honey, but there's something about the location of this shop that's making it feel less than sweet. And I can't put my finger on why.

But if her taking me to the bookshop isn't a surprise, the shop itself is a revelation. I had expected to see a room very similar to that of the main shop. A room that despite Maureen's best efforts still manages to look somewhat like an aircraft hangar. But this is very different.

For one, there's a huge window along the back wall. I had imagined a dark space, but this is light and airy, and utterly charming. And the view from the window is stunning. Not of the sea but, instead, masses of flowers. They stand in pots on a small patio outside the shop. They're planted in the small garden that borders it, and they're wild in the stretch of grassland that disappears into the distance. The room needs no other decoration.

Even so, the walls are freshly whitewashed and hung with simple pen-and-ink drawings of the island and, in one corner, there's an armchair beside a square, squat table. It's a place for browsing, and lingering, for enjoyment.

I look at Maureen, who smiles at the astonishment on my face.

'It used to be an outhouse,' she explains. 'The garden you can see is ours, or part of it anyway. Our cottage is tucked out of sight, just off there to the left. So, when we needed to find another space to house the books, this seemed an obvious choice.'

'It's incredible.' Now I've finished gazing at the room in admiration, I turn my attention to the books themselves. Rustic shelves are filled with them and a display table in the centre of the space is piled high with even more titles. I smile at the sight of some familiar faces.

'What do you think?' asks Maureen.

'I'm surprised,' I reply. 'I really hadn't imagined anything like this.' I give her a sheepish look. 'Sorry. For some reason I thought there'd be just a few rather scruffy and well-thumbed paperbacks.'

'You'll recognise some of them,' she says.

'Yes, you've got a really good range.'

She gives me a warm smile. 'No, I rather meant that you'd *actually* recognise them, seeing as some of them came from your shop.'

I look at her, puzzled, until the light suddenly dawns.

'Cam,' I say.

'Aye. When he was alive he couldn't bear to be parted from most of them, but he did let us have a few.'

I'm beginning to feel choked again, surrounded by so many books which are such a big part of my life and were Cam's too. They were the thing that bound us together.

Maureen gives a wry smile. 'I don't think I realised he had quite so many though. Morag has offered them to me, saying that's what Cam would have wanted, but between you and me, I'm rather glad Alfie is taking so long to sort through them. I'm really not sure where I'd put them at the moment.' She gives me a long look.

I look around again, walking over to inspect one particular shelf and running my fingers along the tops of the volumes. 'Thank you,' I say, turning around. 'It's lovely of you to show this to me, Maureen. I'm really touched, and I think it will be wonderful for the rest of Cam's books to come here eventually. He had very good taste, although perhaps I would say that. Anyway, it's nice that other people will get the opportunity to read them.'

But Maureen doesn't reply, she simply stands there, looking at me expectantly. It strikes me that I could do as Alfie suggested and ask Maureen if I can supply her with stock on a more regular basis, but it feels wrong somehow, as if I'd be taking advantage of her.

'How long have you been selling books?' I ask instead.

'About eighteen months,' she replies. 'And you're right, to start with it was just a pile of scruffy novels. They were donated by some holidaymakers with the suggestion that we should sell even more and it's kind of grown from there. In fact, it's rather taken us by surprise. The literary festival was the catalyst, of course, but even so.'

'Well, I think it's brilliant. It's certainly not something I expected to find when I came here. A bookshop at the edge of the world.' I smile. 'Or maybe it just feels that way.'

Maureen gives me an odd look. 'That's kind of the problem,' she says.

And all at once I feel the conversation become something else. 'I don't know whether you're aware,' she continues, 'but everyone in business on these islands belongs to a trade organisation. We set it up ourselves to help us expand and to share our skills and expertise. It helps ensure our survival, not just as a part of the tourist trade, but as a means of sustaining ourselves and our families long-term.'

I smile politely, wondering what's coming next.

Maureen flicks me a nervous glance before fixing her attention on a bookshelf somewhere to her right. 'There's been a huge call to offer book services to the rest of the islands. None of them have anything like we have here, but I simply don't have the time for all the work it would require. None of us do. You see, the problem with living on such a small island is that we have a very static workforce and most of us here do more than one job as it is. Admittedly a lot of them aren't full-time jobs, but if we didn't work this way, we wouldn't have a postman, or a teacher or… Anyway, I wondered if it might be something you could do?'

I stare at her. 'But I don't live here, Maureen. I'm' – I see her gaze flick downward – 'not sure how I can help. I can offer you some stock perhaps but how could I—'

A scarlet bloom begins to creep up her neck. My eyes widen.

'Sorry, did you think I—' I stop, hardly able to get the words out. 'Did you think I was moving here?'

She clears her throat. 'Oh, I… Perhaps I got the wrong end of the stick. I thought…'

But I can see exactly what she thought. And I'm pretty sure who put the idea there. But it isn't Maureen's fault she got it wrong, and neither must she be made to feel bad. She probably imagines she's handing me a gift. Ridiculous.

I find a smile from somewhere. 'That's such a lovely thought,' I reply. 'And God, I wish it could be, but sadly no, it's just not possible. Too many complications back home.'

She's trying hard not to let her face fall.

'But bless you for thinking of me, and that I could help.' I flick a glance back towards the doorway. 'I'd better rescue Beth,' I add. 'But we should stay in touch. I'd be very happy to help you out with stock if that would be useful. I'm sure we could work something out.'

She nods, her cheeks still flushed, and now, I see, almost desperate for me to leave. Which suits me fine. I don't know the exact way to the distillery but I'm sure it can't be that hard to find. I think Beth and I might take a little detour before going to visit the estate gardens. I can feel a head of steam building and it wouldn't be fair to let the pressure release on anyone but Alfie.

I'm not sure what I imagined, but the distillery looks like most of the other buildings on the island. It's no bigger than a large family house and sits nestled in a dip among the wild-flower-covered grassland that flanks both sides of the road. Importantly, it's on the way to the estate house. Of course it is, everywhere is on the way to everywhere else here.

The distillery is open to the public, but even though I have no idea what their hours are, I didn't come here to sample the gin. A small car park at the front spans the width of the buildings and Beth and I cycle across it, heading towards a door at one end. A sign overhead proclaims it to be the reception. I can already see there's no one inside but that suits me fine too; I'd rather not have to explain myself. Music is playing somewhere at the rear and I turn to Beth as I slow the bike to a stop.

'Do you want to wait here?' I say, smiling. 'I won't be long. I just have a message to give Alfie and then we can get going.' I prop my bike against the wall and head towards the sound of fiddles.

The back of the distillery is divided into four distinct sections, two with large roller-shutter doors reaching right to the top of the building and two with regular-sized doors, one of which is standing open. It's from here that the sound of music is drifting. I walk closer.

I'm about to investigate further when the music is abruptly cut off and replaced by the sound of a telephone ringing. I hang back although I can hear immediately that the voice is Alfie's. And he doesn't sound happy. Seconds later, he strides from the building, so lost in his thoughts that he almost collides with me as he pulls a set of keys from his pocket. He looks up, shocked.

'Abby!' It's as if he expects to see a crowd of people behind me. I almost wish there were. 'Is everything okay? Sorry, I have to go. I've—' He stops, eyes darting around, anywhere but at mine. His words from last night surround him like an aura.

'I've just had a very interesting conversation with Maureen,' I begin, not caring whether he has a meeting to get to or not. 'Please can you enlighten me as to why she thinks I'm about to move here? Because if she thinks it, I can imagine half the island do as well. And there's only one person coming to mind who might have given her that idea. How dare you, when—' It's only then, as I bark words at him, that I realise how dreadful he looks. How hard he's having to fight to keep from crumbling under the weight of whatever is on his shoulders.

He opens his mouth and then closes it again. Takes a breath. Sighs. Fiddles with his car keys.

'It wasn't me,' he says eventually, eyes flicking past mine. 'But I think I know who it might have been.'

I stare at him. 'Well, I knew you had something to do with it. You don't have to be bloody Sherlock Holmes to work that one out!'

He visibly sags. 'Look, I mentioned it to Morag, okay? About Cam's house. We were talking about the estate and I said there was a possibility you might want it. That it was what Cam had wanted. I needed to give them something, Abby. Some hope for the future. Cam's death has affected everyone on this island.'

'Do you think I don't know that? I can see it everywhere I go. Even the woman from the tearoom commented on it yesterday – someone else who knows exactly who I am.'

'But that's just it, don't you understand? It's bad enough when someone dies, but now imagine if everyone who knew that person lives within a five-mile radius and had known that person their whole lives. Imagine how that would feel, day in, day out. All that grief concentrated into one singular source of pain. Believe me, you'd do anything to try to lessen it, even a tiny bit.'

'But you still had no right to do that, Alfie. I understand it, of course I do, and I know how much you did for Cam, at huge cost to yourself. But that was in the past and we're talking about the future now. You can't take all that weight of expectation and shove it onto me. It isn't fair.'

'Not expectation, Abby, but hope. The exact same thing you brought to Cam. People can't live without hope in their lives, you should know that.' His jaw clenches. 'Or else why are you here?'

'That's got nothing to do with it. I might hope for all sorts of things, but I don't go around telling people they're definitely going to happen. Because what about when they don't? You just look foolish, or worse. And now, when I turn all this down, I'll be dashing everyone's hopes, burning their dreams to the ground. Thanks a lot.'

Alfie's eyes flash in the sunlight. 'I think you misunderstand the point of hope, Abby. Hope is what you have when you set yourself free. When you pull apart the bars of your cage and wonder what life is like outside of it. When you dare to imagine what the world could be like if possibility were alive and well.'

'Oh, don't be so ridiculous. You can hope for all sorts of things to happen, things which don't stand a chance of coming true. A lottery win, for example. You make it sound as if it's all so easy. As if everything is there for the taking.'

He drops his head a moment, staring at the car keys in his hand. And then he looks up, eyes boring straight into mine. 'Maybe, maybe not. But you have to buy the ticket in the first place.'

Chapter 23

Alfie strides away from me without another word, the memory of the look in his eyes burned into my brain. I stand watching his rapidly retreating back, all my anger evaporating in an instant, leaving me gasping. I stare up at the sky, pushing the tears away, trying to calm my breathing. I have no idea what I'm going to do.

I take a deep breath and walk as slowly as I dare back around the building. Beth is still standing in the car park, holding her bike, watching a car pulling away. I don't need to ask her whose it is.

My face is as bright as I can make it by the time I reach her, but she looks even more subdued than this morning, worried even.

'Mum, is everything okay? What's the matter with Alfie? He looked really cross and he didn't even say goodbye.' She blinks at me. 'Or hello.'

'He's got a lot on his mind, sweetheart. Nothing for you to worry about. And I think he was late for a meeting, that's all.' I climb on my bike. 'Right, I've delivered the message so we can go now.'

Beth doesn't look convinced. 'So how come you weren't talking to him?'

'But I was, inside.'

'But you weren't with him when he came across the car park?'

'No…' I flash her another smile. 'Alfie had to dash off and I was petting the dog. He's such a friendly thing.' It seems a plausible excuse. For all I know Alfie *does* bring his dog to work.

We cycle out to the edge of the car park, slowing momentarily to check for traffic before swinging back out into the road.

'It's such a beautiful day,' I say. 'The gardens are going to be lovely.'

And they were, but the day was trying too hard to be something it wasn't and didn't quite pull it off. I had so many things whirling around my head that I found it hard to relax and take in what I was looking at. The gardens are renowned for their rhododendrons, and they were spectacular, bigger than anything I've ever seen. I hadn't really expected Beth to find them all that exciting, but there were plenty of other things to look at, things which I had thought she would have shown rather more interest in than she did.

I think I'm tired more than anything. Tired and preoccupied. And also feeling incredibly guilty that the holiday I'd planned for us, the holiday I wanted for Beth, hasn't turned out the way I'd hoped at all. We only have one full day left on the island, which is something else I really don't want to think about.

I can't quite put my finger on what's troubling Beth, however. Perhaps she's got that 'day before you go back to school' feeling as well, but it strikes me that there's something else. And whatever it is, it gets worse as the day wears on, almost as if she's waiting for an axe to fall.

As we cycle towards the hotel on our way back to the cottage, my apprehension turns into something far more solid as I catch sight of Fiona and Morag both standing by the gate. They're scanning the road and I know they can only be waiting for us. They both start speaking before we've even drawn level.

'Abby, we're so sorry. We had no idea.'

'How are you feeling? You should have said.'

'We'd have… well, I don't know what we would have done. But *something*.'

'I can't believe my own brother would do such a thing.'

'It's no wonder you looked like you'd seen a ghost when you first arrived…'

'Is there anything we can do?'

I look from one to the other as I try to decipher what each of them is saying, but it's all just a wall of noise. I can't think straight.

Fiona reaches out to Beth, giving her arm a rub. 'It's okay, pet, don't look so worried.' And the glance she gives me is long enough to see the shared familiarity of motherhood in her eye. She *understands*.

And then I see it too. The way Beth's mouth is twisted as if she's about to cry, the fingers clenched tight around the bike's handlebars, knuckles white. The refusal to meet anyone's eye.

It's clear what's happened. I don't know how they found out what Alfie had done, but obviously, it had something to do with Beth.

I nod at Fiona. 'Thank you, but we're fine. Although we'll get back if you don't mind. We're both very tired and—'

'You don't want to come in?' asks Morag. 'Alfie isn't here, you've not to worry about that. Gillie is at home with him, chewing his ear off quite comprehensively, I would imagine.'

I stare at her. Is that what they think will make all this better? And a sudden wave of shame washes over me. This wasn't what I wanted to happen at all. Alfie doesn't deserve this, he— My thoughts come to a sudden stop. Only a few short days ago, I would have been fully supportive of anyone taking Alfie to task, and I wouldn't have cared how they did it either.

'It's really kind of you and I can see that all this has come as a huge shock to you too but…' I give Morag a weak smile. 'I'm sorry.'

I can't say any more and it's Fiona who speaks first, stepping forward to lay a hand on my arm.

'You get off back to Samphire,' she says. 'We understand, don't we, Morag? We just wanted you to know… Well, we're here if you need us,' she adds, flashing her aunt a look that I've seen a few times over the past week. Fiona being as tactful as ever.

I smile warmly. 'Thank you,' I say. Heartfelt. There's no need to say any more. I can see that Fiona really does understand. She takes a step backward and with a touch to Beth's shoulder, I move off, indicating that she should do the same.

We're back at Samphire in moments. Beth drops the bike by the shed and runs for the garden, barely able to contain her anguish any longer. I know exactly where she's gone; to the same spot where I sat only this morning, wanting to draw comfort from the sea. I wheel my bike slowly up the path and put both of them away in the shed before I follow her.

She's sitting in the grass, knees drawn up, with her arms clasped around them, trying literally to hold herself together. Her gaze is out to the horizon, but I know she's not seeing it, her eyes are too full of tears for one. I sit beside her, mirroring her position, and lean in gently against her side.

'Do you want to tell me what happened?' I say quietly.

My voice breaks the dam holding back her words and they pour forth in a torrent, incoherent, before they stop altogether and give way to hiccupping sobs.

I cradle her head in towards me, kissing the top of it. 'It's okay, sweetheart,' I murmur.

And so we sit, arms around one another, until Beth has poured out her sorrow, the soft breeze lifting it away to evaporate in the early evening air.

'I'm sorry, Mum, it was an accident. I didn't mean to.'

'Was it last night?' I prompt, suspecting that her evening with Shona lay at the root of it all.

She nods. 'We were just talking, about singing and stuff and about how Shona had lessons for a while with a lady that lives on the other side of the island. She's done exams and everything, and I'd said how much I'd like to do that too. She told me about the songs she'd had to learn and there was one, that one from the musical that Alfie and I sang when he came to visit.'

'And so you told her?'

'I didn't mean to, Mum. And I didn't really think anything of it because we were just chatting and stuff. I don't think Shona even noticed, she just said "oh" and then talked about something else. But now I think she must have told her mum. Not to get Alfie into trouble or anything, it wasn't like that, just—'

'A slip of the tongue. I know, sweetheart, it's okay. It's easily done.'

Her face is still stricken.

'You know, I did the same thing,' I say. 'Only in my case I got away with it.'

She looks at me, puzzled.

'At the ceilidh,' I tell her. 'I told Morag that Alfie had admired your dungarees, when no one here had seen them yet. Fortunately, though, Morag thought nothing of it. But that's the trouble, you see, when you keep secrets, or aren't honest with people. It's all too easy for the truth to slip out. And even if the lies you tell are well meant, they have a habit of coming to light sooner rather than later.'

'But now Alfie's in such trouble.'

I smile. 'He'll be okay, he's an adult, Beth. But yes, I suspect he *is* in a bit of trouble. But none of this would have happened if... well, never mind. What's done is done. The problem is that this doesn't only affect me and you, you see, but Morag and Gillie, Fiona too. So, it's going to get bigger than Alfie ever intended, or Cam for that matter.' I squeeze her shoulders. 'It's probably a good thing that's it's out in the open now anyway. And *you* mustn't worry. You've done nothing wrong, Beth.'

'Are you sure Alfie won't hate me?' She chews at the side of her lip.

'Oh, love. No, he won't hate you.' I wipe the wet away from her cheeks. 'Alfie's not like that. He's—' And then I stop, biting back what I was about to say. I look at her troubled face. 'You like him, don't you?'

She nods. 'He's really good at singing and dancing and playing musical instruments, but he's funny too, Mum. And he doesn't talk to me like I'm a two-year-old.'

I can't help but smile, thinking back to the time when Patrick and Beth first met. How excruciating it was. It seems like a very long time ago.

'And I don't really understand why everyone is so cross with him,' she continues. 'I mean, I know he did a bad thing, more than one bad thing. And I know what you said about lies and stuff and always telling the truth, but just because Alfie didn't, it doesn't make him a bad person. In fact, if you think about it, it makes him a very good person, because he was doing it to help someone else. And I think that's very brave. He probably knew he was going to get into trouble. I wish I had a friend like Alfie.'

So do I...

I think for a moment about what I'm going to say next, because it isn't fair to let Beth think otherwise.

'I'm really sorry this week hasn't been the kind of holiday we wanted, but—'

'No, Mum, it's been good, really.'

'But that's probably my fault. If I'd thought about it a bit more, I would have realised that coming here wasn't a good idea.'

'Yes, but you didn't know what Alfie had done before.'

'No, I didn't, did I?'

'And he's still a friend, isn't he?'

I think about her words for a moment. About all that's happened since we arrived. I give her a wry smile. 'Yes, but I probably still should have realised. Hindsight is a wonderful thing and one of those stupid things parents always say, but I'm sure that when you're older you won't do half as many daft things as your mum.'

I'm pleased to see Beth smile at that.

'Mu-um.' She nudges me playfully. 'You're not that bad. Besides, if we hadn't come here, I'd never have met Shona. Or been able to play with the puppies. Or sing at a ceilidh.'

My face falls a little.

'You do know that we're going home on Friday, don't you? As much as it sounds lovely to think about staying here, we can't, we have a life back home.'

She nods. 'Yes, I know,' she says, her wistful tone tugging at my heart. 'But Shona understands. She's promised to FaceTime me. Well, as long as they can get a signal. But if they can't, then she'll text, or email. She even said she'd write to me.'

'I'm really pleased that the two of you have hit it off. It would be lovely if you could stay in touch.' I don't want to spoil things by warning her that it might not happen.

'I know, and I actually think she will, Mum. Not like Trudi.'

I squint at her. 'Trudi?' It's the first time I've heard mention of any of her friends since we've been here.

Beth nods, squirming to fish her phone from her pocket. She presses a finger against the screen. 'Trudi was all like, "Wow, a Scottish island is so cool. You'll have to tell me what it's like and send me loads of photos." But that was before we came. Surprise, surprise, she hasn't bothered to reply to any of my messages.'

'Oh, Beth, she probably hasn't got them. Or you haven't got hers. You know what the signal is like here. I haven't heard from Gwen either and she said she'd text me too.'

Beth angles the screen towards me and scrolls with her finger. 'Yeah, but she has had them, look.' And she points to the tiny letters below one of her messages. 'See, it says she's read them. She just hasn't bothered to reply.'

I watch sadly as Beth scrolls with her finger. She's sent at least one text a day to Trudi. All of them read and none of them replied to. I don't know what to say.

Beth shrugs her shoulders. 'I expect she's just been busy.'

This is horrible. I want so much more for her. She deserves so much more, but… I push the thought away, it isn't helping anybody.

'Anyway, we still have one whole day left of the holiday,' she says, wiping the end of her nose. 'What shall we do tomorrow?'

I smile at the thought that my eleven-year-old daughter is playing jolly hockey sticks with me. I stretch out my legs. 'I don't know. What would you like to do?'

She screws up her nose for a moment. 'If the weather's okay, can we go out really early? On our bikes and ride around the whole island? We can stop if we see something we want to look at a bit more, and wander off if we want to, but I'd like to say we've done a whole loop.'

'I think that sounds like a great idea.'

She purses her lips. 'The only thing is that Shona has invited me over in the evening, seeing as it's our last night. But I don't have to go, we could—'

I put out my hand to still her words. 'And I think that's a lovely idea too.'

'But what will *you* do?'

I don't even have to think about it. 'I'll go and visit the lighthouse, I think. The sunset there is incredible apparently.' I pat her leg. 'Come on, I'm starving. Let's go inside and see what we want for tea. Or…' I grin across at her. 'I've had an even better idea. Shall I see if Andrew or Fiona can do us some fish and chips? I know they have them on the menu. We could bring them back here, and eat them on the beach.'

'Oh, could we?' Beth gets to her feet, holding out her arm to me. 'That would be brilliant.'

It only takes a moment to drop our things inside and while Beth goes back out to sit in the garden, I get on the bike again to pedal down to the hotel, my rucksack slung on my back.

It's as I'm crossing the hotel foyer that I hear the noise, one I haven't heard in a while. All week, in fact. It's the sound of a text message arriving. I pull out my phone, wondering if Gwen has finally managed to get through. But it isn't from her, it's from Alfie.

Please don't tell them about Cam, it says.

They know everything else now, that I pretended to be Cam, that I visited you and Beth last summer, and I've told them why, or as much as I'm prepared to anyway. They still don't know how Cam really was in those last few weeks. How much he was suffering. Please don't tell them, Abby. I know you're angry with me, but please, spare them that.

Chapter 24

We don't see a soul the next day. Or rather we do, but no one we know. Just a collection of people, like us, enjoying the island and all that it has to offer.

We did indeed leave early, taking our breakfast with us, which we ate on the beach by Samphire cottage. From there, we cycled up past the turning to Cam's house and on to the next bay, with its wide beach which stretches almost to the horizon. The tide was far away in the distance, only a slender strip of the sea showing below a pale glowing sky the colour of the sand. But as we watched, it deepened, turning first apricot and then soft blushing pink, the underside of a limpet shell, then rose turned back to brightest fiery orange before, almost without our noticing, it had gone, dissipating as the day emerged from its slumber.

We picked our way over rocks, investigated pools, and turned our heads to the wheeling of birds about the sky before sitting for a while to watch a group of seals basking on a distant promontory.

We rustled our way through grassy swathes, marvelled at a patch of delicate wild orchids, no bigger than my hand, and inhaled the damp deep green of woodland. We stopped at the local beekeepers and bought a jar of honey to take home with us, and drank fresh apple juice from a stall beside an orchard.

I don't know how far we walked or cycled, but by the time we're on the final approach to the hotel, my legs are beginning to feel every inch. The sun has pinked my skin, the wind has tied my hair in knots, but more than that, I have shed the city completely now, I am island through and through.

Even if it is just for one last day.

But it's absolutely what's been needed, to spend the kind of day I'd envisaged us having this week. It's felt like a holiday, and it's given me some much-needed perspective. Holidays come to an end, and this one will too. It's been lovely, and in a way, it seems awful to be thinking about going back to work again, to the routines, to the city with its mass of buildings and complicated skyline. To say goodbye to all of this. But I must. It's home, it's where we belong. Everything else is just a dream.

With a slightly heavy heart, I push open the shed door and we stow our bikes for the final time before trooping into the cottage in search of a drink and something to tide us over before dinner. I start to open cupboards, determinedly not packing for home yet, but acknowledging nonetheless that we really don't want to be carrying any food back with us. What's left now will need to be eaten tonight, tomorrow morning, or put out with the rubbish. I spread it all out on the countertop, while I wait for the kettle to boil, and unpack the things from my rucksack.

My phone screen wakes as I lift it from the front pocket, and I peer at it curiously. At some point during the day another message has arrived, and I smile when I see it's from Gwen. She finally manages to get through on the day before we come home. Typical. But the smile falls when I see the first line of her message, which simply reads DON'T PANIC, all in capitals. The one thing guaranteed to make anyone alarmed.

I click through to see the full message, but there isn't much more. It just says 'don't panic', with an apology that none of her messages seem to be getting through. Then, 'Ring me if you can', and a smiley face with a row of kisses.

I've already dialled her number by the time I reach the cottage's front door, the one place where reception seems better than anywhere else. I check my watch: it's a little before six, the shop will be shut and, with any luck, Gwen will be sitting in my kitchen, nursing a welcome cup of tea.

But there's nothing, no dialling clicks, no ringing, just a cold dead silence. I look at the screen and the little red symbol of a telephone receiver. The call is still trying to connect, but even as I watch, the symbol disappears. Call failed. I try again. Nothing.

I can hear the kettle beginning to boil through the doorway so I tell myself that I'll make a drink and by the time I've finished, the signal will have improved. It's bound to have. But just in case Gwen should try to call me again, I leave my phone on the arm of the sofa – it's much closer to the sweet spot than the kitchen.

It doesn't work, of course. I should know better than to try to make bargains with the universe like this. And the call still doesn't connect the third, fourth, fifth or sixth times I try. Beth has gone upstairs to have a shower and change before going to Shona's and I can still hear the water running overhead. Before I know it, I'm in my bedroom, fishing out my iPad from the drawer where I left it when we arrived. I haven't looked at it all week.

The battery's dead, but I plug it in and return to the kitchen to collect my drink. I'd promised myself I wasn't going to do this. I'd promised Gwen too that on no account would I check the shop's emails while I was here. And so far, I haven't. There's been no need and I trust Gwen implicitly – she will have taken care of everything for me, and if there was a particular problem that was urgent and she couldn't deal with it, then she would have sent me a message. But I know she would have done this only as a very last resort. So, does a text headed *Don't Panic* count as a last resort?

The shop and everything that goes with it seems so very far away from me, and it's a struggle to remember what had been going on just one week ago. No doubt the protest against the rate rises will be gathering speed but the thought of having to battle against bureaucracy, knowing that in all likelihood we will fail, isn't a pleasant one. But fight we will have to. There's no other choice if any of us want to survive.

I drink my tea while I wait for the emails to load, it could take quite a while. I hate that I can feel myself being pulled back towards the city, towards work and responsibilities. Despite the events of this week, I realise that the island *has* done what I hoped it would. It's taken Beth and I away from everything, given us new perspective and, hopefully, the strength to face whatever the future holds. But I also always knew that it would only ever be a temporary reprieve. It's time to get back to reality.

And then I see them. Among the orders and the invoice queries and the rubbish are countless emails from Alfie, all of them sent during the week we've been here. It's just like it was before, as if Cam has been emailing me all over again. And then I stop as a tingle ripples through me. Not Cam emailing me, but Alfie. Exactly like he has all along. I click on the first, sent the morning after we arrived, very aware that my heart is thudding in my chest. I start reading and I carry on until I've read them all, each getting progressively harder to decipher as my eyes fill with tears.

Abby, you need to help me, and before you say you're on your own pal, I'm actually on my hands and knees begging at this point. I am. It's quite embarrassing, I'm in my office and my admin assistant, Caroline, already thinks I'm weird. Anyway, I digress... You see, the thing is, I've actually gone and done it – fallen in love with the most beautiful and incredible woman, but because I'm a total and absolute (I'll spare you the rude word), I've completely stuffed it up. WHAT AM I GOING TO DO????? Please help me, Abby, you're my only hope...

Okay, stop it. I need you to be serious and stop laughing for a minute while I tell you what's happened...

And then he has poured out his heart to the void. Said all the things that he wanted to say to me but which I wouldn't let him. And in between all his rather more poignant words are all the other, inconsequential, ordinary, everyday things which are on the one hand, pretty meaningless, and on the other, absolutely the stuff of life. Things which Cam and I shared for months, things which I looked forward to reading, things which had become so much a part of my life that when they weren't there, I missed them like crazy. Things which I had never shared with Cam at all, not really. Because instead they were things I'd shared with Alfie.

And now Alfie has sent these messages, not even knowing if I would read them, simply because he couldn't bear not to. So how would I feel if I never heard from him again? But I don't need to ask myself the question. I already know the answer. I've known it all along. Because it's how I'm feeling now.

I sit back, perched on the edge of the bed with my iPad on my knee and my hands shaking. I don't know what to do, or think, because I'd almost, not completely, but almost got my head around the fact that we're leaving tomorrow, and now this. I almost wish he hadn't sent them.

As I watch, the screen shifts and another email is delivered. Not from Alfie this time, but from an address which seems somehow familiar. I stare at the combination of letters, trying to get my brain to understand what I'm looking at, to make the connection with my memory. And then I see it. The email has come from an address which I've certainly seen before, but never had much cause to use. Why would I, when I see Gwen in the shop every day? So why is she emailing *me*?

Hiya!

Bet you didn't think you'd be hearing from me, did you? But you weren't kidding when you said the island had little to no phone signal, were you? I've been trying to get a text message to you all week, but with no success, so I'm banking on you reneging on your promise not to check work emails and hoping that you're reading this from your tiny little island and not on the train to Glasgow.

The main thing is not to panic! But if you're reading this, then perhaps you've also read the messages from a man called Alfie, who you obviously know a lot better than I do! And I'm really sorry, I didn't mean to read them, but I opened the first one because I thought it was something to do with the shop, and then, well, I got hooked, because, Abby Prendergast, you dark horse you... I don't know the whole story but I can guess, and so there's something I need to say now, before you come home. In case it makes a difference.

And there's no easy way to say this... but I'm PREGNANT...!!!! Pregnant, yes, me! And I can't believe I'm saying it, that I would ever be saying it, you know how it's been, Abby. You've been with me through all the dark days of trying and failing and then the next few years of me and Rhys still trying but not really talking about it so much, but you knowing how it was because you're such a good friend, and then the last year where we'd kind of given up on the idea. But somehow or other, without us really noticing, a little bit of me decided that it liked a little bit of him very much indeed! And so two will become three. You should see me now, I'm sitting here with the biggest grin on my face!!

So, I had to tell you because it changes things, it's going to change things, and if I hadn't seen those messages from Alfie, I wouldn't be telling you now. I'd have waited until you got back, but you see, that's just it. By the time you get back it will be too late. I don't know who this man is, Abby, and I can see that there's something very weird gone on here, but I also remember that email you had from Cam's account; the one you weren't going to answer, and I'm wondering, suspecting, if that's got a lot to do with it. And if it has… What I'm trying to say is that from what I've read, you need to grab hold of this man with both arms and never let him go. And if he's offered you what I think he has then think very carefully before you say no. Don't say no out of loyalty to me or the shop, or because you have a life back here. Things are changing and maybe that's because it's time that they do.

Courage, my friend.
Gwen xxx

P.S. If you should happen to miss the ferry, either accidentally or on purpose, then Lottie and I have next week covered.

As I've been reading, I've only been dimly aware that the shower has stopped running and the bathroom door opened. Beth's voice from the bedroom doorway sounds like a foghorn, pulling me from the hazy delirium of my thoughts back to the clear and present day.

'Are you okay, Mum?'

I whirl around, folding the cover on my iPad. 'Yes, sorry, I was just being naughty, checking work emails,' I finish, dropping my voice to a whisper.

Beth rolls her eyes. 'You promised!'

'I know, I know.' I find a grin for her too. 'Look, I'm putting them away now,' I add, sliding my iPad back in the drawer. I get to my feet. 'Right, I'll go and rustle up some dinner now you're out of the shower. Do you want to come and see what you'd like?'

I follow her down the stairs, surreptitiously wiping my eyes and face, eradicating any trace of my thoughts. *But Gwen, pregnant, oh my God…*

I never make it to the lighthouse. I intended to, but as I walked up the road, I realised that I would have to go past the turning to Cam's house and somehow my feet turned in that direction.

I don't really know why I'm here, except to say goodbye. My head is filled with thoughts of Gwen, of Alfie, of Cam, but they're not helpful at all, instead they're overwhelming; pulling me this way and that, making suggestions, telling me things I already know, trying to persuade me to take one decision over another. And I almost wish they would all go away. Except that this would mean they'd be gone from my life, and I don't want that either.

Despite what Alfie said, I don't really expect the cottage to be open, but the door handle gives as soon as I turn it. Walking in, the whitewashed walls are already beginning to glow from the rays of the setting sun and the empty space is warm and calming. I stand at the window for a few moments before turning back to look at the room. A room where Cam once lay as his friend watched over him. The images flit through my head, flickering ghosts from the past, except that as I look around me I realise that it isn't Cam I see, but Alfie. Asleep on the sofa, sitting in front of the computer. Face creased in a smile as he reads one of my emails. The man whose image I try to conjure up as he lay in the bed really could have been a ghost, he's no more substantial than the shadow on the wall. I've already said goodbye to Cam, but am I really ready to say goodbye to Alfie?

I sigh and walk back through into the other room, to the boxes of books that are stacked on the floor. I lift the flaps on the topmost one and take out a couple of weighty tomes, but they're teaching textbooks, nothing I've sent to him. I flip through one idly but it occurs to me that this was a side of Cam I rarely saw, the teacher, and I feel further away than ever. I'm about to reach in for another book when the front door opens. I don't know who looks the more surprised, Gillie or me.

My hand goes to my heart. 'Oh God, I'm so sorry.' I cast about the room, but I've no real reason to be here. 'I shouldn't have come without asking.'

Gillie, however, simply smiles. 'Yet if folk were unwelcome here, we'd have kept a lock on the door. It's beautiful at this time of the day, isn't it?'

I look at the books in my hand, replacing them in the box. 'I was just… saying goodbye.'

'Aye.' He gives me a sad smile. 'I come here because I don't want to.' He swallows. 'But the island estate can't keep this place empty forever. One day that will change, and that's okay too. It will be time for someone else to make new memories here.'

I nod, unsure what to say, wondering if he thinks that's going to be me. 'I hope so. It's a beautiful place. The light here is fantastic, and the view, but it's more than that, there's a real peace here too.'

'Maybe that's because it's always been such a happy house.'

I fold the flaps back down on the boxes, turning my face away, turning my thoughts away.

'Anyway, I should go,' I say, straightening up. 'Let you be.'

Gillie doesn't reply, but there's a slight tilt to his head. 'I'll see you in the morning, I expect, before you go,' he says. 'I know it hasn't always been easy for you, but it's been good having you here, lass, your young 'un too.'

'Thank you,' I say. 'It's been lovely. Meeting you and Morag. Everything. We've had a great week.' And suddenly there doesn't seem to be much else to say. I smile, walking to the door. 'Bye then, I'll see you tomorrow.'

I'm almost through it when Gillie's voice comes again. 'Abby, before you go…'

I look back to see him holding a hand to his head as if he's deep in thought.

'There's been lots of things said this week, about Alfie, I mean. And Morag and Fiona they… well, they've a right to be cross. Alfie hasn't always behaved the way they might have wanted him to, but his heart has always been in the right place.' He breaks off, smiling as if at some memory. 'And when Cam put ideas in his head, they tended to stay there. So, when Cam asked Alfie to try to cover up how bad things were, what Alfie didn't take into account was that we're Cam's parents so he was never going to fool us. Of *course* we knew how bad Cam's condition was, we'd spent the first few years of his life practically watching every breath he took. Wondering if he was happy, sad, hurt, okay, telling the truth, lying… We knew everything there was to know about him, so he would never be able to hide the truth of how he was feeling. But the fact that Cam lied to us about that doesn't make him a bad person. He was trying to spare us, that's all. That and try to cope with everything himself. The last thing he wanted was everyone weeping and wailing around his bedside, so we went along with it. As best we could anyway, hard though it was. We always understood that, in a way, it was Cam's final wish, so how could we possibly deny him that? And the fact that Alfie tried his hardest to perpetuate Cam's deceit, well, that doesn't make him a bad person either. Quite the reverse, in fact.'

My mouth drops open, thoughts frantically rushing through my head. 'But Alfie has been terrified that you would find out! He thought you would hate him for it.'

'Yes, I know.' Gillie sighs. 'Although it's taken me far too long to realise.'

My heart goes out to him. He looks so helpless, standing there. He's been through so much.

'All I'm really trying to say is that I didn't want you to leave and think too badly of Alfie for the things he got wrong. He only ever did things out of the best of intentions and out of love. He may have been a little misguided at times, and rather naive at others, but love doesn't come with a manual, does it? And let's just say that some of us are a little more well-read than others.'

Chapter 25

One short week ago, Beth and I stood looking at a sea of faces in the bookshop as they waited to wave us goodbye. I never dreamed that in such a short space of time we'd be doing it again, with people who feel just as special. But here they all are, on the quayside, expressions bright, wreathed in smiles, all chattering away nineteen to the dozen: Fiona, Morag, Gillie and Shona. Andrew, bless him, must be running the hotel single-handed.

'Now, you must ring us, the minute you get home, let us know you're safe.' This from Morag.

'Please, please, come back and see us soon. And don't mind if the website says we're booked up, I'll find room for you,' says Fiona as she throws her arms around me.

'I'll send you all the songs,' promises Shona, as she and Beth hug.

'Go on with you, lass,' says Gillie as I lean up to kiss his cheek. 'Stop, or you'll make me cry.' He looks even more emotional than me, if that were possible.

But there's one person missing.

And it feels like there's the biggest hole in my heart.

I wasn't really sure if Alfie would appear this morning. Fiona muttered something about a meeting, but despite everything that's happened, somehow I still thought he'd be here. I thought there'd be time, you see, to root him out and say our goodbyes in private, but more than that to tell him what Gillie had revealed to me last night. That the thing he feared most wasn't something to be afraid of, after all.

But the reality was that by the time we'd packed and cleaned the cottage and made sure that everything was left exactly as we found it, after we'd popped into the shop to buy something to eat on our journey, and left a couple of books for Maureen, the morning had just disappeared. And now it's time to go.

I hadn't answered Gwen's email in the end. I hadn't known what to say. About Alfie's emails, or her pregnancy, or about her reasons for telling me her news, because it didn't feel like it was a conversation that would ever be finished.

I know it's well-meant, but I've found it so hard to deal with everyone's assumptions about me. Assuming that I came to the island as some sort of precursor to moving here permanently. Assuming that I'll take over the bookshop from Maureen and move into Cam's house. That this is such a brilliant opportunity for us, why wouldn't we want to do it? That Alfie and I… But the weight of all that expectation is a heavy burden and it feels as if I've simply swapped one set of assumptions for another. As if it's my mother laying out her blueprint for my life again, that there's nothing I should want more than to be married off and… I quash the thought. It's been round and round in my head so many times, and I'm still no further forward.

We're up on the ferry deck now, leaning against the railings to wave at everyone below us. There are plenty of other folk milling around. Holidaymakers like us, leaving for home with fond memories to take with them. People loading goods that are destined for the mainland. Islanders travelling for business or for pleasure in Oban or Glasgow.

But, try as I might, scanning the figures, searching through the faces, none of them belong to Alfie. Perhaps it's better this way.

The weather is calm out at sea, thankfully, and it's quite pleasant here, up on deck, particularly if you can find yourself a seat tucked out of the wind. I reach into my bag and take out the sandwiches that we bought from Maureen earlier, offering one to Beth. She has her head firmly in her book, a stance she adopted pretty much from the moment the ferry set sail. I don't blame her, I don't feel much like talking either.

She tucks her bookmark inside the book and bends to rest it on her bag. As she leans down, I catch a glimpse of a man sitting in the row behind us. There's something about the way he's holding a book of his own that seems so familiar somehow.

'What?' asks Beth, catching me looking. She takes the sandwich from me and begins to unwrap it.

'Nothing. I just…' I angle my head backwards, cranking my body round to see past Beth's shoulders. But there's not much to go on. The same colour jacket, collar turned up against the wind, the back of his head, dark-haired, but it's the way he holds open the pages of his book that looks familiar, not just with his thumb, but with his little finger too.

'I thought I saw Mr Ridley,' I whisper. 'But it can't be him.'

Beth frowns at me. 'Mr Ridley?'

'Yes, you know, from the shop.'

'Yes, but what would *he* be doing here?'

'Exactly, he wouldn't. Just…' I smile at the memory of our one and only proper conversation. 'I got chatting to him a few weeks ago and he mentioned how he and his wife used to travel a lot. He told me how much he loved the countryside, and wished that he could visit it again, just like he used to when his wife was alive. For a minute there I thought that perhaps…' I shake my head. No, that's a silly idea.

'But, Mum, he's *ancient*,' replies Beth, like only an eleven-year-old can. 'He wouldn't have been on holiday way out here, it's far too far away.'

I nod and smile as his words come back to me. *The middle of nowhere is much nicer*. And he said something else too, what was it? And then it comes to me.

You mustn't let hope stand in the way of things. You can wait too long in the hope of something coming to you. Sometimes you have to get on and do. And then he'd told me that he'd wasted too many years hoping that his Lily would come back.

I recall that it had struck me as a little odd at the time, because how can hope stand in the way of something? But then I'd been thinking about Patrick and Gwen had come back and Mr Ridley's words had all but been forgotten. I stare out at the horizon, pondering his wisdom anew, and I think perhaps I *can* see what he meant. That you can be so busy hoping that something might happen that you don't realise when something is. The hope itself has become what's important, not the possibilities that it can bring.

Was that what I had done? Had I locked myself in the shop, given myself the perfect opportunity to be forever hopeful, but never fulfilled? I'm struck forcibly by some of the last words Alfie had said to me: *Hope is what you have when you set yourself free.*

He saw someone who was so determined to stay in her cage that she saw everything she was being offered as obligation, instead of friendship. Friendship and understanding from a bunch of people who took me and Beth to their hearts and simply wanted to keep us around. How could I ever have thought that was wrong?

I'd been so determined to see the wrongs that Alfie had done that I couldn't see the things that were right. I was so busy pushing everything away from me that I couldn't even see what was missing from my life.

And now it's too late.

It seems as if days have passed before the ferry finally docks and we feel solid ground beneath our feet once more. The intervening hours have dragged almost unbearably and I've willed them to pass as quickly as possible. But time never listens, of course, it simply goes at its own pace regardless. It's only your perception of it that's different. Just like a lot of things.

But as I step from the ferry I know I've made the right decision, the only one I can, and I turn my face to the sun, to the future. I feel quite lightheaded. I slip my hand into Beth's, giving it a squeeze as I feel her tremble a little beside me. She's been quiet the whole journey, lost in her thoughts the same as I, the pages of her book unturned and unread. Now, she looks close to tears. But I'm doing the right thing, I know I am.

I give her hand another squeeze and start walking, wheeling our cases along the quayside, as we manoeuvre our way around the other holidaymakers and day-trippers. I can't help but look at them as they mill around, wondering whether they're coming or going; lives crossing, lives intersecting, all of us trying to do the best we can for whatever time we have left to us.

I can hardly see where I'm going now, my eyes are so full of tears, but it isn't too far to walk. I just have to keep putting one foot in front of the other and in a few minutes we'll be at the hotel where I'm hoping we can stay for the night. After that, well, we've a long journey ahead of us, but the sooner we're there, the sooner we can get on with our lives.

I smile at Beth, as I pull open the hotel door, seeing her expression mirror my own, and with a deep breath, we walk inside. There's no going back now. No time for second thoughts.

For a moment all is still and the seconds seem to take an eternity to tick past but then we're spotted, just as we were before, by Fiona coming through the lounge. And like it did the first time, her shout brings everyone running.

Shona comes hurtling across the hotel foyer from behind her, throwing her arms around Beth, who drops the handle of her suitcase and returns the hug just as fiercely, the two of them jumping up and down in excitement. Gillie appears to my right, a worried expression on his face until he catches sight of us, whereupon he turns on his heel and rushes off, his wife's name on his lips.

Seconds later, they're gathered around, Morag, Andrew, Gillie and Fiona, faces wreathed in grins as they hug us like they'll never let us go, all until Fiona suddenly throws up her hands and shouts for everyone to stop. She looks around her, as I am, straining for a glimpse, looking from one person to the next and still not finding who she hopes to see.

'Oh for goodness' sake, will someone *please* go and fetch Alfie! He was here a minute ago.' She catches my eye as Shona races off, through the small lounge and into the hall.

The puppies come first, streaking through the open doorway, making the most of their unexpected freedom, and then hot on their tails is Alfie, a bag of dog food still in his hand as he falls over his feet in his haste to get to us. He doesn't know whether to chase the dogs or let them go, or do something else entirely. And then he stops. And his eyes fly to mine, wide and disbelieving, until he sees that I'm really here. That I've come back. And everything else melts away. He thrusts the bag of dog food at Fiona, and the next heartbeat he's standing before me. And he's just the same Alfie he always was; the one I first met, the one I fell in love with. The one I *am* in love with.

'How are you even here?' he asks, breath catching in his throat as he takes my hands in his, pulling me closer. 'I'm not sure I can quite believe it. I thought...' But he's unable to finish.

'Well, we got off the ferry in Oban, and then we got straight back on it. It's really quite simple. I thought my shop, the flat, our life was everything I ever wanted, until I realised I'd been telling myself that for so long, I'd started to believe something that could never be true. Because there would have always been something missing.' I break off to thread my fingers through his. 'I was like Brown Bear, waiting for the impossible to come along, ever hopeful, but actually just a part of the furniture.'

The surprise is dropping from Alfie's face, it's being replaced by another emotion, something hopeful, something just waiting to burst into life. Much like myself. 'I need new horizons, Alfie. New challenges in my life, new people... you, actually. Only I'm not quite sure what I should do now.'

A slow smile works its way up his face, the slanting evening sun catching the edge of those green eyes I thought I'd never see again.

'Well then, how about this?' And he leans across the small distance between us and presses his lips against mine. Softly and absolutely perfectly. 'Hello, Abby Prendergast. It's absolutely delightful to meet you. Again...' He touches his forehead to mine. 'I thought I'd lost you,' he says, eyes roving my face, drinking me in. 'Once was hard enough, I wasn't sure how I was going to bear it for a second time.'

'I thought I'd lost you too,' I reply. 'Until I realised that it was never you I lost. That you were right here all along. That you've always been here.'

'Well, you're lucky you caught me,' he says. 'A few more minutes and I'd have been on my way home.'

I smile, touching my lips against his one more time. 'That's funny,' I reply. 'Because that's exactly where I'm going.'

Epilogue

August

I think it's a trait we second-hand booksellers have, to give each new book that crosses our path a little shake, or a flick through, just to check there's been nothing left inside. And I always check for inscriptions, they're my favourite thing to find. But I wasn't expecting to find anything, even as the envelope drops into my lap.

I pick it up from where it's fallen on the floor, illuminated by the shaft of sunlight that slants across the room. Is my heart supposed to be beating this hard? I turn it over, breath catching in my throat as I see what's written there. I don't recognise the handwriting, but then why would I? Cam only ever emailed, I've never even thought about the way his hand would form the letters of my name. But they're rounded, comfortable, friendly. And I lay my fingers on them, reaching across time to feel the hand that wrote them.

My fingers begin to tremble, fumbling with the flap, desperate not to tear it in my haste to get to the letter the envelope contains. I'm holding my breath, knowing that once I have read the words within, the possibility of what they might say will be gone. They will *become*.

But even as my eyes fix on the first line, a smile starts at the corners of my mouth, one that reaches all the way down to my heart.

Dear Abby,

So, this is one of those 'if you're reading this then I'm dead' kind of letters. Only this time there's no murder mystery, no conniving family hell-bent on getting their hands on my fortune. Just plain old life, I'm afraid. It gets to everyone in the end, doesn't it?

But don't be sad, Abby, not least of all because you've made me very happy. Especially now. Because if you're reading this letter, it means that it's found its way to you, or, as I hope, you've found your way to it. And that's something that has kept me going during these final dark weeks, the thought that one day, my Abby would be here.

And I am sorry. Of course I have to say that – because it's true, obviously – but also because I promised Alfie that I would tell you myself how sorry I am. I'm sorry for dying, but I'm also so very sorry for keeping from you everything I have. But believe me, it's better this way. Everyone says, 'Oh, you should have told me, I'd have wanted to be with you.' But they wouldn't, Abby, not really. There's nothing pleasant or worthwhile about being with someone who's dying. It's ugly and undignified and one way to spoil a perfectly good relationship. Trust me.

So that brings me rather neatly to Alfie, without whom the end would have been so much harder. The most amazing person I know, aside from myself, of course (ha ha!). Because Alfie is all the things I aspired to be. And just so you know, this isn't one of those things that people say when they're fishing for compliments; I achieved some of the things I wanted to be, and some of the others, well, I have to hope that I would have got around to them. But I guess what I'm really trying to say is that, even though you might want to hang Alfie from the lighthouse and leave the cruel sea to have its way with him, please don't.

Not only will he not deserve it, because none of this was ever his fault, but it would rather spoil the point of this letter, or one of them anyway. Because you see, I mentioned right at the off that I'm glad you're reading this letter, because it means that you've found your way to us here on the island. In fact, it was a dream of mine that you would come here. I think Alfie might have told you that himself? What he probably didn't tell you, mainly because I didn't tell him, was that in my dreams I never saw you here alone. I always saw you with him; sitting out in the garden on a summer evening, watching the sun set over the sea. I know, I'm such a soppy romantic fool. But so is he, that's definitely what you'd be doing…

I knew quite early on that he was in love with you. And when I realised, for a second, just a second… possibly three or four, I wanted to mash his face against the wall, but then I realised that anyone in their right mind would fall in love with you, Abby Prendergast, so how could I possibly blame him? He does have impeccably good taste. Once I knew this though, it put me in rather a quandary. Because Alfie and I have talked about everything over the years, and you wouldn't believe the conversations we had in the last few months of my life, but then again you probably would. But the one thing we never spoke about was you. Or rather you and him. Him and you. He never let on that he was in love with you. Ever. He wouldn't do that to me. Just as he never took advantage of my condition to further his own advances.

So there, now you've heard what I have to say, my last will and testament as it were. And maybe I didn't get everything I wanted in life, but I reckon I didn't do too badly, after all. As for you, you have your whole life ahead of you, so make it a good one, Abby Prendergast, it's been an absolute pleasure. And remember, when it comes to Alfie, everything he did, he did because I asked him to. Praying that one way or another, this whole thing called life might find its happy ending.

I hope so.

With all my love, Cam xxx

I look up, letting the room gradually come back into focus as it swims through my tears. They're happy tears, though. It seems as if I've been waiting for this day all my life.

It's almost finished now. All my pieces of furniture in place and some of Cam's too, including his bookcases. But it won't be a home until all the books are unpacked, and I left his till last, wanting them to be the final pieces that will make everything complete.

Through the window I can hear shouts of laughter. Beth is playing on the lawn with one of the puppies, though not so little now, of course. And, as I look up, I can see Nipper dancing around her in delight, or *Juniper*, as I now know. Quite an appropriate name for the dog that belongs to a man who distils gin for a living. But she's beautiful and Beth has never looked happier. Of course, the dog is not the only reason…

It's taken a few months to get this far, to make all the arrangements that will knit our lives together, but although at times it felt as if it would never happen, now that it has, it's all been worth it. Never in a million years did I ever dream that this tiny gem of an island could be my home. But it is. Seven miles long by two miles wide; a chunk of land nestling amid sparkling blue waters and home to just one hundred and thirty-five people. One hundred and thirty-seven now, I correct myself.

My shop has been sold, Gwen is absolutely blooming, but looking forward excitedly to her new life. My mother and sister, well, they have open invitations to come for a visit. If they want to, that is. My mother told me I was mad, of course, and I certainly felt it that day when I got off the ferry in Oban and told Beth we were getting straight back on it again in a few hours. And that's exactly what we did. I don't think I'll ever forget the look on Alfie's face as he spotted us in the hotel. Fiona hugged me so hard I couldn't breathe, but as for the rest, well…

I fold up the single sheet of paper, still in my hand, and slide it back inside its envelope. I might have known Cam would tuck it between the covers of the book that started it all, the story of a man called William Stoner. And in a way the letter it now holds is the story of Cam's life too. He really was a soppy romantic fool, and absolutely right about his best friend. I might have fallen in love with Cam first, but then I fell in love with Alfie. It's so simple, I'm amazed it took me so long to see it.

I add the book to the shelf, just as the door opens beside me. Alfie is home, his work for the day done, and just as Cam said we would, very soon we'll be sitting in the garden with a mug of tea, watching the sun set over the sea.

He comes over and wraps a warm hug around me, nuzzling his face into the side of my neck. And I breathe in the scent of him as my lips find his.

'I still can't get over the sight of you here,' he murmurs. 'Whoever would have thought it?'

'Oh, I don't know… I can think of a few people.'

He pulls away, a query on his face, but then he catches sight of the bookcase beside me and I see his eyes rove the shelves. When he looks back, they're shining with emotion.

'What do you think?' he asks. 'It looks good, doesn't it?'

I look around the room, at the view outside, at Beth and at the man standing beside me. 'It does. It's all absolutely perfect.'

A Letter from Emma

Hello, and thank you so much for choosing to read *The Little Island Secret*. I hope you enjoy reading my stories as much as I enjoy writing them. So, if you'd like to stay updated on what's coming next, please do sign up to my newsletter here and you'll be the first to know!

www.bookouture.com/emma-davies

It's a well-known fact among my friends that I'm a bit of a sucker for a Scottish accent. Just as well-known is my fantasy of living on a remote Scottish island, so it's not really any surprise that eventually one of my leading men would be a Scot who just happens to be an island dweller. There is something so wonderfully romantic and majestic about these wild and wide-open spaces. Places where the world seems to slow right down and catch its breath, where timeless time exists. And they call to me just as loudly as the tree-filled sanctuaries around my home, where I spend as much of my free time as I can. It's that sense of the world being so incredibly vast, while you're so incredibly small, and I love that feeling. It was something I wanted Abby to discover about her life – that the one she had in Cambridge was busy and confining and, even though she loved it, her soul really longed for something wild and free. And so did Beth's, incidentally.

But along with my love of the landscape is also my love for the music that is so much a part of people's lives in these communities. I spent several years in Ireland as a child, frequently exposed to music that came seemingly as naturally as breathing, and indeed sprang up at a moment's notice whenever a group of people came together. And perhaps that's why I love it so much. The music is elemental, and for me speaks of something ancient and permanent, but what I love the most is its folkloric element; the stories that grew up were passed on from one generation to the next and are still sung and played today. And maybe that's why I love telling stories of my own too.

A few years ago, a friend of mine sent me a clip of music, primarily because it was performed live in a Scottish glen. It seemed so organic, cementing the world of nature with our daily lives, and from there it spawned a reawakening of my love for folk music and in particular for the music of fiddle player, Duncan Chisholm. The piece was called 'A Precious Place' and taken from his spectacular album, *Sandwood*. Do have a listen if you get the chance. It might not be your cup of tea, but it's the perfect accompaniment for *The Little Island Secret*, and played virtually on repeat while I was writing it!

Of course none of this would be possible without the support of my wonderful editor, Jessie Botterill. Huge thanks to her and also the incredible team of people at Bookouture, who take my stories and transform them with the utmost skill and care, delivering them into your hands. And finally, to you, lovely readers, the biggest thanks of them all for continuing to read my books, and without which none of this would be possible. You really do make everything worthwhile.

Having folks take the time to get in touch really does make my day, and if you'd like to contact me then I'd love to hear from you. The easiest way to do this is by finding me on Twitter and Facebook, or you could also pop by my website, where you can read about my love of Pringles among other things…

I hope to see you again very soon and, in the meantime, if you've enjoyed reading *The Little Island Secret*, I would really appreciate a few minutes of your time to leave a review or post on social media. Every single review makes a massive difference and is very much appreciated!

Until next time,
Love, Emma xx

Printed in Great Britain
by Amazon